Little Dolls

JANE BLYTHE

Cover designed by Q Designs

✵ Created with Vellum

Acknowledgments

I'd like to thank everyone who played a part in bringing this story to life. Particularly my mom who is always there to share her thoughts and opinions with me. My wonderful cover designer Amy who did an amazing job with this stunning cover. My fabulous editor Lisa for all the hard work she puts into polishing my work. My awesome team, Sophie, Robyn, and Clayr, without your help I'd never be able to run my street team. And my fantastic street team members who help share my books with every share, comment, and like!

And of course a big thank you to all of you, my readers! Without you I wouldn't be living my dreams of sharing the stories in my head with the world!

CHAPTER

One

February 7th
4:12 P.M.

Clara's heart was beating so hard and fast; it felt like a hammer against her ribs.

In the rearview mirror, she could see red and blue lights swirling. Whirling sirens filled the air. They were close—too close. They were going to catch her.

She cast a quick glance at the gas gauge; it was nearing empty. She couldn't keep going much longer.

She should stop.

Pull over.

But she didn't.

Instead, she pressed her foot harder on the accelerator. The car sped up, as did the police car following her. So did the police car behind that. And the one behind that. And the many other police cars that were in the long black and white snake tailing her.

She wanted to stop, tell them what had happened, but she was too scared. What if they didn't understand? What if they blamed her? What if they dragged her off to jail?

This was all her fault. What was wrong with her? She was usually so careful; she was *always* so careful. Today, however, for some stupid reason she had been distracted. If only she'd been paying attention, then this wouldn't have happened.

Now she was stuck.

She had no choice but to just keep going for as long as she could and hope for the best. Another glance at the gas gauge showed the red line was hovering on empty. She had *maybe* another couple of minutes before it was all over.

Clara didn't bother to try and hold back tears as they began to trickle down her cheeks. She was so afraid. More afraid than she'd ever been in her life. She felt trapped. Trapped and helpless. She wanted a way out, but at that moment it didn't seem like one was going to present itself.

Again she sped the car up; she was beyond glad she had let her sister pressure her to take a defensive driving course a couple of years ago. As she drove, she scanned the area, looking for someplace to hide. Of course, that was ridiculous. There had to be at least eight or nine police cars chasing her. There was nowhere to hide.

Turning onto a freeway, perhaps she could make one quick burst for freedom and outrun the cops before her car ran out of gas.

She'd made it only a half mile or so when the car suddenly slowed and then rolled to a stop.

Red and blue spun around her. Cars were everywhere. Sirens were wailing. Voices were screaming at her, but she couldn't make out their words.

Clara felt weird.

Floaty.

The air in the car was stifling.

She needed some fresh air.

Why did she feel so dazed?

On wobbly legs, she climbed from the car.

∾

4:21 P.M.

Something was wrong.

Detective Jonathon Dawson knew it as soon as the woman climbed from the car.

At first, he thought drugs; she was swaying, and her eyes looked glazed. But then he caught sight of the blood on her neck, and he immediately thought victim. If this woman had been assaulted, she might be in shock, which could explain why she had just spent the last ninety minutes driving through the city seemingly oblivious to the dozen police cars tailing her.

Catching his partner's eye, he pointed at his neck and Allina nodded that she too had noticed the woman's injury. While his partner gestured to the other cops surrounding the woman and her car to keep back, Jonathon lowered his gun and took a tentative step forward.

"Ma'am?" he called out. He would have liked to have kept his voice as quiet and calming as possible, but sirens were still whining, and cars were whizzing past on the other side of the freeway.

The woman didn't appear to have heard him. She was staring at the scene before her as though unable to comprehend it.

Jonathon put his gun away. He didn't think she was a threat, and even if he'd read her wrong, there were enough cops on the scene with guns to neutralize her if the need arose.

"Ma'am," he said again, moving toward her.

Up close she looked frail and vulnerable. She was thin—a little too thin. Her skin was as white as freshly fallen snow, and out in the cold—for which she wasn't properly dressed—it looked nearly translucent. She had enormous green eyes, which would have been beautiful if they weren't dulled by shock. Her hair hung several inches past her shoulders and shimmered like gold as it caught the late afternoon sun. His heart did a strange little pitter-patter. She was gorgeous. Before he got too carried away, his gaze was drawn to her bloody neck. There was a gash—maybe five inches long—which looked deep enough to need stitches. Blood had poured down her neck, soaking her china blue sweater, but the bleeding appeared to have slowed—or maybe even stopped completely. She had probably received the wound shortly before the car chase began.

His movements seemed to capture her attention, and she turned toward him in extreme slow motion. For a moment, her face was blank, but then her eyes began to clear a little. Shock faded to fear, and her mouth moved, but no sound came out.

"Ma'am, I'm here to help you. Can you tell me who hurt you?"

She took a stumbling step toward him. "He has a gun," she whispered.

As her words hit him, his gaze snapped from the woman to the car, knowing instinctively that whoever hurt this woman was still in there. Jonathon had time to yell a warning to his colleagues then fling himself at the woman, tackling her to the ground, before gunfire filled the air.

Using his body as a shield, he pressed her down, keeping her firmly in place and out of the line of fire. They were virtually sitting ducks here. They were right beside the car, guns firing on either side of them, and he couldn't get to his gun without leaving the woman vulnerable. She felt small beneath him; her whole body was trembling. Jonathon could practically feel the bullets flying above him from the still-open driver's door of the car. His colleagues returned fire, but he heard several grunts of pain and knew that people were being hit. Helpless to do anything about it, all he could do was stay where he was, protect this woman, and pray that none of the cops on the scene were badly hurt.

Eventually, everything stopped.

The woman hadn't tried to fight him off, and he didn't move a muscle until he heard confirmation that the shooter was down. Slowly, he levered his body off hers. Her eyes were closed, and she didn't acknowledge him in any way. Concerned that she may have hit her head when he'd knocked her to the ground, he quickly ran his hands over her scalp. He didn't find any bumps, and when he brought his hands away, he didn't see any blood. Her head might not be bleeding, but the tackle seemed to have caused the wound on her neck to start gushing again.

Yanking a handkerchief from his pocket, he pressed it to the cut and yelled over his shoulder, "I need an ambulance!"

"Already on the way," Allina dropped down beside him. "Is she okay?"

"In shock, I think," he replied. "Ma'am, can you hear me?"

The woman gave a tiny nod of her head.

Relieved that she was at least conscious, he tried to question her further. "Can you tell me your name?"

"Clara."

The word was whispered so quietly, he hardly heard her. "Are you hurt any place else, Clara?" He had no idea what else the man who'd obviously carjacked her had inflicted upon her.

"Is . . . is . . . is he . . . dead?" Her eyes fluttered open to stare up at him imploringly.

He glanced sideways. The shooter was slumped half outside the car. The top of the man's head—what was left of it—was resting on the road. A bullet had entered through his left eye and taken half his face with it. That was not a sight Clara needed to have seared in her mind, so Jonathon surreptitiously maneuvered himself so he fully blocked her view of the shooter's body. "He's dead," he assured her.

A long sigh escaped her lips, and her eyes fell closed again.

"Clara, an ambulance is coming, but I need to know if you're hurt anywhere else," he prompted since she had neglected to answer him.

Perhaps she wasn't even aware of any injuries she might have—she was clearly badly shaken up. When again she offered no response, he took it upon himself to run his hands up and down her body in search of injuries. Clara didn't protest, nor did she wince at his movements. She was beginning to shake in earnest now—a combination of shock and cold, he presumed. There wasn't much he could do about her going into shock; the paramedics would deal with that when they got here, but he could at least wrap her up in some blankets and put her in his car. Shrugging out of his jacket, he eased her shoulders off the ground and slid it under her, then buttoned it up in front.

"I'm going to take her to the car," he told Allina.

His partner nodded then hurried to their car, opening the back door, then the trunk where she retrieved some blankets. Jonathon gently hooked his arms under Clara's knees and behind her back and scooped her up. As he stood, he took in the scene for the first time. There were three cops down; two were sitting up and talking, but one looked serious. A stray bullet must have caused a car on the other side of the freeway to crash, or the driver had been distracted by all the shooting and hit a pole. Four people stood around the vehicle, none appeared to have sustained more than minor injuries.

Carrying Clara to the car, he slid into the backseat and settled her on his lap. The idea of leaving her alone never even entered his mind. Nor did the idea of simply setting her down and sitting beside her. It was purely practical, he assured himself. She was cold, and his body heat would help to warm her. It had nothing at all to do with the initial jolt of attraction that had shot through him the moment he'd gotten close to her.

"Here you go." Allina passed him the blankets and gave him a look he decided he didn't want to decipher.

Wrapping Clara in the blankets, he tucked her head under his chin and tried hard not to like it when she snuggled closer.

~

4:32 P.M.

Someone was cradling her gently. Their hand was stroking her hair, and they were murmuring soothingly in her ear.

Knowledge of where she was and what had happened eluded her.

All she knew was that something was wrong with her.

She felt odd.

The voice whispering in her ear was calming, and the body she rested against was warm. Clara snuggled closer, seeking reassurance. Her body was shaking, she couldn't stop it, and her throat ached horribly. She lifted a hand to her neck to try to find out why, but someone grasped it.

"Just rest, Clara," the words rumbled in the chest she was slumped against. "The paramedics will be here soon; they'll stitch your neck and give you some painkillers."

Stitch her neck? Was it cut? Is that why it hurt?

Panic sliced through her, and she opened her eyes, trying to push herself into an upright position, but hampered by the fact that her arms were tucked inside a buttoned coat. Why didn't she remember someone cutting her neck? What was wrong with her?

Seemingly reading her mind, the man who held her spoke softly, "You're in shock, Clara. The paramedics will be able to help you with that, too."

In shock?

A stab of pain in her neck made her moan, but it also jolted her memory. The man in her car had held a knife to her throat. Sliced the tip of the blade through her skin. So much blood had flowed out that she'd been afraid she would pass out. But there was more. "He . . . he . . . He had a gun?" she tilted her gaze up so she could see the man's face.

"Yeah, he did," the man agreed.

Trying to make her sluggish mind remember, she asked, "He's dead, though?"

"He's dead," the man assured her.

The affirmation had her sinking back down against his hard chest. He was so warm, and she was so cold. When he lifted a hand, and began to smooth her hair again, she felt a rush of contentment flood through her. The man was handsome—his eyes were a lovely warm light brown, his hair was dark brown, and he wore it a little long, so it hung just above his eyes. There was something about him that soothed her. She knew that was strange—and stupid—she didn't even know his name. At least she thought she didn't. But maybe he'd told her already and she'd just forgotten.

"Clara? Do you think you can tell me what happened to you?"

"Wh . . . what's your name?" she asked without lifting her head. She was so tired.

"Jonathon. Detective Jonathon Dawson. Clara, what happened?"

She shuddered and shook her head, burrowing her face into the detective's sweater. She didn't want to think about what had happened. She felt numb all over, heavy too, and stuck, like when you're unable to move in a dream.

Jostling her a little, Jonathon said, "Clara, I need you to tell me."

She liked the way her name sounded coming from his lips.

"Clara, I need you to tell me," he repeated patiently when she didn't speak.

Jonathon clearly wasn't going to give up. Maybe she should just tell him, then he'd leave her alone, and she could close her eyes and sleep. "He was waiting for me."

"Where were you coming from?"

"Work."

"What do you do?"

"'Do'?" she repeated. She felt stunned, just concentrating for a few moments was a struggle.

Taking hold of her shoulders, Jonathon sat her up. "Where do you work?" he repeated.

"Work?" she echoed.

"Clara." He shook her, the movement sending her head snapping back, which made her neck sting sharply, but it also cleared away a few of the cobwebs. "I know it's hard, but try to focus. Where do you work?"

"I own a business. A bookstore." She tried hard to do as he asked and focus.

He gave her an encouraging smile. "Where do you park your car?"

"There's a parking lot around back."

"Do you always park there?"

She nodded; her head was starting to feel heavy, and she wanted more than anything to rest it back down on Jonathon's shoulder.

"Was anyone else around when you went to your car?" the detective continued with his relentless questions.

"Just him."

"Was he waiting for you in your car, or outside it?"

Clara paused, unsure. "I . . . I don't know."

"Yes, you do," Jonathon contradicted firmly. "Think. Did you see him as you walked to your car or did he surprise you once you got in?"

Closing her eyes, she tried to think. "Inside the car," she said at last. "He . . . He had a . . . a knife." Her teeth were beginning to chatter, and she knew it wasn't from the cold. "He cut me." She said it like she couldn't believe it. She *didn't* believe it, didn't believe any of what had happened this afternoon.

"He cut you, but you're okay, Clara; you're safe here."

His firm but gentle tone gave her something to hold on to. She clutched at it desperately, tried to use it to still her trembling body and clear her foggy mind.

"Did he say anything to you?"

"He told me to drive. He kept telling me to drive faster. He wouldn't let me stop. I saw the lights, heard the sirens, and I begged him to let me pull over but he wouldn't. He wouldn't." The last was a sob as tears came in a sudden rush, catching her by surprise. Clara would have been embarrassed if she had enough energy left. Jonathon's arms came around her, and he resumed stroking her hair. Voices bumbled above her like buzzing bees. She didn't bother to attempt to decipher them; her overwhelmed mind was seeking the blissfulness of sleep.

"Clara, the paramedics are here," Jonathon announced as he slid sideways and climbed out of the car.

As the cold air hit her, the shaking intensified. She was starting to feel a little light-headed, and the world swirled around her in a very disconcerting manner. She was carried to an ambulance, set down on a gurney, and quickly covered in blankets. Clara protested with a muted moan when Jonathon went to move away from her. For some reason, he made her feel safe and she didn't want him to leave.

"It's okay, Clara. I can ride with you to the hospital if you like," he soothed.

At the word *hospital*, she snapped out of her shock-induced daze. She was *not* going to the hospital. No way, no how. "I don't need a hospital," she said, trying to make her voice sound strong.

"You're in shock," Jonathon reminded her, his brow creasing in a small frown. "You need to be checked out."

"The paramedics can do that here," she countered.

"Your neck needs to be stitched," Jonathon argued.

"They can do that here," she repeated. The topic wasn't up for discussion. She simply wasn't going to go to a hospital.

"Clara," Jonathon's tone now sounded like he was dealing with a recalcitrant child. "You need medical attention; you probably need to be observed overnight ..."

"I'm okay; I'm feeling much better." To the paramedics, she asked, "Can you stitch the cut for me here?"

One of the paramedics looked curiously from her to Jonathon, probably wondering if there was something between them, given the intimacy their argument implied. "Yes, we can, but it'd be better to get it done at the hospital, get yourself checked out thoroughly."

She forced her lips to curve into a small smile. "Thank you, but I really am okay. If you could just stitch the cut, then I'll be on my way." It occurred to her that she had no way of getting home. Her car was almost definitely evidence, and her purse had been in it. She'd have to ask Jonathon to retrieve it for her, and once he did, she would have her phone to call a cab and money to pay for it.

Shrugging, the paramedic retrieved some supplies and perched beside her. At the sight of the needle he produced, Clara's courage waned. She hated needles even more than she hated hospitals. A terrified little moan slipped from her lips.

"Here." Jonathon was suddenly beside her, holding out his hand. "Squeeze as hard as you need to."

Clara hesitated for a moment. This man made her feel safe, but she didn't know anything about him other than his name and occupation. She'd felt a sudden attraction to him when she'd opened her eyes to find him looming over her. The physical attraction had been reinforced by how kind and gentle he'd been with her. But they didn't know each other, and after today she'd probably never see him again. Getting attached was probably not the smartest of ideas. However, as the para- medic swiped her neck with an alcohol swab and pierced the skin with the needle, she grabbed Jonathon's hand and did indeed squeeze as hard as she could.

"Local anesthetic should have it numb in a moment," the medic informed her.

Scrunching her eyes closed, Clara tried to pretend she was anywhere but here.

"What are your favorite books?" Jonathon's voice asked, close to her ear.

She opened her eyes to stare blankly at him. Books? Why was he asking her about books?

"You said you own a bookshop, I'm guessing because you love to read. What are your favorite books?"

Allowing him to distract her, she could afford to lean on him just a little longer. "I like romances," she admitted, feeling her cheeks heat in embarrassment to be talking about romance with a guy she found herself attracted to.

Jonathon simply smiled at her and asked, "Have you always wanted to own a bookshop?"

Flinching as the medic started to stitch her wound, then coherent thought flew from her mind. Surely the cut wasn't so bad it needed stitches, and it would heal on its own—maybe she should just leave now and go straight home.

"Clara, look at me," Jonathon ordered gently.

Reluctantly, she complied. His face was close to hers; his warm breath brushed her cold cheeks. His eyes were calm and seemed to ooze comfort and control. She let both wash over her and her thumping heart slowed a little.

"Did you always want to own a bookshop?"

She wondered whether he was tired of having to repeat things to her. He didn't appear to be, but surely he must be growing weary of it by now. "Yes." She tried to keep her focus on Jonathon and not on the paramedic and his horrible needle. "I've loved books since I was a very little girl." As a child, books had been her salvation; if she hadn't had them, she didn't know what would have happened to her.

"I love books, too." Jonathon smiled again.

She liked his smile. He said something else, but she couldn't hear it. Everything was getting kind of blurry, and the sensation that she was floating had returned. She'd been doing okay, holding it together, and now suddenly she was quickly losing control. Her overwhelmed mind seemed to have reached its limit, and now it was ready to crash.

Above her, Jonathon's forehead furrowed in concern. "Clara, stay with me."

The words sounded faraway, as though there were miles between them instead of inches.

Jonathon's gaze shifted to the paramedic. "She's going to faint."

He was right; she was going to faint.

And she did.

~

6:58 P.M.

"So you know who he is, right?"

Jonathon glanced up at his partner as she sat down at her desk. Allina Bennett looked less like a cop than any other police officer he'd ever met. They'd been partners for almost a year now, and he was embarrassed to admit that at first, he'd had some doubts about being paired up with her. Allina was in her mid-thirties but looked at least ten years younger—she was barely five-foot-one, with big blue eyes, curly blonde hair, and freckles. Despite her small stature and appearance, Allina was probably the toughest woman he'd ever met.

"Jon?" Allina prodded. She was the only person who called him by that nickname; everyone else used his full name.

"Yeah, I know who he is," he replied. When they'd done a background check on the carjacker, Thomas Karl, they had learned all about his past.

"Do you think it's related to the case?" Allina asked.

His partner was referring to one of their open cases. "Maybe," he answered, thinking it was indeed more than likely, but right now, they had no proof.

At the age of six, Thomas Karl had been abducted by a pair of serial killers who abducted small children, made them pretend to be dolls, and then killed them. The bodies had all been left in the park and had been accompanied by a doll that resembled them. The couple always took a boy and a girl together—the children were always blondes with blue or green eyes, just like the dolls. Over a ten-year span, the couple had killed eighteen children.

Then the killings had abruptly stopped.

Because two of the children had managed to escape.

One of the two children who got away was Thomas Karl.

A couple of months ago, the killings had started up again. Two children had gone missing—both blondes—within days of each other. Then about a month later, their bodies were found in the park with dolls. Shortly after, another little boy and girl had been taken, and so far, their bodies hadn't turned up. They were hoping the children were still alive.

Twenty years between killings, they weren't sure whether the original killing pair had returned or whether a copycat had taken their place. Now that Thomas Karl, one of the only two people who knew the identities of the couple, had turned up on their radar, carjacking someone, then shooting three cops, it seemed plausible that he could be the one replicating the original crimes. Especially since . . .

"And you know who she is?" Allina continued.

He drew in a slow breath. "She's the other one," he murmured.

Clara Candella was the other child who had escaped the Doll Killers alongside Thomas Karl. She too had been six when she'd been abducted, and she and Thomas had been missing almost six weeks before they were found, badly malnourished and dehydrated, wandering alone at the side of a road.

"They were together, the only two surviving victims, just months after the killings started up again," Allina stated the obvious.

Narrowing his eyes at her, he replied, "He carjacked her."

"As far as we know."

"He cut her, she was bleeding; you saw that yourself," he reminded his partner.

"Did she mention that she knew the man who carjacked her?"

"She was in shock, getting anything out of her was a struggle." He'd been concerned about Clara from the moment she'd first stepped from her vehicle. In his car, when he'd been questioning her, he'd had to repeat things to her several times to get answers. Her eyes had been glassy and vacant, her voice soft and far away, and she had struggled to focus on anything he'd said to her. And then in the ambulance, just when he'd thought her mind was starting to clear, and she was starting to pull it together, she had fainted. He had seen it coming—all of a sudden her already pale face had drained of color, her eyes had gone all unfocused, and then she was gone. In a way, he'd been glad she'd passed out because then she hadn't been able to protest being taken to the hospital.

Before that, though, he had noticed something in her that indicated the attraction he'd felt for her was mutual. The way she'd looked at him, been comforted by him, the way her cheeks had turned pink with embarrassment when she'd told him she liked romance books. Perhaps, depending on what her relationship to Thomas Karl turned out to be, he would think about asking her out. The carjacking case was closed. Thomas was dead, and she wouldn't be a victim in an open case he was working on—there was nothing preventing him pursuing things with her.

"The two of them together, though, right when the doll murders have started up again; we can't deny the possibility that Thomas and Clara were working together and they were the ones behind the latest abductions and murders," Allina pointed out.

"Then why would he carjack and hurt her?" Jonathon felt it in his bones that Clara was nothing more than an innocent victim. Again.

Allina shrugged. "Maybe they were working together and then she got cold feet, wanted to pull out, and he wouldn't let her. Or since the original killings were committed by a pair, maybe Thomas started on his own but wanted to replicate things properly so he tracked down his old doll partner and tried to force her to help him and she refused, so he hurt her," she suggested.

To Jonathon, that sounded a lot more plausible. He didn't like the idea of anyone being a threat to Clara's safety. Although if Thomas had appointed himself the reincarnation of the Doll Killers, now that he was dead, that meant the two children he'd recently abducted were left all alone. Which meant that Clara was their best bet at learning anything that might help them find the children before it was too late. She'd been the last person to talk to Thomas before he died—hopefully, he'd said something that would help them.

As if reading his mind, Allina said, "We need to talk to Clara."

Clara had still been unconscious when the ambulance had left to take her to the hospital. Jonathon doubted that they would get anything useful out of her tonight, but first thing tomorrow morning, they'd visit her. He may be physically attracted to Clara Candella, but absolutely nothing was going to stop him from getting the answers he needed to solve this case.

CHAPTER

Two

February 8th
1:30 A.M.

She was so cold.

Cold and hungry and thirsty, and she just wanted to go home.

Clara knew she'd made a mistake when she'd walked away from her mother at the supermarket, but now she didn't know how to make it right.

She wanted her mother.

Tommy did, too. He was always crying for his mom. She tried to help him, but she didn't know what to do.

Clara shivered.

The room was too cold.

It was dark in here, too, and Clara was scared of the dark.

Footsteps sounded on the stairs.

They were coming.

She was so frightened; she wanted to hide, but there wasn't

anywhere to go up here where they wouldn't find her, and she should know she'd been here for so long.

The lock turned, and the sound seemed so loud—too loud.

The door creaked open, but no one was there.

Surprised, Clara took a step toward the open door—perhaps she could escape through it and finally go home.

She took another step but something stopped her. Something cold and sharp at her neck.

She wasn't in the attic anymore. Now she was in a car.

"I'm sorry, Clara."

Something wet and sticky began to flow down her neck.

Blood.

A bang as loud as an explosion resonated through the vehicle.

For some reason, Clara knew what she was going to see even before she turned around.

She didn't want to turn. She didn't want to see it. And yet, turn she did.

Tommy was lying on the backseat covered in blood.

So much blood.

It was everywhere.

Flooding the car.

"Tommy!" she screamed.

He didn't respond.

"Why, Tommy, why?" she sobbed.

"Clara!"

Someone was shaking her.

"Clara!"

She woke up with a gasp and bolted upright, panting and disoriented.

"Clara, are you with me?"

The room faded in and out a couple of times before stilling, and she realized it was her bedroom. She wasn't still trapped in that horrible attic, or in her car with Tommy.

"Clara? Are you okay?"

She focused her gaze on the face in front of her. She half expected it to be Tommy's, but it was her sister's instead.

Naomi's brown eyes were brimming with concern as they searched her face. "You with me, Clara? Are you okay?"

"Yeah," it came out all shaky, probably because she wasn't okay, but she didn't want to worry her sister further. When she'd woken up in the hospital emergency room, her sister had been by her side. Naomi had stayed with her when she'd gone for a head scan. Clara had been adamant that she hadn't hit her head when Jonathon had tackled her, but given that she'd been unconscious for almost thirty minutes, the doctors had insisted. Of course, the scan had been clear—the reason she'd passed out was Tommy. When she had finally been released, Naomi had driven her home and insisted on spending the night despite Clara's protestations that she would be perfectly okay on her own.

"It was just a nightmare, honey." Naomi reached over and tucked Clara's hair behind her ear.

Tears were brimming in her eyes, and she shook her head. "No, it wasn't—Tommy really is dead."

Her sister didn't say anything, just hugged her. Naomi was always so calm, so in control. Clara wished that they'd always been part of each other's lives, but they'd only gotten to know one another in the last ten years. She and Naomi were half-sisters; they had the same father but different mothers. Her mother had had an affair that produced Clara. The affair had broken up her mother's marriage, and she'd been divorced before Clara's first birthday. As a child, she had spent most of her time with her mother and two older half-brothers, but she had spent one weekend a month with her father. On visits to her father, she was never allowed to go to his home—his wife wouldn't allow it. Instead, the two of them would stay at a hotel. As such, she never got to know her father's three other children. Naomi's mother had also cheated on her husband, an act that produced Naomi. Unlike Clara's family, Naomi's had stayed together after the affair, but her experience with their father was the same.

Clara lifted her head from her sister's shoulder. She wiped the tears from her cold and clammy face. "Why would Tommy do that?" she begged Naomi.

"I don't know, honey," Naomi replied. "You were the one who was with him in the car."

When she'd asked her sister at the hospital how long the car chase had lasted, she'd been surprised to learn it was only an hour and a half. She could have sworn it was so much longer. Those ninety minutes had felt more like ninety hours.

"Did he say anything to you?"

"Just that he wanted to show me something." Clara could feel fresh tears building, and a hysterical swirling was beginning in her stomach. "He was waiting for me in my car with a knife and a gun. He told me to drive but I said no, and I asked him what was wrong. He didn't answer, he just cut me," she finished in disbelief. "How could Tommy hurt me? He was my friend—at least I thought he was my friend."

"I don't know why he hurt you. What about while you were driving, did he say anything then?"

"Just to go faster and that I couldn't stop even though the cops were chasing us. He shot at them, Naomi. He hit three cops. He had to know they'd shoot back."

"Maybe he wanted them to," Naomi suggested gently.

Her shock-dulled mind hadn't thought of that. "You think he committed suicide by cop?" she gasped.

"I don't know. Sorry I keep saying that, but I don't have any answers for you. I wish I did, but I don't." Naomi looked pained. Clara knew her sister always wanted to fix everything for everyone.

"Maybe I could have stopped it ..."

"Clara, no . . ."

"Yes," she contradicted. "In the car, I should have tried harder to get him to talk. I should have made more of an effort to spend time with him lately, only I've been so busy with work. I should have stopped him from shooting at the cops. He's dead—Tommy's dead because of me."

"Clara, that's ridiculous, and you know it," Naomi sternly rebuked.

"No, it's not." The hysteria in her stomach was bubbling up. Tommy was one of her best friends; they'd been through something horrific together, and they'd survived—the bond between them could never be broken. But she'd let him down. Tommy had obviously needed help, and she hadn't even noticed. "It's my fault. If I'd done something differently, then Tommy might still be alive."

Why hadn't she insisted that Tommy tell her where he wanted to take her?

Why hadn't she insisted that she wasn't going anywhere with him? Why hadn't she insisted that he put the gun and knife away?

Why hadn't she said something to Jonathon the second she stepped out of the car so he could stop Tommy before he even started shooting?

"I don't like to hear you talk that way," her sister reprimanded. "Tommy is an adult; he's responsible for his own choices. He couldn't use what happened to him as a kid as an excuse for poor decision making forever. You went through the same thing, and you've never used it as an excuse not to continue with your life."

That sobered Clara a little. She had indeed used what happened to her as an excuse for not doing lots of things—she just didn't share that with her family. She wanted them to think that she was strong, that she'd been able to move past her childhood trauma. Of course, in a lot of ways she had moved on—but how could something so big not make an impact on her and on her life?

"How about I get you some painkillers, and then you try and get some more sleep?" Naomi suggested.

"No, I can't go back to sleep now." Clara knew sleep would almost certainly bring with it more nightmares. She hadn't dreamed of what had happened to her as a child in years, but Tommy carjacking her and his subsequent death must have unlocked the door holding those dreams at bay, allowing them to seep back in. The painkillers, however, were negotiable. She hadn't been seriously hurt when Jonathon had tackled her, but she must have gotten some bruises. She hadn't noticed them yesterday, but her body had stiffened while she'd been sleeping and now it was achy all over. Not that she was complaining. If Jonathon hadn't tackled her when he did, then she almost definitely would have been hit by one of the bullets from Tommy's gun.

Naomi looked like she wanted to protest, but instead, she said, "Okay then, I'll go and put the kettle on and make some tea, and we can watch some old movies."

"You don't have to stay up with me; you should go back to bed. I'll be okay."

Her sister just looked at her like she was an idiot and moved to stand. "I'll go pick out something from your Disney collection."

Clara grabbed her hand. "Thanks, Naomi. I'm really lucky to have a sister like you."

She was, she thought, as she dragged herself from the bed and reached for her robe. Naomi would help her find out what had made Tommy behave in such a bizarre manner. And Clara needed to know. She and Tommy had shared a traumatic experience, they'd become friends, spent lots of time together over the years, helped each other forget their childhood ordeal—she owed it to her friend to find out what had happened to him.

∽

9:11 A.M.

"You're attracted to Clara Candella, aren't you?" Allina asked as they climbed from their car in front of Clara's house.

"Yes," Jonathon admitted. "But right now, nothing is more important to me than solving this case."

"She might be involved," his partner reminded him.

"If she is, then I'll cross that bridge when I come to it. Right now, though, she's nothing more than a victim. And we don't even know if she has had anything to do with Thomas Karl in the twenty-three years since they were kidnapped. For all we know, it's the first time she'd seen him since they were children."

"Well, until we know more, just keep things professional," Allina warned.

Jonathon feared it was already too late for professional. He'd held the woman in his arms yesterday. He hadn't held her out of necessity or as part of his professional responsibilities—he'd held her because he wanted to. Last night he'd lain in bed for hours thinking about her. About how his words and his touch had calmed her. About how she'd suffered as a child and he hated the thought of her suffering all over again. Still, despite all that, he meant what he'd just told his partner—

nothing in the world right now was more important to him than finding the Doll Killers, regardless of whether Thomas Karl was involved. He had a vested interest in this case, and he was going to see to it that no other children suffered because of a sick obsession with dolls.

"Jonathon?" Allina prodded.

"Yeah, professional." He nodded vaguely, studying Clara's house. It looked like something out of a fairy tale. The house was small, double story, built from stone, with vines crawling over half of it. The garden was elaborate, full of bushes and shrubs and trees, and Jonathon guessed that in the spring it would be a virtual rainbow of colorful flowers. He thought the house perfectly suited Clara.

"I think it would be best if I lead the interview," Allina was saying. "From what I saw yesterday, Clara is already too attached to you, and given that you're attracted to her, I'm not sure that you're going to be able to push her in the event that she isn't forthcoming with answers."

Jonathon didn't agree—attracted to Clara or not, nothing was going to stop him from getting the information he needed to help him solve this case, but he'd let Allina take the lead if that was what she wanted. "Sure." He nodded as he rapped on the door. It inched open a moment later. "Clara, we need . . . Oh," he broke off. "You're not Clara."

"What an astute observation," the woman at the door said dryly. She looked identical to Clara—around the same height, only she was toned and muscled, had the same blonde hair except it only hung to her shoulders, and her facial features were the same, only her eyes were brown instead of green.

"I didn't know Clara had a twin sister," he said.

"She doesn't; we aren't twins. More like some kind of weird variant on triplets," the woman replied.

"Care to explain?" he asked when it became clear she wasn't going to say more.

She shrugged disinterestedly. "Clara and I have the same father, but different mothers—both of us were conceived when our mothers cheated on their husbands. Even though we're half-sisters, we were born on the same day, as was our father's legitimate daughter. All three of us look the same and share a birthday, so we're triplets, but we aren't."

Interesting family dynamics. "And your name is?"

"Naomi Candella."

"You both have your father's last name?" That seemed unusual given the circumstances of their conceptions.

"Yep. Apparently, our father was most insistent that we take his name."

So far Naomi hadn't allowed them entrance to the house and it didn't seem as though she were inclined to do so of her own volition. "May we come in? We need to speak with your sister."

Somewhat reluctantly, she opened the door and allowed them to enter. The downstairs was one big room. To their left was a kitchen and a door that Jonathon presumed led to a laundry room; immediately in front of them was a large dining table, and the right half of the room had three couches grouped in front of a large fireplace. Doors on the opposite wall led out to a decked area, beyond which was a garden that was just as beautiful as the front one. By every available bit of wall that wasn't occupied by a window or a door, there was a bookcase. Jonathon counted at least eleven—each one filled to the brim with books.

Just as the outside of the house had suited Clara, so did the inside. All the furniture appeared to be antique, but nothing matched. Each of the eight chairs at the table were a different style and made from a different type of wood. Same with the bookcases; he spotted some in oak, walnut, maple, and mahogany. The couches were all different, and although there were probably six or seven little tables about the large room, none of them were the same. Even the walls were all painted a different color. It was like Clara took a piece of each of the books she loved and made them a part of her life.

All the wood was making him nostalgic. As a kid, he'd spent hours in his grandfather's shed helping the old man build things. His papa had been an enthusiastic carpenter. He didn't care what he made; he just loved using his hands to create something that his family could enjoy. Together they had built chairs and tables, beds and dressers, boxes and birdhouses. His grandfather had passed away when Jonathon was fourteen, and he hadn't built anything since. But standing here in Clara's home, the desire to build something for her was making him glad he'd kept his grandfather's tools.

"You may as well sit," Naomi told them, closing the front door.

"Where's Clara?" he asked.

"Upstairs, taking a shower. Look, she's still really shaken up about yesterday. Can't you come back and question her another time?" her sister asked, looking genuinely concerned.

"I wish we could, but we really need to talk to her now—we weren't able to get a lot out of her yesterday," he replied sympathetically.

"I'm just not sure she's up to it," Naomi protested.

"I'm up to it."

The voice on the stairs had all three of their heads swiveling to face it. Clara was slowly making her way downstairs, her blonde hair still wet, she was dressed in sweats, and the bright white bandage on her neck was the same color as her too pale skin. She looked like she should be in bed, and Jonathon's desire to get answers from her wavered.

"Really, I'm fine, Naomi," Clara assured her sister as she came and took a seat at the table. "Go, ask your questions." Despite her obvious fatigue, her green eyes were clear and alert.

Taking the seat beside her, Jonathon said, "You didn't tell me yesterday that you knew the man who carjacked you." He could feel his partner's frustration that he'd begun the questioning, but Allina didn't say anything; she just took a seat at the table.

Rubbing her fingers on her temple, Clara responded, "I'm sorry, I don't really remember much of anything after I got in my car yesterday afternoon. I know that I talked with you, but it was all fuzzy. I couldn't concentrate properly."

"You were in shock," he reminded her.

"She's still in shock," Naomi muttered, but nobody—including her sister—paid her any attention.

"Yesterday you said that all Thomas said to you was to drive, and that he wouldn't let you stop when you wanted to when we started following you."

Clara nodded slowly.

"Did he say anything else?"

"Just that he wanted to show me something." A shudder wracked her thin frame.

"But you knew it was Thomas Karl?" he confirmed.

She nodded again, as her eyes started to grow misty with a mixture of tears and dismay.

"How did you know Thomas?" he continued.

At the question, her eyes cleared instantly. "If you're asking me that, then you already know."

"What happened to her as a child is off limits," Naomi quipped, her brown eyes shooting arrows at them.

"I wish it were, but unfortunately the doll murders have started up again," he said gently.

At his words, Clara went completely still; her eyes glazed over, and she barely even looked like she was breathing. Her sister, on the other hand, bounded to her feet and began to pace, running her hands through her hair and shaking her head.

"It's been over twenty years," Naomi protested. "Why would they start killing again? It doesn't make any sense."

Jonathon ignored her for the moment. Clara's stillness was scaring him. He reached for her shoulder and gave her a small shake. "Clara? Can you hear me?"

Her eyes turned to his, and she began to tremble. "No. It's over. They stopped," she said, her voice heartbreakingly childlike, and he hated himself for making her relive her worst nightmare.

"I'm sorry, Clara. They did stop, but they started again a few months ago."

"How many so far?" Naomi asked.

"Two dead, another two taken," he replied.

"The dolls?" Naomi stopped her frenetic pacing to pierce him with a horrified glare.

"They were found with the bodies," he confirmed.

Wrapping her arms around her middle, Clara whispered, "I don't understand. Why start again now?"

"We're not sure it is the original killers," he ventured, unsure how she would take the accusation against Thomas.

Her reaction was so instantaneous that it caught him off guard. Clara bounded to her feet so quickly her chair clattered to the floor. "You think *Thomas* has been abducting and killing children in the same way as the people who took us?" her voice brimmed with incredulity.

"Tommy would *never* hurt anyone. How dare you even suggest such a thing! You don't even know Tommy."

"You're right, I don't, but you do..."

"I am *not* helping you pin this on my friend," she interrupted. "Besides, the people who took us worked as a team—if someone started up the murders again, then wouldn't they be working as a team? So why would Tommy be doing this alone?" she demanded.

This time it was Naomi who caught on first. "Get out," she said as she stalked to the door and threw it open.

"What?" Clara cast her sister a confused glance.

"They think it's you," Naomi ground out. "They think you're Tommy's partner."

Clara recoiled as though she'd been slapped. Pain and betrayal filled her eyes, and pink splashed her pale cheeks. "You . . . You think I'm a killer? You think I'd hurt children? After what happened to me?"

"We have more questions, Clara," Allina spoke for the first time. "Maybe it would be best if we ask them down at the station."

Naomi snapped immediately into protective mode. "Is my sister under arrest?" she demanded.

"No," Jonathon answered firmly. "No," he repeated, this time directing it to Clara.

"Then we're not going anywhere with you," Naomi challenged.

"It's okay, Naomi," Clara's voice was now icy cold and chillingly calm. "I want to go. I want to answer their questions, so I never have to see them again. I'll get dressed, and we'll meet you there in an hour."

With that, she turned and headed back upstairs. The finality with which she said that she never wanted to see him again left Jonathon feeling horribly empty. He'd thought he wanted to solve this case no matter what the cost. If the cost turned out to be losing his chance with Clara, could he live with that?

~

9:46 A.M.

. . .

Katie was bored.

She hated having to tag along with her mom and baby brother running errands. But this was the price she had to pay to get a day off school. She'd told her mom she had a sore tummy, but really she just hadn't wanted to go to school.

It was all Becca Stevens' fault.

Becca and her family had moved away at the end of first grade. That would have been fine; only it messed things up with their friends. Now there were three of them. And three was an odd number; they'd learned about odd and even numbers in math class. Even numbers went together in pairs, but odd numbers meant someone was always left out. And right now, *she* was the one who kept getting left out.

It wasn't fair.

Jasmine was *her* best friend. They'd been best friends since kindergarten, but now that Becca was gone, Kelly wanted Jasmine to be her best friend. It wasn't her fault that Becca had moved; why should she lose her best friend because of it?

And Katie was scared that she *was* going to lose her best friend.

Jasmine and Kelly were always whispering secrets to each other. They sat next to each other in class. They were working on a project together while she was stuck working with Missy Fendrake. Missy Fendrake! The weird girl that no one played with because she hardly ever talked, but was always laughing at everything, and Katie was going to have to be her partner! Maybe she'd even have to go to Missy's house or have Missy come to hers! Everyone in their class was going to tease her.

And then yesterday, as if being Missy's project partner wasn't enough, Jasmine and Kelly said she couldn't play with them. Katie had been so shocked; she hadn't known what to do. She had just stood there and then Jasmine and Kelly had laughed at her. Embarrassed, she had gone running off and hid in the library for the rest of lunchtime.

How could she go back to school now?

She couldn't.

She hated second grade.

She hated school.

If she could manage it, she would never set foot in that place again.

"Katie," her mom's angry voice broke into her thoughts.

Blinking, she found her mom frowning at her. She had been too busy thinking about her problems at school that she couldn't even remember what shop they were in. They'd been to so many already this morning; now they were in the bank. Katie hated the bank most of all. There was always a long line, and there was nothing fun to look at while you waited.

"Would you stop daydreaming?" her mom snapped. "I need you to watch Kevin while I wait in line; he's tired of sitting in his stroller."

Kevin's sticky little hand was thrust into hers, and her mom moved off to take her place at the end of the line. Katie didn't like her little brother. Her dad kept telling her that one day she would, one day she'd love him, one day she'd be glad to have a sibling, but so far that day hadn't arrived.

Things had been better when it was just her and her parents—they hadn't needed anyone else. Only her mommy had disagreed. After Katie was born, her mom wanted more kids, but for some reason, she couldn't have them. So, when Katie was five, they had decided to adopt, and that's how Kevin had joined their family. Kevin was eighteen months old now, and he was all her mom ever talked about.

Kevin was all her mom wanted.

She and her mom never did things together anymore; her mom was always too busy with Kevin. All Katie ever heard was Kevin this or Kevin that. Since Kevin came to live with them, her mom hadn't read her stories or helped her with her homework or curled up on the couch on Saturday mornings to watch cartoons and have a pajama day. She wanted her mom back.

It just wasn't fair, Katie sulked.

Her brother was tugging on her hand, trying to free his from her grip, and squealing miserably because she wouldn't let him go. Annoyed, she released his hand. Why should she have to watch him anyway? That was her mom's job. Her mom was the one who wanted Kevin; not her. And so what if he didn't want to sit in his stroller anymore? She had to do things all the time that she didn't want to do. Why should Kevin be any different?

Free at last, Kevin toddled off and crawled under a table, picking up something from the floor. Glancing at her mother, when she saw there were still seven people ahead of her in the line, Katie wandered to the window. The parking lot was full. Everyone seemed to be out today running errands. She watched the cars as they parked and circled the busy lot.

Katie couldn't wait until she was old enough to learn to drive. Sometimes, when her mommy was busy with Kevin, her daddy would let her sit on his lap in the car and pretend to drive it up and down their driveway. When she had a license and her own car, she'd be able to do whatever she wanted, whenever she wanted to do it. She wouldn't have to wait for her mom or dad to take her places; she'd be free.

Wondering whether her mother would consider homeschooling her, Katie turned to check on Kevin and her heart stopped.

He was gone.

Terror welled up inside her and she looked to her mom to see if she'd noticed. But her mother hadn't. She had her phone out and was busily typing away.

That gave her time.

Kevin couldn't have gone far; he was only a baby.

Scanning the bank, she couldn't see him anywhere.

Why, oh, why hadn't she watched him?

He wasn't so bad as far as annoying, attention-hogging babies went. Sometimes he wanted to sit in her lap and listen to her read him stories. Sometimes he cried because she wouldn't sit down and play trains with him. And sometimes he gave her great big, wet, sticky kisses on her cheek. She pretended not to like it when he did that, always complained and went running off to wash her face, but deep down she did kind of like it.

Where was he?

Maybe he'd gone outside? Kevin loved the snow. He was always sneaking out of the house whenever someone, usually her, left a door open so he could crawl through it and hold it in his chubby little hands and study it.

Running outside, Katie looked up and down the strip mall and let out a gigantic sigh of relief.

There he was.

An old lady was holding Kevin and looking around as though searching for who he belonged to.

Katie ran up to her and threw her arms around the lady's waist. "Oh thank you, thank you, thank you," she gushed.

"Does he belong to you, dear?" the lady asked.

"Yes, I was supposed to be watching him for my mom while she was in line in the bank, but I got distracted for just a second, and when I looked up, he was gone," Katie rambled, grabbing hold of Kevin's hand as he grabbed at her hair.

"Tsk, tsk," the lady shook her head. "Children watching children, what is the world coming to?"

"Thank you so much for finding him," she said as she reached for her brother, but the woman didn't release him.

"He's your brother is he, dear?"

"Yes." She wanted to just grab Kevin and run back inside before their mother noticed they were missing, but this woman had saved her brother before he'd been able to crawl into the road and get hit by a car. She couldn't just run off without being polite.

"He doesn't look much like you."

"He's adopted," she explained, unsure why the woman cared that they didn't look alike. Because Kevin was adopted, they didn't share any physical features. Katie was pale-skinned with blonde hair and blue eyes; her brother had olive skin with dark hair and eyes. Maybe the old lady thought Katie was lying and Kevin wasn't her brother after all.

"Perhaps I should talk to your mother about the dangers of leaving a little girl to watch over her baby brother," the old lady said, and took a step toward the bank.

"No, please don't tell her. I'll get in trouble," Katie begged. Why couldn't the woman just give her Kevin and let her go? An uneasy feeling began to brew in her tummy. Something felt wrong; she just couldn't figure out what it was.

Then it hit her.

Kevin's knees were dry.

Her brother could walk, but when he wanted to get someplace fast, he crawled. And whenever he escaped from their house to look at the snow, he always moved quickly. He would have crawled out of the bank.

Therefore, his knees should be wet from crawling along the wet, snowy, footpath. But his knees were dry. Kevin hadn't crawled from the bank on his own. Someone had carried him out.

Eyes growing wide, she looked up at the old lady and was about to demand she give her Kevin back, or she was going to scream for help when something jabbed her in the arm.

The world went swirling around her.

And then she fell.

~

10:17 A.M.

"Let me make this perfectly clear," Jonathon announced as he entered the small interview room that someone had set them up in when they'd arrived at the police station twenty minutes ago. "I do *not* think that you are involved in the recent copycat doll killer abduction and murders. But you and Thomas Karl were the only two victims who survived. After you escaped, the murders stopped. Then suddenly, after twenty years, the killings start again, and then you get carjacked by the other survivor, who gets himself killed by shooting at the police. You're all that's left; you're the only link that we have. Surely you can understand why we need to talk to you?"

Clara simply glowered at him. What a jerk. How could her opinion of Detective Jonathon Dawson change so dramatically in less than twenty-four hours? Just yesterday he had been the only thing keeping her anchored when her world had been swirling around her, and now she viewed him as possibly the most despicable person on the planet.

How could his touch, his voice, have ever calmed her? Now both grated on her nerves like fingernails on a chalkboard. She didn't want to be sitting here listening to him, but what choice did she have? They were going to interview her at some point, so she may as well just get it over with.

Naomi had insisted on coming with her, much to Clara's relief. She didn't think she could face Jonathon and his partner on her own, especially given the topic they wanted to question her about. Her sister was annoyed that she'd agreed to come. They'd argued about it on the drive here, but no matter how frustrated Naomi was, Clara knew her sister would support her in whatever way she could.

"Clara, you understand, don't you?" Jonathon looked pained by the idea she might hold this against him.

Well too bad for him, she did hold it against him. He couldn't go from cradling her in his arms to all but accusing her of replicating the crimes she had been a victim of over twenty years ago.

"Clara?" Jonathon prodded, his gaze intent.

"Sure, whatever. Can we just get on with it?" She was tired and sore, and she had to stop by the bookshop to catch up on a few things before she could go home and get some rest.

Jonathon looked hurt but nodded and turned his expression professional. "Why don't we start by going over your abduction? I'm sorry, I know it must be hard to talk about, but we need to know if we're dealing with a copycat or the same perpetrators."

"No." She wasn't going to relive that horror again. She'd boxed it away many years ago and she had no intention of opening the lid.

Confused, Jonathon asked, "No, what?"

"No, I'm not going to talk about what happened to me when I was six. You have access to the case files, which include the statement I gave to the police at the time. I see no need for you to ask me questions when you already have my answers." She had to fight to keep her voice calm, but she managed it.

"If we thought we could get all the information we needed from your statement, we wouldn't have asked you to come down here, Ms. Candella." Jonathon's partner looked annoyed.

"I'm sorry, I don't think I got your name," she addressed the other woman. Jonathon's partner looked too young to be a cop, in every way except her eyes. Her eyes looked old. Old and there was something else there. Deep in the blue depths was pain. Haunted pain.

"Detective Bennett."

"Detective Bennett, I don't know what else you want me to tell you that isn't already in my statement."

"Your statement was vague," Jonathon noted. "Both yours and

Thomas'. You hardly said anything, either about your time there, or how you managed to escape."

"I told what I remembered," she replied.

"You were gone for six weeks, Clara," Jonathon reminded her as if she didn't know that already. "You must know more than you told the police."

So you would think, at least. "I told everything I know."

"So all you remember is being cold and hungry and locked in an attic?" Detective Bennett raised a suspicious blonde eyebrow.

"Yes." And those memories had haunted her dreams every night those first few months after she had returned home.

"And you have no idea how you and Thomas escaped?"

"No." All she remembered was being scared as footsteps sounded on the stairs and then the next thing she knew she and Tommy were walking down a road, and someone was stopping to ask if they were okay.

"My sister has answered your questions. Look at her, she should be home resting. Come on, Clara; we're leaving," Naomi stood, tugging on Clara's arm as she did so.

"Wait, just look at this."

Jonathon thrust the picture at her, and she took it without thinking.

And immediately wished she hadn't.

With the photo clutched in her hand, she sunk back down into her seat.

"That was low," Naomi growled at the detectives as she saw what Clara clutched in her hands.

"I'm sorry." Jonathon did indeed sound contrite. "I don't want to upset your sister, but those children deserve justice, and so does she."

Clara couldn't tear her gaze from the photo. Two little blonde children sat side by side on a park bench. A boy and a girl. Each had a doll perched on their lap. The dolls resembled the children, or perhaps it was the other way around, and the children resembled the dolls.

The children were dead.

They'd been murdered by the Doll Killers.

Without saying a word, Jonathon lay two other pictures down in front of her.

Against her will, her hand moved to pick them up.

Unfortunately, they showed exactly what she thought they would.

"Clara, don't; they're trying to manipulate you," Naomi protested.

She knew that and yet still she couldn't take her eyes off the smiling little faces. The children were alive in these pictures, their happy little faces full of energy and life. "How old?" she asked, her voice sounding hollow and shaky and nothing like she usually sounded.

"Eight and seven," Jonathon answered softly.

"Names?"

"Clara, don't torture yourself," Naomi begged.

"Lottie Hatcher and Paul Owen."

Two more children killed by the same people who would have ended her life if she hadn't escaped. Or by someone depraved enough to want to copy the crimes.

Jonathon laid another two pictures down on the table, and another two beaming little children looked up at her.

"That's Lindsey Peters and Kent Mason; they're both eight. They've been missing almost a month."

A month. To a child, it felt more like a year. She knew. Just like she knew what it was like to be trapped and praying that someone would come and find you, save you, only no one ever came. Only *them*.

"Do you see now, Clara, why we need to know anything you can tell us?"

Squeezing her eyes close, Clara responded, "I'm sorry, I don't know anything else."

"You really don't remember?" Jonathon sounded surprised.

"I'm sorry." She'd always been glad her brain had closed off those memories, but now for the first time in twenty-three years she was wishing it hadn't.

"You have nothing to be sorry for, Clara," her sister rebuked. "You were six years old and traumatized; your mind did what it had to so that you could function."

"Clara." Jonathon moved closer to her, and she was beyond irritated with herself when his proximity comforted her. "Look at me," he prompted.

Reluctantly, she did, and the raw understanding in his eyes warmed her heart in a way it shouldn't. It was as if he put her under some spell.

"What about Thomas? His statement is as vague as yours. Did you two discuss not telling the police anything, or did he not remember what happened as well?"

"We didn't discuss anything, at least that I remember. I really don't know what Thomas told the police."

"But you kept in contact with Thomas?" Continuing when she nodded, he asked, "Did you two ever discuss it?"

"No, never. I never talked to anyone about it, not even Naomi or my brothers."

"Tell us about Thomas," Detective Bennett all but demanded.

Narrowing her eyes at the woman, Clara snapped, "I'm not helping you pin this on my friend."

"We're not asking you to," Jonathon soothed. "Just tell us about him."

"Tommy really struggled to fit in," Clara began, still suspicious of their motives, but perhaps if they came to understand Tommy, they would realize he wasn't a killer. "He was very sensitive and emotional and he got teased a lot at school. He was very smart, but for a while, he didn't know what he wanted to do with his life. His dad wanted him to become an accountant, like him, but Tommy didn't love numbers; he loved art. Once he got into that, things finally settled down for him."

"Have you met Thomas?" Detective Bennett asked Naomi.

"A couple of times, but he was pretty shy; he never really said more than hello," Naomi replied.

"Did he ever see a psychiatrist? Take medication? Suffer from depression?" Jonathon asked.

"We both did," she said softly. The darkest time in her life had been just after graduating high school. Her brothers were both busy with their lives, she hadn't known what she wanted to do with her own life, and she'd quickly started falling into a deep depression. But then she'd met Naomi, and the two of them had hit it off, instantly feeling the sisterly bond even though they'd just met. It had been her sister who had encouraged her to follow her dream and open a book-store. That had given her focus and drive, and she had managed to shake off the dark bonds of depression that had been holding her down.

"Before yesterday, when was the last time you saw Thomas?" Detective Bennett asked.

"Maybe six months ago," she guessed. She'd been busy lately and hadn't had time for anything, even friends. "Tommy suffered because of what they did to us, but he would *never* hurt another kid. If the killings have started up again, then it must be *them*. The ones who took us, who killed all those other kids."

"It's been twenty-three years since the killings stopped, and they'd been going ten years before that, that makes thirty-three years, depending on how old the killers were when the first pair of children were taken, they may be too old to have committed the most recent murders," Jonathon explained.

"You said you don't remember much about your time being held captive, and you don't remember how you managed to escape, but do you remember your abductors?" Detective Bennett's blue eyes clearly said she believed that Clara was lying and remembered a whole lot more than she was saying.

"No."

"But you remembered enough to tell the police that there were two of them," Jonathon reminded her. "Before that, they were working under the assumption that it was a single killer. You and Thomas told them that it was a male and female pair who took you."

"A man and woman, that's all I can tell you about them."

"We just need an age," Detective Bennett persisted. "You say that Thomas wouldn't have committed these crimes, that it was the original killers, so we need to know whether that's a viable possibility. If you can give us an approximate age of the people who took you, then it will help us discount or confirm your theory."

"Old, but I was six; everyone over the age of about thirteen looked old." She desperately wanted to convince them that Thomas was not their killer, no matter how sick it made her to think that the people who hurt her were still out there hurting other children. But she sincerely didn't remember anything about the people who held her prisoner for six weeks beyond that they were a man and a woman.

"What about the abduction itself?" Jonathon asked.

Her whole body froze as though it had been turned to ice. "What about it?" she tried to keep her voice steady but feared she failed.

"You don't remember much about anything else. Do you remember how you were taken?"

Clara could feel herself shutting down. There was no way on earth she was talking about that. With anyone. Ever.

~

10:48 A.M.

"Come on, hurry up," Daniel urged his girlfriend.

"I'm coming," Tamara snapped.

"We don't have long," he reminded her. His wife would notice if he was gone for longer than ten to fifteen minutes.

"I said, I'm coming," Tamara growled again.

Not liking the look on her face, Daniel quickly gentled his voice, "I'm sorry, Tam. It won't always be like this; I promise." If he didn't stay on Tamara's good side, then she wasn't going to put out. And he already had that problem with his wife. What was the point of having a girlfriend if she wasn't going to be willing to have sex all the time?

"You keep saying that," Tamara grumbled. "But when are you going to leave her so we can be together?"

"Soon, baby, real soon." He reached for her hand and squeezed. Daniel was happy to tell her whatever she wanted to hear, but he had no intention of leaving his wife. That would cost him *way* too much money. Too bad he'd made his money after he was married—if he'd made it big before, he would have gone with a pre-nuptial agreement. It wasn't fair. His lazy wife hadn't contributed a single thing to his business; all she did was hang around the house all day. Their kid was seven, and he was in school most of the time. Why couldn't she get a job? She said that cooking and cleaning and laundry were a job, but she wasn't even good at any of those things.

And even if he did ditch his wife, what good would it do him to hook straight up with someone else? That would just be exchanging one set of problems for another. Women were all the same. They were all lazy, complaining losers. Good for only one thing. And since his wife had lost interest in him after their son was born, he'd had to start looking elsewhere to get his needs attended to. Hence the need for a girl-friend. Unfortunately, the downside to having a mistress was that time with her was limited. He worked long hours, had obligations at home, and very little time for fun.

Today, though, he'd needed some relaxation time. Tamara had been hounding him to spend time with her, and the wife had been hounding him to spend some time with her and the kid, so he had come up with the brilliant idea of bringing the two together. He'd told his wife to take their son out of school for the day so they could have family time at the park. Then once they'd gotten here, he'd said he'd forgotten about an important phone call he had to make. That bought him about fifteen minutes. And he intended to make the most of it.

"How soon?" Tamara pouted.

"Very soon," he replied, fighting to keep his annoyance from showing in his voice. Sometimes Tamara could be such a whiner. She was almost more trouble than she was worth. Almost.

"Promise?"

He pushed her up against a tree. "Promise," he murmured before hungrily devouring her mouth as though he were starving. Tamara kissed him back just as hungrily.

Daniel broke away from her long enough to grab the blanket Tamara had brought with her. Last time they'd done it in the park she'd complained endlessly about the grass, and the bugs, and the sticks that had cut into her flesh. He'd told her next time to be more prepared, and it seemed she'd listened to him. When he'd joined her in the wooded area by the playground, she'd had the blanket in hand.

Deciding they were in a quiet enough place to have a quickie without anyone happening upon them, Daniel spread the blanket out and then pushed Tamara down onto it. He probably should have been a bit gentler, but he was already primed and ready to go. And Tamara didn't seem to mind. She was turned on too and already reaching for his belt.

Neither of them noticed the cold as they tore off each other's clothes. Coats, scarves, gloves, sweaters, pants, shoes, socks all thrown into a scattered pile surrounding the blanket. It wasn't until they were down to underwear that he noticed it.

Footprints.

Leading to their left.

Distractedly, his eyes followed the trail.

And he froze.

Someone was sitting on a bench just yards away. Why hadn't they said anything?

Tamara's hands slipped inside his underwear, but he stopped her. "Someone is watching us," he whispered.

"So what? If they want to watch, let's give them a really good show."

With that, she bit his nipple, and he was about to give in and keep going when a thought occurred to him. What if the person on the bench was a private investigator hired by his wife? What if she'd learned of his affairs and wanted proof that he was cheating so she could divorce him and take half of everything he had worked so hard for? There was no way he was letting that happen.

"Tamara, stop," he insisted, pushing away her hands and reaching for his pants.

"Daniel," Tamara whined.

He ignored her; he was the one with something to lose if the private investigator got pictures of the two of them having sex, not Tamara. Once he'd yanked his pants on, he stood and pushed aside the branches of the bush partially separating them from whoever was on the other side and then paused uncertainly.

It didn't look like a private investigator.

It looked like two people. Small people.

Children, perhaps?

Cautiously now, he walked toward the bench—his bare feet felt like they were being stabbed by a million tiny needles as he walked through patches of snow. What were a couple of kids doing out here? It was quiet and wooded, exactly why he'd chosen it for his rendezvous with Tamara. But it wasn't a place kids should be on their own, and there didn't appear to be an adult nearby. The lake was just on the other side of a thick grouping of trees, and at this time of year, it was partially frozen. What if the kids were to wander onto it, not realizing the dangers? Daniel knew he wasn't the world's best father—not even close —but he'd never let his son play around here on his own.

The children didn't move as he approached. That was odd. Maybe the kids were homeless? They could be suffering from hypothermia. What if they were dead? He'd never seen a dead body before; the thought of it creeped him out. Whenever he went to a funeral where there was an open casket, he always made sure he stayed as far away from the coffin as possible.

Rounding the bench, he stopped abruptly.

The kids weren't homeless.

Nor had they succumbed to hypothermia.

Although they weren't properly dressed for the icy winter weather.

But that didn't matter because the children were indeed dead.

A little blonde-haired girl sat beside a little blond-haired boy.

In the lap of the little girl was a little blonde girl doll.

In the lap of the little boy was a little blond boy doll.

These children had been killed by the Doll Killers.

His wife had told him about the crimes because their little boy was a seven-year-old blond, exactly the kind of child the killers were targeting. She'd been scared that their son would be taken from them. He'd thought it was a silly thing to worry about, nothing like that was going to happen to their family.

But here, less than a mile from where his son was playing, the killers had left two dead bodies. The same killers had murdered another pair of children a month or so ago before taking the children who now sat dead before him.

They'd be looking for their next victims.

His son.

Oblivious to the cold or the fact that he was wearing nothing but his pants, he began to run.

"Daniel? What are you doing? Who was it? Where are you going? Daniel, you can't just leave me here," Tamara wailed.

Ignoring her, Daniel just ran. He was desperate to get to his son, make sure he was safe.

As he ran, he prayed.

Promising God that if his son was safe, he'd stop with the affairs. He'd be a better father, a better husband. He'd spend more time at home and less time at work.

If God just made sure his son was safe, he'd do anything.

∼

11:03 A.M.

"Let me take you home, Clara."

Clara almost protested that she didn't need to go home. That she had work at the bookstore that needed to be attended to. That she was fine. But that would have been a lie—well, not the work part, she did have a whole list of tasks to attend to at her shop—but the rest of it. Jonathon and Detective Bennett had left the room about ten minutes ago after peppering her relentlessly with questions about her abduction and Tommy. They had been so persistent, so unyielding, that her head had started to spin.

Too many questions.

Questions she didn't want to answer. Questions she didn't even want to think about. As soon as the detectives had gone, she'd folded her arms on the table and rested her head on them. Naomi had let her be and paced the room in an attempt to work off her own frustrations. Her sister always paced when she was annoyed, and she always got annoyed when she couldn't make things better for someone she loved.

"Come on, Clara," Naomi wheedled. "You need to get some rest. Yesterday would have been bad enough even if it wasn't Tommy who carjacked you. You were hurt, you barely slept last night, you've had to answer questions about what happened to you as a kid—you really need to get some rest."

Clara debated with herself. She was feeling a little woozy, perhaps going home and getting some rest wasn't a horrible idea. She should probably eat something, too; she'd skipped breakfast because her stomach had still been too queasy; it still was, but she couldn't put off eating forever.

"You need to eat something, too," Naomi added, as though reading her mind.

She was about to agree when the door suddenly swung open. She knew without lifting her head that it was Jonathon who had entered the room. Part of her didn't want to ever see his face again, and part of her wanted to see it one last time. The part that wanted to see it again won out, and she slowly lifted her head.

"You can go, Clara." His bright brown eyes locked onto hers, he looked like he had more to say but wasn't sure if he should say it or not.

"I'm not a suspect anymore?" That anyone, especially someone that she'd felt some connection to, could think that she would replicate the crimes that nearly cost her her life was devastating. Those six weeks that she'd spent locked in the attic had changed her forever. She'd become quiet and serious, preferring the company of characters in books to real people. When the real world was too hard to live in, she had found herself inhabiting a fantasy world. She'd become much pickier about who she allowed herself to grow close to. Most relationships she kept shallow and superficial, but the people that she let into her heart were there for life. Her circle may be small, but between her sister, her brothers, and a couple of very close and supportive friends, she never felt alone.

"You were never a suspect, Clara."

"Maybe not to you," she reluctantly conceded. She hadn't seen even a hint of distrust or suspicion toward her in his face or his words. "But I was to your partner."

"Not anymore."

The way he said it had her mind bucking in refusal. "They're dead," she said dully. "Lindsey and Kent, the children in the pictures you showed me earlier."

"Yes. I'm sorry, Clara. They were just found on a park bench. I wish this weren't happening again. For those children and their families, and for you."

But it *was* happening again. And last time the police hadn't known who the killers were. They hadn't even had any suspects. And then after she and Tommy escaped, the killers just stopped. They'd been smart enough to stay off the police radar all these years; surely they'd be smart enough to stay off it now. Clara was sure it was the same people. It *had* to be. She knew in her heart it wasn't Tommy.

"Are you okay?" Jonathon stepped toward her in concern. "You've gone all pale."

Waving him off, Naomi sat back down beside her. "You don't look so good, Clara. Let me take you home; you can have something to eat, then take some painkillers and a sleeping pill and get some sleep."

She ignored both of them. "Have they taken another child?"

"A seven-year-old girl, Katie Logan, went missing this morning while at the bank with her mother and little brother," Jonathon replied. "We're not sure if it's connected yet, but she's the right age, and she has blonde hair and blue eyes. For the moment, we're working it as related, especially given they've killed the children they had, but we don't want to count something else out by jumping to conclusions."

They all knew that Katie Logan was the Doll Killers' next victim. And what was worse was knowing that a little boy was about to join her. Then something occurred to her, and she looked up hopefully. "That means Tommy couldn't have done it. He died yesterday—he couldn't have left the children's bodies to be found in the park, and he couldn't have kidnapped that little girl."

"The Doll Killers work as a team—you know that, Clara," he reminded her patiently. "Tommy is dead, but his partner is still out there somewhere."

Tommy wasn't the killer, but otherwise, he was right. The killers were still out there somewhere. How many more children were going to die?

"Let's go, Clara. There's nothing more you can do here." Naomi took her arm and tugged her to her feet.

Feeling like she was trapped in a hazy stupor, Clara allowed her sister to help her stand, glad of Naomi's steadying hand on her arm as the world shimmied around her. Any thoughts of going to work had flown away. She couldn't concentrate on anything right now. She'd let her sister take her home and ask her to stay in case she had nightmares.

"Before you go, may I have a minute alone with Clara?" Jonathon directed the question to Naomi.

Her sister turned to her, "Clara?"

"It's okay," she assured Naomi; it was better to get this over and done with now. Say her goodbyes to whatever might have been so she could get closure and move on. "I'll meet you at the car in a few minutes."

"Okay. A couple of minutes though or I'm coming to find you." Naomi shot Jonathon a threatening glare as she stalked from the room.

"Your sister is pretty protective of you," Jonathon observed, somewhat hesitantly taking a seat at the table and gesturing for her to sit beside him.

"Naomi's a protector. She does personal security," she explained.

"I can picture her as a bodyguard," Jonathon smiled.

"Yeah, she's pretty tough. She's a black belt in Taekwondo and a perfect shot, and she never lets anyone push her around." Sometimes Clara was jealous of her sister's strength, but she knew that Naomi's had come at a price. A high price.

"You're tough, too." Jonathon leaned closer, invading her personal space.

Running her hands through her hair, tucking and re-tucking it behind her ears. Jonathon made her feel self-conscious. "Not really."

"Yes, you are," he contradicted. "You went through something horrific as a child, and yet you didn't let it define you. You built a life for yourself."

Shrugging dismissively, she said, "Kids are resilient."

He gave her a small frown, "Don't downplay it. I'm sure rebuilding your life was no small feat, but you did it. You graduated high school, you got your MBA, you run a successful business. I'd say you had to be pretty tough to accomplish all of that."

Clara felt uncomfortable that he knew so much more about her than she knew about him. She also felt uncomfortable with his obvious admiration. Just because she had been abducted as a child didn't mean that she deserved any special treatment in any area of her life.

"Clara, no one, not even my partner, thinks that you are involved in this beyond being a victim of both the Doll Killers and Thomas Karl.

Since you're not a suspect, your carjacking case is closed, and while your old case is active, I'm not in any way involved with it, so I don't see any conflict of interest in what I'm about to ask you. Would you like to have dinner with me sometime?"

The earnestness with which he asked almost made her regret her answer. "No."

Surprise and disappointment flooded his face. "No?"

Nodding slowly, she repeated, "No."

"Why? When we met, there was something there. Something between us. Attraction, a spark, whatever you want to call it; but I know you felt it, too."

Unfortunately, she had. It still didn't change the facts. Softening her tone, she said, "I'm sorry, but I can't go out with you."

"Why? I know you're attracted to me. And I know it's not because you think I thought you were a killer, because I know deep down you know I never doubted you. So, what's the problem?"

"Tommy," she answered softly. "You think he did this. You're determined to prove that he did. I know he wouldn't, but you don't believe me."

For a long moment, he just stared at her as though trying to figure her out. Then his eyes shuttered, and he stood. "Okay. Fair enough."

"You're okay with that?" Surprised, and all right, she admitted, a little disappointed that he'd given up on her so easily. Surely he could have fought for her at least a little bit.

"No, but I'm not going to force you to go out with me when you don't want to. I wish you all the best, Clara." Jonathon paused at the door. "And if you ever change your mind, you know where to find me."

With that, he was gone.

And Clara was left alone with her thoughts. Had she just made a mistake? Would the connection she'd felt with Jonathon fade? Should she go after him? Would she ever go after him? Or would she be a coward and walk away from the first man she'd ever met who she thought she even had a chance of falling in love with?

The only question that never entered her mind was what if she was wrong about Tommy? She was one hundred percent convicted of her friend's innocence. And somehow she'd prove she was right.

∾

4:29 P.M.

It had been a productive day.

Lindsey and Kent had moved on to a better life. Now they could live on forever in the form of dolls. Those children had been given the gift of immortality. What more could a person ask for?

Dolls.

They were so perfect. So amazing. Humanity captured in a perfect little entity that could never be destroyed, never be corrupted.

The nickname the press had chosen wasn't correct. Doll Killers. Who would ever kill a doll? Who *could* kill a doll? They were eternal.

What they were doing wasn't killing; it was creating. Transferring life from one being to another. These children were being given a beautiful gift. If only everyone could be so lucky. If only she could be so lucky.

The love affair with dolls had started early in childhood. Now her doll collection was vast, and it contained several very rare and expensive pieces. It had taken her many years to build it up, and each carefully chosen contribution made her collection even more exquisite. She loved them all, of course, but she also couldn't deny that she had her favorites. There was something so intriguing about them; they were so lifelike and yet not. They were so beautiful—the smooth, clear skin, the sparkling eyes, the perfectly styled hair. No real life child could compare. She certainly couldn't. All her life she had been told that. Told it so many times that she had come to believe it.

To her, the story of Pinocchio had always seemed like an odd one. What doll would ever give that up to become a mere mortal? Who gave up perfection to be plain and ordinary? As a child, she had spent hours playing with her dolls, wishing that she could become one. Each night she would wait anxiously at her bedroom window to catch sight of the first star so she could make her wish. She had loved that poem—still did. There were still many a night that she would sit at her window, watch for that first star, and recite the poem: *Star light, star bright, first star I see tonight, I wish I may, I wish I might, have the wish I wish tonight.* The words were so magical and held so much meaning. And in a way, her wish had finally come true.

She had found a way to help others do what she had never managed. She had helped them to achieve perfection. Now those pretty little children would never lose magnificence. Now it could last forever. They would never grow old; they would never be corrupted—either inside or out—and they would never suffer as she had suffered.

Plain and ordinary had been a big part of her life. But it wasn't now. Now her life was full of beauty and magic. Creating perfect little dolls that would live on for all eternity. And through her creations, she too would live on forever. A part of her became a part of them.

Her next little creation was waiting for her in the attic. Tomorrow, the little girl would be joined by her partner. A perfect little boy to create another perfect little couple. She never made them make the journey alone. She wouldn't do that. She always made sure that they went together. She knew children sometimes got scared when they were alone. And she would *never* want to make a child afraid. She loved children—she would never hurt one. In fact, she insisted that when the time came for them to make the transition from human child to living doll, it was a painless journey.

He never fought her on that. He understood. Understood what it meant to create something so utterly perfect it almost shouldn't exist in a world that was so full of ugliness. He understood because he knew what it was like to be ugly. And only ugliness could truly comprehend the beauty of perfection.

Perfection.

That was what life was all about.

Achieving perfection.

And she had done it.

～

5:39 P.M.

. . .

"Catch me up, guys," Captain Heidi Kramer ordered as he and Allina sat at the desk in their boss' office.

"Well," Jonathon began slowly, "we're waiting for the official report, but Lindsey Peters and Kent Mason appear to have died in the same manner as the other children—both the recent murders and the ones from thirty years ago."

"What about the man who found the bodies? Is he a possible suspect?" Heidi asked.

"I don't think so," he answered. "He'd been having a secret meeting with his girlfriend while his wife was at the playground with their son. When he first saw someone on the park bench, he thought his wife had caught on to his cheating ways and hired a private investigator. Then when he got closer, he realized it was children and because they weren't moving he thought they might be homeless and had possibly died from hypothermia. Once he saw the dolls, he realized what was going on and went running straight for the playground, concerned the killers may go after his son. He was so concerned he forgot he was only wearing a pair of pants. When his wife saw him, she realized what he had been up to. When we interviewed them, he was begging for forgiveness, and she was talking divorce. But given the way he reacted upon finding the children, I don't think he's a suspect, if for no other reason than if his wife does divorce him she's going to take half of his considerable fortune. So if he were going to plant the bodies then pretend to be scared about it, he would have gotten dressed before he went running off."

"Check out him and his girlfriend just to be certain. What about the dolls?"

"They appear to be the same as all the others. This time is was a Kestner 167 with Lindsey, and a Bahr and Proschild 585 with Kent. Both dolls are German . . ."

"Not all of them were, though, correct?" Heidi interrupted.

"Correct. A couple of the dolls from the original killings were French, but almost all were German made," he replied. "All of the dolls from the first time around and this time are from around the turn of the last century."

"But they never used the same doll twice," Allina noted.

"No, but we still get a feel for their tastes. Size obviously wasn't important; the dolls ranged from eleven to thirty-two inches. The material used doesn't appear to be crucial, all have bisque heads, most composition bodies, but a couple had cloth bodies. Maker didn't seem to matter, a couple of times they doubled up, but most of the dolls were made by different companies. But the appearance of the doll seemed extremely important; all have blonde hair and blue eyes, just like the children. There are plenty of other dolls out there, and yet they never once used one with brown eyes, or brown, black, or red hair."

"But did the kids fit the dolls or the dolls fit the kids?" Heidi's stern face looked thoughtful. Jonathon didn't think he'd ever seen her smile at work; she appeared perpetually austere. But get her away from the precinct and into a social setting, and she was like a completely different person and a surprisingly jovial one. Heidi was in her fifties, just over six feet tall, with an angular and bony face, and as skinny as a stick. She was a tightly bound up ball of energy who was constantly on the move; even when she was still, she was fiddling with something. Right now she was squeezing a stress ball in the shape of a bumblebee.

"If we knew that, then we'd know their motivation," Allina replied. "If the dolls come first, then they're the focus. If it's the kids, then they're the focus."

"I think that the dolls come first," Jonathon stated. "If the kids came first, then they would have had to find a doll that looked like each one of them."

"They had each of the kids for at least a month," Heidi noted. "Plenty of time to purchase a doll before killing them."

"Then there are Clara's eyes," he continued. "They're green, not blue. I know we never knew what her doll looked like, but there were a couple of other children with green eyes, and they were found with blue-eyed dolls. If they got the dolls to match the children, then they would have made sure to get dolls with the correct color eyes."

"Can you find antique dolls with green eyes?" Heidi asked.

"Not sure. It wasn't in any of the research we did on antique dolls, but I'll look into it," he replied.

"Blue or green eyes can be hard to distinguish from a distance," Allina pointed out. "Perhaps they thought they were taking blue-eyed kids and didn't realize till they already had them that they, in fact, had green eyes. Maybe it was close enough, and they didn't worry about that slight difference."

"If the kids were the Doll Killers' focus, then I think they would have been found in their own clothes, and the dolls would be dressed accordingly," Jonathon addressed his next argument. "Instead, the killers went to all the trouble of perfectly recreating the costumes the dolls were wearing—right down to undergarments, socks, and shoes. Hair was also done to match the dolls, too, including hair ribbons."

Heidi nodded. "That all makes sense."

"I agree," Allina concurred. "And don't forget the markings."

Jonathon wished he had, but he hadn't.

"The children each had markings on them identical to those on the dolls they were found with. Those whose dolls had two sets of markings, on the head and the body, also had two sets of markings. No need to go to all that trouble if the dolls were simply found to go with the kids."

They had no idea if the children had been branded shortly after they were taken or just before death. Both medical examiners, the one from thirty years ago and the current one, had noted that it had been done before death—the wounds had started to heal but hadn't healed completely—but they couldn't determine exactly how long before. Had Clara been branded? The thought of some sick monster burning her flesh to match markings on a doll filled him with a deep protective rage and anger that he'd never encountered before.

"Let's focus on the doll aspect, get in contact with any store that sells antique dolls, focus on the four dolls found with our most recent victims, see if that leads us anywhere. And that brings us to Clara Candella." Heidi's brown eyes sought his and held his gaze. "Jonathon?"

"She's not involved," he replied, willing his voice to remain neutral, and pleased with the results.

She moved her gaze to his partner. "Allina?"

"She couldn't have left the bodies in the park or abducted Katie Logan because she was here at the station, so it seems unlikely that she's Thomas Karl's partner. Assuming he is involved. I suppose it could be the original Doll Killers, plus her and Thomas, all working together, but she was fairly convincingly horrified by the entire ordeal."

"So, she's out as a suspect?" Heidi clarified.

Leaving it up to his partner to confirm, Jonathon looked at Allina. She rolled her eyes at him in response. "Yeah, she's out."

"So, how does she fit into all of this? Did you get anything else out of her when you interviewed her?"

"She says she doesn't remember what happened to her in the six weeks she was missing, or how she and Thomas escaped," Allina replied.

"Do you believe her?"

"Yes," Allina confirmed. "She seems truly devastated about the children. I think if she knew anything that could help us find Katie then she'd tell us."

"She remembers the abduction itself, though," Jonathon spoke up. "Her reaction when we asked about that was different than her reaction when we asked about everything else."

Allina nodded approvingly at him, liked he'd just passed some test he hadn't known he'd been sitting. "I picked up on that, too. I think she remembers it, but she's scared to talk about it for some reason."

"Well get her to talk." Heidi set the stress ball down, picked up a pen and began to twirl it between her fingers. "If she remembers the abduction, then she remembers something about the kidnappers and the way they operate. We need to know. Last time these killers managed to slip away; I'm not having that happen again. Eighteen victims back then, plus two who survived, another five already...I don't want any more kids dying while we sit here and try and figure this out."

"We have the doll angle. The statements from Clara and Thomas after they were found are basically useless—neither of them say much about anything. I think our best bet is to try and get Clara to remember. Maybe we can convince her to try hypnotism or something. With Thomas dead, she's the only living person left who knows the identity of the original killers." Jonathon wasn't sure how he was going to convince her to try getting help to get her memories back. He hadn't even been able to convince her to go on a date with him; she'd turned him down flat. It had stung. A lot. But this wasn't about the two of them. This was about children in danger. And if Clara thought that they wanted to prove the original killers were still involved, then she might be willing to give hypnosis a try.

"So, do we think original killers or Thomas Karl working with a partner?" Heidi asked.

"Thomas Karl is involved," Jonathon answered confidently. "It is way too much of a coincidence that Clara stops hearing from him around the time the murders start, and then out of the blue he turns up in her car with a knife and a gun, carjacks her and tells her he has to show her something. And the carjacking was deliberately targeting Clara, he was waiting for her *inside* her car, so it was not random. It makes him look even more suspicious that he'd rather die than have to talk to us. When Clara's car finally ran out of gas, he knew it was over. He knew that if he talked to us, we'd find out what he'd been up to. He knew shooting at cops was going to get him killed, and he'd rather die than get found out."

"He's replicated everything else, so it seems logical that he's also working with a partner," Allina added. "Tomorrow Jon and I are going to check out his apartment and then speak with his mother."

"I like that plan. And if the original killers are working with Thomas, I think when we find proof that he's involved, we'll also find the identities of the Doll Killers. Then no one else will get hurt, and the victims and their families get their justice."

Jonathon agreed one hundred percent with his boss' words. Those children deserved justice. And so did their families. And he was determined to get it for them. Even if it meant hurting Clara. This case needed to be solved; the killers needed to be stopped, and if Clara reliving what she endured in those missing weeks helped make that happen, then her pain was a regrettable yet unavoidable consequence.

That didn't mean he wouldn't feel guilty. Or that he wouldn't feel Clara's pain as sharply as though it were his own.

But this case consumed him.

The Doll Killers *would* be stopped.

CHAPTER
Three

February 9th
4:57 A.M.

"Wait," he yelled.

But she didn't wait.

She never waited.

Why didn't she?

Why wouldn't she?

Didn't she know what was going to happen?

If only *he'd* known what was going to happen, then perhaps he could have stopped it.

He would have given anything to stop it.

"Dora, wait," he begged.

She paused and turned to look at him. Her big blue eyes were bright and sparkling like jewels in the sunshine, her blonde braids were untidy from playing outdoors, and her yellow sundress was stained brown from climbing trees and making mud pies.

She looked so pretty, so sweet, so innocent.

She was so young.

She hadn't deserved what had happened to her.

It just wasn't fair.

"Dora, wait there; I'm coming for you."

He started to run toward her.

He ran as fast as he could, but it was taking him forever to reach her.

Then Dora giggled and began to run in the opposite direction.

"Dora. No. Wait," he screamed.

Why was she running?

Did she think they were playing?

He was running as fast as he could. Faster than he ever had before. Why wasn't he catching up to her? He was ten, she was only six. Usually he could catch her without even trying. But today it didn't seem to matter how fast he went, she only got farther and farther away from him.

Then abruptly, Dora stopped.

She was talking to someone. He couldn't see who, they were hidden behind a tree, but he could hear his sister's voice. He strained to make out the words. Maybe if he knew what they'd said to her, what she'd said to them, he'd know where to look for her.

Then she disappeared.

Poof.

Gone.

Just like that.

"Dora." His screamed echoed, growing exponentially louder until it was deafening.

Finally, he reached the place where he'd last spied his sister. Only there was no sign of her anywhere.

Then he saw someone sitting on a picnic blanket.

Someone with blonde braids and a yellow sundress.

"Dora?"

There was no answer.

He walked slower now, a sense of foreboding welling up inside him, filling him slowly like when he'd filled water balloons with Dora earlier in the summer.

Why was she so still and quiet? Those were two words he would never have associated with his effervescent little sister.

When he'd circled so he was in front of her, he saw why she wasn't moving.

She was dead.

Dora was dead.

She looked like she was sleeping but he knew she wasn't.

In her lap sat a doll.

He screamed.

Someone was laughing, but he couldn't see anyone about.

The fear and horror and guilt inside him kept growing, filling him to the brim until he exploded with an enormous bang.

Jonathon woke with a start.

He was drenched in sweat, even though he was wearing only a pair of sweatpants and had thrown all his covers on the floor while he slept. His heart was rocketing in his heaving chest, and his hands were shaking.

Of course, he'd never actually seen his sister's dead body, either at the park, at the morgue, or at the funeral. It didn't matter to his mind, though. In his dreams, he always pictured her as she must have looked when she was found on that picnic blanket. Beautiful, her skin unmarred, her eyes closed as though simply asleep.

Jonathon hadn't seen her disappear, either. She had just been there and then she hadn't. If he'd noticed her wandering off, then perhaps he would have been able to tell the cops something that helped them find her. But he hadn't. He hadn't witnessed what had caused his sister to leave the playground, even though she knew never to go off on her own, and especially not with a stranger.

Wanting to shake off the dream, he climbed from his bed and padded barefoot down the stairs to the living room, where he settled down in his rocking chair. For some reason, the rocking motion still soothed him, just as it had when he was a colicky baby, and his mother had sat in this very chair to attempt to get him to sleep.

He remembered perfectly the day his little sister disappeared.

The two of them had been playing at the park. They were meant to be home by dark, but he'd begged to be allowed to stay until dark because he and his friends had wanted to play some game. Twenty-three years later he couldn't even remember what it was. Of course, Dora had begged to stay, too. Whatever he did, she wanted to do, as well. Back then it had been so annoying. Dora had been practically a baby, only six, although as she had repeatedly reminded him she was almost seven and would be starting second grade after the summer.

Their mom had reluctantly agreed to let them stay late, on the provision that their dad met them there after work. Only he'd never turned up. Jonathon had known that he should take his sister home, that their mom wouldn't like them being there without a parent after dark. But he'd wanted to stay with his friends.

One minute Dora, all muddy and disheveled from a day at the park, had been swinging on the swings. The next she'd been gone.

Those awful hours were seared into his mind, and he could see them playing out with crystal clarity as though they were happening this very minute.

Realizing Dora was gone.

Looking everywhere for her.

Running home, just a street from the park, hoping the whole way that Dora would be there waiting for him. Jonathon had known if she was there, he was in for the punishment of a lifetime, but it would be worth it just to see his sister safe and sound.

But she wasn't there and telling his mother he'd lost her was the single worst moment of his life.

That night their home was a hive of activity.

Police officers came, and neighbors, friends, and family.

Everyone searched the streets for Dora, but she was nowhere to be found.

What came next was somehow worse.

Stillness.

Complete and utter stillness.

As the days ticked by and no progress was made in finding Dora, it was like his family died.

They were both alive and dead.

His dad went to work. He left early in the morning and didn't return home until well after dark.

His mother puttered aimlessly around the house. Cleaning and re-cleaning it. Cooking and baking more food than three people could eat. Cooking and baking more food than three hundred people could eat.

And as for him, he didn't do anything. He didn't go to the park and play with his friends. He didn't play video games or read or play with his toys or watch TV. He just hung around the house, unsure what to do or say.

Then came the phone call.

Dora's body had been found.

She was a victim of the serial killer dubbed the Doll Killer.

And with his sister's death, his family was changed forever.

Although he hadn't known it at the time, his sister and the little boy killed alongside her were the last children the Doll Killers would murder. Their next victims were Clara Candella and Thomas Karl, the two children who had escaped. Then the killings had stopped—until now.

Was it fate that had brought Clara into his life when he was determined to fix the mistake he'd made back then? He couldn't bring Dora back, but he could do everything within his power to make sure another child never suffered the same fate, and he could get closure for his mother by finding the people responsible for her daughter's death.

As much as Clara was the key to all of that, what he felt for her ran a lot deeper.

Had it been a mistake to agree to her terms?

He wanted her. Badly. Almost more than he wanted to catch the Doll Killers.

But she said she wasn't interested. Well, more accurately, she had all but said that she *was* indeed interested, but that she didn't intend to do anything about it because he suspected her friend as the new Doll Killer.

Jonathon supposed he could understand that. This case was personal for her, too. She'd lived it firsthand. Lived it with Thomas Karl, so it made sense that her brain couldn't fathom the thought that he was anything other than the same as her—a victim.

Just because he understood didn't mean he agreed.

He admired Clara. He thought she was strong, and he respected her.

He was certainly attracted to her, but he was not going to force her into a relationship she didn't want.

He'd been there, done that, and it hadn't worked.

His first marriage had ended in divorce; if he were to get married again, he wanted it to work. And if he pursued things with Clara and he was more into it than she was, then their relationship would be doomed.

Last time he'd gone in with blinders on. That had been a mistake. One he was determined not to replicate.

Garnet had been pretty and smart and sexy. Everything he thought he wanted, everything he still wanted, but there had been something missing. He and Garnet hadn't been on the same wavelength. She'd wanted fun and adventure and excitement—a life of frivolity. He'd wanted kids, stable jobs, pets, a mortgage. Garnet had balked at the idea of so much responsibility.

So, their marriage had quickly started dissolving. She had yelled and screamed that she was young and beautiful and didn't want to be tied down. He had sulked that they were married and all he wanted were the rest of the things that were supposed to come with that.

Still, despite the disaster his marriage had become, he had been shocked when Garnet presented him with divorce papers. She'd said he could have the house, the furniture, the cars—she just wanted out.

For a while he had considered fighting for their marriage, but what would have been the point? They wanted different things out of life. So, he hadn't contested the divorce, although he'd moved out of their house. He couldn't stay there; it was simply a reminder that he still didn't have, and may never have, the family he wanted.

Jonathon still wanted it all. A wife, kids, dogs, cats, family meals, family holidays, little league and dance classes, sleepless nights, toddler tantrums, teenage dramas.

What was killing him about Clara was that he was pretty sure that she wanted it all, too. He'd only known her a couple of days, and they hadn't even had a chance to sit down and get to know one another, and what he knew of her life was mostly what he'd gleaned from researching her for deciding whether she could be Thomas Karl's partner. He couldn't claim that he was in love; he wasn't. It was way too soon, but that connection was there, and he wanted a chance to explore it. He wanted to learn if he and Clara wanted the same things out of life. He wanted to see if they were compatible. He wanted to know if he could fall in love with her.

But the ball was in her court now.

What happened next was up to her, and he had to find a way to live with that.

It shouldn't be too hard; right now the Doll Killer case would keep him plenty occupied. And to that end, he stood and stretched. It was almost six o'clock, no point in going back to bed, it was almost his usual get up time, and he'd managed to get a good few hours' sleep before his nightmare. Instead, he dragged himself back upstairs to grab some clothes. He'd go for a run, then a shower, then breakfast, and off to work.

Plenty to do to keep his mind off Clara.

Plenty.

Really.

Only, he knew he was lying to himself. He fully expected thoughts of Clara to fill his head while he ran, showered, ate, and worked.

~

7:12 A.M.

"How did you sleep?"

Before she could answer, a large yawn nearly split her head in two and Clara supposed that in and of itself was an answer to her sister's question. When they'd gotten home from the police station early yesterday afternoon, she had taken a sleeping pill and gone to bed. She'd gotten maybe three or four hours of sleep before another nightmare had woken her. She and Naomi had eaten dinner and watched a movie, and then, at her sister's urging, she'd gone back to bed.

All night she had tossed and turned. Sleeping in little fits and bursts, punctuated by horrible dreams. She'd thought about giving up and just getting up, but that wouldn't have changed anything. Then she would have just been stuck in the awake version of her nightmare.

Katie Logan had been in her dreams. That poor little girl was suffering so horribly—she would be so scared, all alone in that attic. Clara felt that she was partly responsible for the child's affliction. If only she could remember. If she could only recall more about what her abductors had done to her and how she escaped, then she might know something that could help Jonathon and his partner find the little girl before it was too late.

"Don't do that, Clara," Naomi's voice penetrated her thoughts. "Pushing yourself isn't going to make your memories come back."

Cocking her head inquisitively, Clara asked, "How do you always know what I'm thinking?" Naomi was great at reading her, and it wasn't because they were kind of triplets, her sister somehow had an uncanny knack of knowing exactly what was going on inside her head.

Naomi smiled. "Because it's always written all over your face. You couldn't hide what you're thinking if your life depended on it."

Unlike Naomi. Clara often found it extremely difficult to figure out what was going on behind her sister's brown eyes. She wasn't having that problem at the moment, though; right now Naomi's face was screaming exhausted. She'd probably stayed awake last night and the night before, wanting to be available should Clara need her. "You should get some sleep, Nay; you look tired."

Straightening in her chair as though the comment had been a criticism, Naomi quickly replied, "I'm fine. I slept last night."

Not for more than an hour or so spread over the whole night, if Naomi's pale face and the dark circles under her eyes were anything to go by. Naomi always thought she had to be perfect, but try as she might, Clara could not pry the reason why out of her.

"So, are you going to work today?" Naomi asked, ignoring the topic of the rest she clearly needed.

"Nope." Her neck was causing her a lot less pain today; the stitches were even starting to itch a little. However, she had other, much more pressing, plans for the day.

"You're going to stay home and take it easy?" Naomi asked, surprised.

"Nope."

Suspicion laced her next words. "Then what *are* you planning on doing today?"

Naomi looked like she expected not to like the answer. Clara suspected that she was right. "I want to prove that Tommy is not the new Doll Killer."

"Really, Clara?" Naomi looked irritated. "Don't you think you should leave that up to the police?"

"Leave it up to the police?" she echoed incredulously. Had her sister forgotten that the detectives wanted to prove Tommy *was* the killer, not that he *wasn't*? "How is that going to help anything?"

"How is you trying to solve a murder case on your own going to help anything?" Naomi shot back. "You're likely to get yourself killed."

"I'm not going to get myself killed," Clara contradicted.

"Murder investigations can be dangerous things," Naomi reminded her.

"I'm not stupid, Naomi. I know that. But I can't let them pin this on Tommy. Besides, I was hoping I wouldn't be trying to solve a murder case on my own." She raised a hopeful eyebrow at her sister.

Naomi rolled her eyes. "You want me to help you."

"Please, Naomi," she begged. "You graduated from the police academy; you'll know what questions I should be asking. And you work as a bodyguard, so I'll be completely safe with you," she wheedled.

"Clara," Naomi complained.

"Please."

"Fine. But I still think this is a bad idea," Naomi grumbled.

"Thank you!" She kissed her sister's cheek.

"I don't think that Jonathon Dawson is going to like you messing with his investigation," Naomi warned.

Clara didn't want to think about Jonathon right now. He was an added complication in her life that she didn't need. Once she sorted out clearing Tommy's name, then she could sit down and evaluate the pros and cons of dating Jonathon. "So?" she aimed for nonchalance but wasn't convinced she achieved it.

Her sister's smirk confirmed she wasn't fooled by the faked indifference. "So you like him, don't you?"

"I guess."

"You guess?"

"Okay, fine. I may be physically attracted to him. So, what? You saw him, he's good-looking, right?"

Naomi chuckled. "He's not really my type. And I don't think you're just attracted to him. It runs deeper than that. I saw the way you reacted when he came close to you. He calms you, comforts you—you must feel something for him."

"I don't know. Maybe you're right," she admitted.

"Not maybe; you know I'm right. You know how you feel. Why are you fighting it?"

"I'm not," she protested. "I just ... I just... Okay," Clara sighed. "You're right. For some reason, he makes me feel safe. I like that. I just don't know if I'm at a place in my life right now where I'm looking for something serious."

"Why not?"

"Why aren't you?" she retorted.

"I like being alone," Naomi said seriously.

"Well, so do I."

Naomi was studying her. "It's not the same, Clara, and you know it."

"I worry about you sometimes, Naomi."

"You don't need to worry about me, Clara," Naomi said, visibly withdrawing inside herself, she hated to be the center of anyone's scrutiny.

"Stop it. I'm allowed to worry about you. You're my sister. I love you. I want you to be happy. I don't want what happened to stop you from being happy. You don't have to be perfect all the time, Nay. It's okay to fail sometimes."

"I don't need a shrink." Naomi's brown eyes had shuttered.

Clara hated when her sister did that. She understood her sister was afraid for anyone to think she couldn't do something perfectly, but Naomi wasn't perfect—no one was—and the pressure Naomi put on herself was going to end up crushing her. "I'm not being a shrink; I'm being your sister."

Naomi's voice softened, "I know you are. I'm sorry. I don't like to fail. I've failed enough people in my life. I don't want to fail anyone else. So, Jonathon asked you out?"

Taking the admission as enough for now, Clara resisted the urge to remind her sister that she hadn't failed anyone and instead allowed the conversation to veer back to herself. "Yes, he asked me out to dinner."

"And you said no."

"I said no."

"Well, next time he asks, say yes."

"Actually, he said he wasn't going to ask again. He said it's up to me. That if I changed my mind, I knew where to find him."

Brightening, Naomi replied, "Perfect. Next time you see him, you can tell him you've changed your mind."

"Have I?"

"You tell me."

The tingling in her stomach said she had. The tingling in her heart warned her that Jonathon Dawson might be someone she could fall in love with. Maybe she was ready to take that step, as terrifying as it may be. "I changed my mind."

"I'm happy for you, Clara. I really am. I hope it works out." Naomi stood. "I'm going to go grab a quick shower, and I'm going to have to wear something of yours—I'm all out of clean clothes. I'll have to go by my place sometime today to pack a few things. I'm staying here with you until this whole Doll Killer thing is resolved. When I'm done, you can tell me your plans for convincing the cops Tommy isn't a killer.

Clara hadn't missed the hint of sadness in her sister's voice. She hoped someday soon everything worked out for Naomi, too.

9:34 A.M.

"Wow, nice apartment building," Allina said appreciatively. She'd thought the townhouse where she and her husband lived was nice, but this place was like a luxury hotel.

"Sure is." Jonathon was staring in awe at the large apartment complex.

It was a magnificent place. Forty stories high, gleaming white in the winter sunshine. There was a gorgeous pool and spa area, a gym, a coffee shop, and a fancy restaurant.

"Come on, Ali."

Surprised, she turned to her partner. "Ali?" He hadn't called her by that nickname in the year they'd been partners.

His light-brown eyes crinkled in concern, as though he'd offended her. "Sorry, I heard your husband call you that the other day. I thought since we work together you wouldn't mind, but if I've offended you..."

Allina felt bad. She must have been hard to work with the last year if Jonathon was afraid he'd upset her over something as trivial as a nickname. She hadn't meant to be distant with him. She liked Jonathon. He was smart, thoughtful, good with victims, good with suspects, and a perfect shot; everything she wanted and needed in a partner. But her family life was stressful, and sometimes it leaked over into her work life.

He gave a small disappointed sigh. "Let's go, Allina," Jonathon amended.

She stopped him with a hand on his arm. "Ali is fine. I'm sorry, I haven't been hard to get close to on purpose. I just have a lot going on."

"I'd like us to be friends." Jonathon cast her a cautious glance as they entered the lobby. "If you need help with something, I want you to be comfortable with me to just ask—we are partners, after all."

Allina gave a sigh of her own. She hated thinking about it, and yet it consumed most of her waking thoughts, most of her sleeping ones too. Maybe Jonathon should know. They were partners, and it was hardly a secret—everyone knew about it. "I'm surprised you haven't heard. Maybe because you weren't around when it happened. It's been three years now. Which is totally shocking. It doesn't feel like it. And yet at the same time, it feels like it's been ten times that long . . ."

Jonathon stopped walking and stood in front of her so that she had to stop too. "You're rambling, Ali; just tell me."

He was right; she was rambling. It shouldn't be so hard to just say the words. She and her husband talked about it every day. Other than work, talk about it was pretty much all her family did.

"You're scaring me, Ali. Just say it; it can't be that bad."

Unfortunately, he was right; it wasn't *that bad*—it was way worse. Forcing the words out, she said, "Three years ago my sister-in-law was taken from her home. There was a broken window and blood on the floor in her kitchen. That was it. She hasn't been seen again. There was no ransom, and her body was never found—she just disappeared. She was more like my sister than my sister-in-law. Our parents were best friends; we grew up next door to each other. She's twenty-four, fifteen years younger than my sister and I, and her brothers. We basically helped raise her." Allina could feel tears brimming in her eyes. "I don't know what's worse—believing she's dead or believing she's still alive."

Her partner clucked sympathetically. "I guess I was wrong; it *is* that bad. I'm so sorry. Is there anything I can do to help? Do you have any leads?"

While Allina and her family prayed every day that Grace was still alive and would somehow come back to them, they also knew that if she was still alive, then she was suffering. They'd all lost sleep knowing just how she was most likely suffering. And being cops meant they knew more details about what Grace was probably experiencing than any of them wanted to. Her husband was a cop, and so was her sister; her brother-in-law was a forensic psychiatrist who regularly consulted with the police, and her brother was in the military—they worked Grace's case every spare second they had. "Thanks, Jon. No, there were never any leads. She was just gone. I hate knowing that if she's alive, whoever has her is hurting her."

"You don't know that, Ali."

She shook off his attempts to console her. They both knew she was right. "He's hurting her. Raping her at least, maybe physically assaulting her, too." That knowledge haunted her daily, hovering in the background, tormenting her, like an oversized mosquito bite.

"Anything I can do, Ali, don't hesitate to ask. I mean it." His hand on her shoulder squeezed reassuringly.

"Thanks, Jon, I know you do. Maybe a fresh pair of eyes going through her case file would help." Allina wondered why she hadn't opened up to her partner before now.

"We can swing by your place at the end of the day, and I'll pick up the files."

"Thanks." Allina pushed away thoughts of Grace, setting them at the back of her mind. They never went away, but if she let them overwhelm her, she'd never be able to function.

Sensing the change in her, Jonathon strode towards the lifts. "Thomas' apartment is on the thirtieth floor. He must make good money to afford this place."

"I think he sold some of his drawings to an advertising company to use in some national campaign," she said as they traveled up in the lift.

"Too bad I can't draw anything beyond stick figures," Jonathon joked.

"I can't even manage that." Allina offered up a small smile. Smiling didn't come easy these days, but sometimes it was necessary. She didn't want to let herself get depressed over Grace's situation—her sister-in-law was counting on them to rescue her, and they couldn't do that if they let themselves fall apart.

"I wasn't expecting this," Jonathon said as they opened Thomas' door.

The place was as messy as the apartment building was luxurious. The apartment itself was large; they were in a huge open plan living room, dining room, and kitchen. There wasn't much furniture, a large table that was strewn with papers, and shelves that were full of paints and pencils and other art supplies. The kitchen benches were full of plates of leftover food, and the sink was piled high with dirty dishes. There was no TV, no couch, no dining table. It seemed like all Thomas did was draw, and that when he did stop for a meal, it was a quick one in the kitchen that he rarely managed to finish. The apartment had beautiful hardwood floors, which were barely visible through the mass of discarded papers. Hundreds of pieces of paper full of drawings in various stages of completion were tacked to the walls.

"I'll check out the bedroom," she announced as she headed toward a door on the opposite wall.

"I'll do the spare bedroom," Jonathon headed for the other door.

Thomas' bedroom was as sparsely furnished as the rest of the apartment. There was a bed and a small night table beside it. That was it. The closet was open, and in it she could see a few items of clothing hanging on coat hangers, but most of his wardrobe appeared to be scattered about on the floor.

"Anything?" Jonathon appeared in the doorway.

"Looks like just clothes. Anything in the spare room?"

"Nope. It's completely empty. Bathroom just has a few basic toiletries. If we're going to find anything incriminating here, it's going to be in his drawings."

"I agree," Allina returned to the main room. "We may as well get started; there's a lot here."

"You take the chair and go through what's on the table; I'll do the floor," Jonathon offered.

"Chivalry isn't dead, I see." She grinned and took the only chair, beginning her examination of the table's contents. The drawings were dark. Full of dragons, demons, trolls, and monsters. Allina couldn't help but feel sorry for Thomas Karl. He was obviously suffering. To him, the world was a fearful, gloomy, evil place. If these pictures were anything to go by, then Thomas was a sad, bleak young man.

This insight into his mind also hinted toward the darkness he had brought into the lives of others. Perhaps he suffered from depression; perhaps he suffered from post-traumatic stress disorder; perhaps his childhood had warped his mind so dramatically that it no longer functioned correctly—

"Ali."

Her head snapped up at the tone in her partner's voice. "What did you find?"

"Pictures of the children."

"Which children?"

"The victims."

Joining Jonathon on the floor, he handed her a book. The first page had extremely lifelike drawings of Lindsey Peters and Kent Mason. In the pictures, the children were perched on a plain white chair, each with a doll clasped in their laps. It looked like the children were posing for the picture. The next page contained pictures of Lottie Hatcher and Paul Owen, posed in the same manner as the one of Lindsey and Kent.

"This isn't necessarily proof he was involved," Jonathon stated.

"The children's pictures were all over the TV and the Internet when they went missing."

"Except the clothes," she said softly. "The dolls are wearing identical clothes to the ones that were found with the children. How could he have known that if he wasn't there?"

"The pictures are all drawn in black; a defense attorney could argue he simply drew doll's clothes that happened to look similar to the ones the doll was wearing."

"Lucky we don't need to convince a judge or jury. Thomas is dead— we just needed proof he was involved. Now we have it." Allina turned the next page in the book and cast a concerned glance at Jonathon. "It's Clara."

"I know," he replied tightly, refusing to look at the picture. "They're all there. All eighteen of them."

Flipping quickly through the book, Allina discovered her partner was correct. All eighteen children who had died at the hands of the Doll Killers were featured in the book. Did that mean that Thomas had met the original killers as an adult? Or had he found pictures of the children someplace else?

Now they knew Thomas was involved, they just needed to find his partner and hopefully, Katie Logan, and then they could put an end to these crimes for good.

∽

10:47 A.M.

"Yes," Clara answered before her sister could even ask the question.

"I thought you were supposed to be the easy-to-read one," Naomi grumbled.

Clara laughed at the look on her sister's face. "Don't worry, you're not easy to read, Nay, just predictable. You're always worried about everyone else." Clara barely managed to keep from adding, *everyone except yourself.* Instead, she said, "But I'm sure that I want to do this. Positive, in fact."

"Okay," Naomi sighed. "Well I still think you should leave it to Jonathon and his partner, but since you seem determined not to, I'll help you see this through. But I want it noted that I have a bad feeling about this."

"Noted," she nodded, but not taking her sister all that seriously; Naomi tended to be a bit pessimistic. "Turn left at the next street. Tommy's mother's house is about halfway down on our right."

"I didn't realize Tommy grew up so close to where you lived as a kid," Naomi commented as she turned the corner.

"Just a few streets over," Clara agreed.

"Did you know him before?"

"No. We'd never met."

"Had you seen him at the park or anything?"

"I don't know. You know how kids are, they don't pay attention to anyone or anything around them."

"I suppose," Naomi replied.

Clara wondered whether her sister had ever truly been a child. She suspected that Naomi had been one of those children who was an adult in a tiny little body. "That house there," she pointed to a pretty two-story weatherboard painted white with blue shutters and trim around the windows and front door. The garden was simple but neat and tidy, mostly grass with the odd tree. When she'd first started coming here twenty years ago, the garden had been a mass of color, but Mrs. Karl suffered from arthritis and these days couldn't manage the upkeep, so she'd taken out the bushes and shrubs and replaced them with grass.

"How long since you've seen Tommy's mother?" Naomi asked as they walked down the path to the front door.

"Too long," she admitted. "Maybe a year."

"You're nervous," Naomi observed.

"She just lost her son."

"Which is *not* your fault," Naomi said sternly.

"Maybe, or maybe not." Clara still felt there might have been something she could have done to prevent Tommy's death. "But either way, I feel responsible. I don't know what to say to her."

"You'll figure it out."

Naomi pressed the doorbell, and they waited in silence for the door to open. Barely thirty seconds later, it inched open. Mrs. Karl peered nervously out at them, but then threw the door open wider and all but crushed Clara in a fierce hug.

"Oh, dear, I'm so sorry. I'm so sorry," Mrs. Karl sobbed.

Clara also began to cry and tightly squeezed the old woman. She loved Tommy's mother, who had often been more of a mother to her than her own. "I'm sorry," she wept into the woman's shoulder.

At her apology Mrs. Karl abruptly pulled back, her gray eyes snapping fire. "Don't you apologize to me, dear. You did nothing wrong. Do you hear me?"

She nodded meekly.

"Did my son really do that to you?" Mrs. Karl brushed a hand gently over the bandage on Clara's neck.

Giving another nod, she felt very much like a vulnerable little girl again in the presence of a woman she held in such high esteem.

"I'm so sorry, dear," she murmured. "I don't know what would possess him to hurt you. He was a little in love with you, you know."

She staggered back in shock. Clara hadn't known that. She'd never once thought of Tommy as a potential love interest. He was a good friend, almost like a brother to her. How had she missed that Tommy was in love with her?

Offering a half smile, Mrs. Karl murmured, "I take it you didn't know." Noticing Naomi for the first time, she said, "You must be one of Clara's sisters. Naomi or Agape?"

"Naomi. Nice to meet you, Mrs. Karl."

From the look on her sister's face, Clara could tell that Naomi was thinking about the third sister in their weird little set of triplets. After she and Naomi had connected, they had reached out to Agape, but she hadn't wanted anything to do with them. Maybe they should try again; they'd talked about it, both of them wanted a relationship with their sister.

"Call me Donna, dear. I'm always telling Clara to call me that, but she won't."

"Because you're Tommy's mom," she protested.

"May we come in?" Naomi asked.

"Oh, of course, I'm sorry dears, when I heard the doorbell I thought you were the police. They said they were coming by this morning. They want to talk to me about Tommy."

Clara clearly got the message Naomi's eyes all but screamed at her. Don't mention the Doll Killer case. She wanted to, but if Naomi thought it was better not to, then she would go with that—for now at least.

"I still can't believe he carjacked you," Mrs. Karl muttered as she led them to the cozy lounge room. "Why would he do that?"

The old lady, who had been so kind to her, looked so forlorn that Clara hated that Jonathon and his partner were going to hurt her by telling her they thought Tommy had started abducting and killing children. She wanted to be the one to break the bad news. She would do it much more gently than Jonathon would. Naomi gave her a warning nudge, and Clara kept her mouth closed, instead sitting beside Mrs. Karl and wrapping an arm around the woman's shoulders. She had spent so many happy hours with Tommy and his mother in this very room. Watching movies, playing board games, drawing pictures, and building things with Lego blocks. This place had been a safe haven for her in the months and years following her kidnapping—it was the one place she had *always* felt safe. And that was solely because of Mrs. Karl.

"I'm sorry," she whispered. The part she had played in Tommy's death and the pain it had caused his mother ate at her.

"No, dear, you have nothing to be sorry for. I just don't understand. Did Tommy say anything to you?"

"Just that he wanted to show me something."

"I was wondering," Mrs. Karl began nervously, "if maybe he tried to show you how he felt about you, and you rejected him, and that's why he hurt you, why he shot at the cops knowing they'd shoot back. I know you said you didn't know that Tommy had a crush on you, but if you were just trying to protect my feelings, because . . ."

"No, nothing like that," Clara assured her. "I didn't know Tommy had a crush on me. And I truly don't know why he carjacked me. But I want to understand; I thought you might be able to help me."

"Help you?" Mrs. Karl echoed listlessly.

For a moment, anger at Tommy flashed through her. How could he be so selfish? Hurting her, hurting his mother. He should have known better. Mrs. Karl and her husband had struggled for years to have a baby before finally conceiving and carrying Tommy to term when they were in their mid-forties. From what Tommy had told her he had been quite spoiled as a child, even before his abduction, and following it, he was treated like a prince who could do no wrong—his every whim catered to. After his father's sudden death about ten years ago, Tommy had grown even closer to his mother. Clara couldn't imagine him causing her pain. "The Tommy I knew would never pull a gun on me or cut me or put me in danger by making me run from the police, and yet he did all those things. I need to know why. Have you noticed anything different about him lately? Something that would explain this sudden change in behavior?"

"Well . . ." Mrs. Karl looked around nervously.

"We're not the cops," Clara reminded her. "I'm Tommy's friend. Please, if you know something, then please tell me. I need to know."

"A couple of months ago I got a call from his doctor—his psychiatrist—to ask if I'd heard from Tommy because he'd skipped his last appointment and hadn't returned any of the doctor's calls. I was the emergency contact that Tommy gave, so he called me to make sure Tommy was okay."

"He'd been seeing a psychiatrist again? Why didn't he tell me?" That he hadn't confided in her, hurt her deeply. She and Tommy had always been completely open and honest with one another about how they were feeling, and both of them had talked the other out of a deep, dark hole more than once. Why wouldn't he have come to her if he was facing another battle with depression? Instead, this time he'd pulled away from her. She hadn't heard from him in months. Was he embarrassed that he was struggling again? She saw no reason why he should be embarrassed around her.

"I don't know, dear," Mrs. Karl patted her knee comfortingly. "He didn't tell me, either."

"There was more, though," Naomi spoke up. "The doctor told you something else, didn't he?"

Surprised, Mrs. Karl turned to her with a wry smile. "Now I see why you brought your sister."

"Naomi's good at things like that," Clara acknowledged. "Is she right? Did the doctor tell you something else?"

After another hesitation, Mrs. Karl began, "The doctor was concerned because Tommy hadn't picked up his prescription."

"He was back on antidepressants?"

"I think he was supposed to be. But I was cleaning his old room the other day, and I found something."

"Found what?" she prompted when the old woman didn't continue.

"He'd hidden them in a dresser drawer. They were all unopened. There were eight bottles of antidepressants. He hadn't been taking his medication in at least six months."

~

11:31 A.M.

"Is that who I think it is?" Jonathon growled as he pulled to a stop outside Donna Karl's house.

"Yep," Allina agreed, a small smile tugging at the corners of her mouth.

Jonathon was at least glad that his predicament with Clara was distracting his partner enough to get her to smile. He was also glad that she had finally told him about her sister-in-law. And it certainly explained her distance and the weariness in her eyes that she tried so hard to hide. Jonathon couldn't imagine living for three minutes—let alone three years—with the knowledge that someone you loved was either dead or suffering horrendously. But despite his partner's amusement, his displeasure at seeing Clara leaving Tommy's mother's house wasn't of a personal nature but rather a professional one. He didn't want her meddling with his investigation.

As soon as he'd parked, he bounded from the car, storming toward Clara and her sister.

"Think before you speak," Allina warned quietly as she followed him.

The sight of Clara, upon reaching her, put a slight dent in his anger. She was too pale, and her eyes were dull. Still, he couldn't help snapping, "I don't like you interfering with my case."

The dullness left her eyes, anger taking its place. "I won't stop," she all but pouted. "You're trying to prove that Tommy is a killer, but he's not. And I won't stop until I prove you wrong."

"Thomas *is* a killer. One of the officers he shot died," he informed her softly.

Clara looked stricken and staggered backward. Concerned she might collapse, Jonathon reached for her, but her sister grabbed her first.

"Not your fault, Clara," Naomi insisted.

Her devastated green eyes looked up at him. "What was his name? How old was he? Did he have a wife? Kids?"

Naomi muttered something about Clara torturing herself, but Jonathon wasn't listening—he was debating whether to answer Clara's questions. He decided he would; perhaps if she accepted Thomas was capable of violence, she would let go of this notion of attempting to prove his innocence. "His name was Martin Hine. He was married with two adult kids and four grandchildren. He was a month away from retiring."

She absorbed this, her eyes full of pain but her voice was even when she spoke, "I'm sorry Tommy did that. I'm sorry that I didn't warn you as soon as I got out of the car." She waved him off when he would have reminded her that she'd been injured and in shock. "I don't know why Tommy did that, but I do know that he would never abduct and kill children."

"You're free to think whatever you want; just don't put yourself in the middle of my investigation," he ordered. He wanted to be more understanding; he knew that Thomas was her friend. He knew she was grieving him, and he knew she was still shaken up by the carjacking. But she'd upset him by turning down his offer of dinner, and as such, his feelings toward her were too churned up at the moment. It was best to just keep his focus on the case. "What did Mrs. Karl say to you?"

"Nothing," Clara answered quickly. Too quickly. She was clearly lying—it was written all over her face.

"What did she say?" he repeated, frustration making him enunciate each word.

"We just talked about the funeral. Tommy doesn't have many friends, and other than his mother, there are only a few distant cousins. I didn't want his mother to have to deal with making all the arrangements on her own. She hasn't been well, so I came over to discuss what she wanted for the funeral."

He doubted that was all that had been discussed, but for now, he let it go. "I mean it, Clara—stay away from anything related to this case. If you're right and Thomas had nothing to do with this, then we'll find that out. We're not out to frame anyone; we want to find who's started up the doll murders and put a stop to it. Now go home, get some rest; you look tired. You do, too," he told Naomi, who he could have sworn was fighting the urge to poke her tongue out at him.

Ready to dismiss the sisters and get on to interviewing Thomas' mother, he was turning his back on them when he noticed Naomi give Clara a nudge. "Jonathon, wait."

Suspicious, he asked, "What?"

"Can I talk to you for a moment? Alone." Clara shot a pointed glance at Allina.

"I'll just check my phone." Allina walked a short distance away.

Naomi too had left them alone, and Jonathon wondered whether Clara intended to try and convince him to leave Thomas' mother alone. "Look, Clara, I know you—"

"I changed my mind," she blurted out.

The words he'd said to her the day before floated through his head, but he didn't want to make the mistake of jumping to conclusions—he needed to hear her spell it out. "Oh?" was all he said.

"I shouldn't have said no when you asked me out. I agree that there's a spark between us, and I'd like to see where it leads. So, if your invitation to dinner still stands, then I accept."

Jonathon was almost tempted to make her squirm a little, but the nervousness that was rolling off her in waves stopped him. Smiling, he reached for her hand. His day had suddenly improved dramatically. He'd hoped she'd change her mind—suspected she might—but he hadn't expected her to do it so quickly. "Of course the offer still stands, and I'm delighted you accepted. Let's try for tonight."

It was Clara's turn to look surprised. "Tonight?"

"Unless that's too soon. If you prefer, we can wait until this case is over."

Clara smiled, and her whole face was transformed. She looked stunning; her green eyes sparkled, her cheeks tinted a pretty shade of pink, and her lips looked so tempting that he had to force himself to resist the urge to kiss her right here and now. "Tonight is fine. Perfect," she added.

"Okay, I'll call you later, and we can fix the details," he smiled, feeling like he couldn't stop.

Clara stood on tiptoe and kissed his cheek and then hurried off to her sister's car. Jonathon stood staring after her, long after the car had disappeared up the street, until Allina poked him in the side.

"She's watching us from the window," his partner informed him.

He snapped himself back into work mode. Clara's decision to go out with him had thrown him, but now it was time to focus on the task at hand. At the front door, he gave a brisk knock, and a moment later it was cautiously opened. "Good morning, Mrs. Karl. I'm Detective Dawson, and this is Detective Bennett."

"Come in," the woman said in a resigned tone.

Wordlessly, she led them through the house and into a small but homey lounge room. Jonathon wondered whether she knew they were here to talk about more than the carjacking. He didn't think Clara would have said anything—if for no other reason than her sister, who seemed to have a sensible head on her shoulders, would have told her not to.

"You think my Tommy is involved, don't you? In the Doll Killer copycat murders?"

"Did Clara say that to you?" Jonathon asked, sharper than he intended to, but if Clara had done that she was going to get a real talking to at dinner tonight.

"No. But Tommy's dead; there isn't really any need for you to talk to me about the carjacking. And the crimes started up a few months ago, and then Tommy goes after Clara. I'm not stupid, Detective; I can put the pieces together."

"Do you think he could be involved?" he asked, intrigued by the woman's attitude. Mrs. Karl seemed more resigned than angry or adamantly maintaining her son's innocence.

"What about Clara? Could she be involved?" Allina added.

"Clara? My goodness, no," Mrs. Karl looked horrified by even the possibility.

"But you think Thomas might be?" he pressed gently.

Looking miserable, she responded, "Maybe. I didn't have the heart to say it to Clara though."

"Why do you think your son might be involved?" Allina asked.

The woman looked conflicted, and Jonathon took pity on her and asked instead, "Was Thomas different after the abduction?"

"Yes, he regressed. Started wetting the bed, had nightmares, became very clingy, cried a lot—all things his therapist said were normal," she finished defensively.

"And at school?"

"He was teased a lot. Bullied. Because he was so emotional. He started to withdraw."

"How did he cope with the bullying?"

"Drawing. It became his life after the abduction. It was basically all he'd do. I could hardly ever pry him away from his pencils and paints."

"Did he ever talk to you about the abduction or the bullying?"

"No, he kept all that in. I tried to encourage him to be open about it all, but he wouldn't. I think he'd talk to Clara, though. They were very close."

He caught the hidden meaning there. Thomas Karl had had a crush on Clara, and he was fairly sure it wasn't reciprocated. "When did the bullying stop?"

"Probably after high school. In college, he was quiet, kept to himself. He was a very polite boy, and very sensitive, but he wasn't confident in forming bonds with people. He made a few friends once he started his art degree, but I don't really know any of them."

"What did the bullying involve?"

"Tommy didn't have good control over some of his emotions after he came home. Not anger; he was never one to get angry about anything, but he'd cry at the drop of a hat, and he'd get real embarrassed about it. The boys at his school would call him a sissy, steal his clothes during gym class and replace them with dresses. They would call him Tammy, corner him in the playground and try to convince him to fight them to prove he was a real man. The school was supportive, but whenever they did anything to punish the boys involved, they'd stop for a while, wait for things to die down, and then start up again. That was almost worse because Tommy would start to relax, thinking it was finally over." Mrs. Karl's voice was a mixture of fury and helplessness.

"Did Thomas date?"

"Yes, from time to time. It never usually lasted too long. Although there was one young lady. I thought it might have been the real thing; from what he said, she seemed to truly understand him. But Tommy was very secretive about the whole thing. I think he was worried about failing and somehow letting me down. But I didn't want Tommy to find someone to love for my benefit. I wanted it for him."

Hopefully, since Clara was the person Thomas usually opened up to she might know the identity of this woman. "What about the last few months? Has Thomas' behavior changed?"

"I haven't seen him in six months," Donna Karl admitted. "Which I suppose is a change. Tommy would usually come by at least once a month; often, more regularly."

"Did he answer phone calls or emails? Keep up his social media profiles?"

"Tommy didn't use the Internet. He had a cell phone which he used for phone calls, but lately, whenever he returned my calls, he was always in a hurry. He'd assure me he was fine, just busy, and that he'd come around to visit soon. He never did." Tears welled in the woman's eyes.

The timeline fit both with what Clara had told them and with the crimes. Tommy had virtually cut off contact with his family and friends a couple of months before he abducted the first pair of children. Now if they could just find out who he had been spending his time with the last six months, then they'd find his partner and the missing little girl.

∼

4:09 P.M.

. . .

The hardest thing about collecting the next precious little person to be given the gift of immortality was timing everything perfectly.

So many things could go wrong. So far, they'd been lucky—every single time things had gone smoothly. But she always knew the risks were high. Particularly the longer things went on. The more children that made the trip to eternity, the more people became paranoid and kept a closer watch on their little ones.

It was because they didn't understand.

If they understood what she was doing for these children, then they wouldn't try to hide them away. Instead, they would be lining up to bring their children to her—begging her to choose their child next.

But people didn't understand, so they were afraid. Which meant that she needed to keep on her toes. Be constantly aware of what was happening around her.

Today she was on the lookout for a little boy to be a partner for Katie. The child was in desperate need of a mate. She had been crying for the last twenty-four hours straight. It was starting to get annoying. Ever since the child had woken up, tucked securely away in the specially designed attic, she had been a mess of tears. Katie should be grateful; soon her transformation would take place. She'd tried to explain that to the girl, but she just continued to sob and ask if her brother was safe. If the child cared about her little brother, then she would have been watching him and noticed when a stranger carried him from the bank. But the girl hadn't noticed.

Neither had the mother.

What kind of mother allowed her seven-year-old to watch a baby?

How irresponsible. The lady hadn't even been keeping a vague eye on the children. She hadn't noticed a stranger carrying her toddler away. She hadn't noticed her little girl go running off in search of the baby. She hadn't noticed her unconscious daughter being carried away. She hadn't noticed her toddler being returned to the bank. She clearly didn't deserve her children.

So many parents didn't.

Anyway, it would be a relief to give Katie Logan someone to talk to and play with because she was starting to get fed up with the constant weeping.

Scanning the library, it seemed like a good place to go looking for the perfect kid. She was surprised she hadn't thought of it before.

It didn't take long.

She spotted the perfect child almost immediately.

He was a handsome little boy. His blond hair was cut shorter than she liked, but otherwise, he was just what she was looking for. His skin was delightfully pale, with just a sprinkling of freckles across his nose and cheeks. His eyes were big and brilliantly blue, framed by lovely long dark lashes. His lips were beautifully defined and a wonderful shade of red. The child almost looked like a doll already. That haircut was bothersome, though; she might have to keep these two for a little longer than usual to let it grow out. She would hate to send the child into infinity with an awful hairdo.

Now she just needed a plan on how best to isolate and then remove the little boy from the library without being detected.

First things first. She needed to find out who his mother was and how attentive she was. The boy was in the children's area, curled up on one of the large beanbag chairs, with his nose buried in a book. There were at least five other children in the area, but none of them were blondes, so she didn't think any were relatives. Three adults lingered around the children, half paying attention to them, half flicking through books of their own. Again, none of the adults were blondes, so she didn't think any were the boy's parent.

Next, she needed to find where the boy's mother was. She didn't want to be right in the middle of luring the boy only to have the mother come and interfere and ruin things. Taking her time, she wandered the library, pretending to peruse the books as she went. Finally, she identified the woman she presumed to be the boy's mother. The woman appeared to be in her thirties and was sitting at a computer typing madly, a mess of textbooks spread out around her.

Reassured that the mom was occupied writing her paper, she moved on to the next task: finding out the child's name. Lying beside the boy was a schoolbag. Edging closer she noticed a name written in bright colors on the front. Jimmy Wallander. Jimmy. What a beautiful name.

She was so glad that this child had been placed in front of her today; he was going to make her most beautiful doll thus far.

Already a plan was formulating in her head. She knew just how best to quickly gain the child's confidence and spirit him away.

"Excuse me, young man," she sidled to a stop in front of the boy.

Startled, the boy's eyes snapped from his book to her, wary for a moment, but then he assessed her and decided she wasn't a threat. Wariness changed to shyness, and his pale cheeks heated.

"How old are you, young man?"

"Eight," his voice was soft and sweet.

Beaming a mega smile at him, she responded, "That's perfect. My little grandson is exactly your age. He's coming to stay with me for a couple of weeks while his mom and dad go on a holiday; he loves to read, and I wanted to choose some books for him to read. Do you read a lot?"

Eager now, the boy replied, "Yes, I love reading."

"Would you mind helping me pick out a few books that my grandson might like?"

He hesitated for a moment, probably replaying his parents' warnings to never talk to strangers. But the fact that she looked like an old lady, and that he probably felt safe in the library, he quickly brushed his concerns aside and bounced to his feet. Following him, he hurried to some shelves and began pulling out books.

Fate was on her side today. The shelves he'd chosen were partially hidden from view, and close to one of the exits—again, as fate would have it, it was the quieter one. Carefully, she extracted the vial of sedatives and syringe from her purse.

"These are my favorites," the boy was saying, holding out several books.

"That's nice, dear," she murmured as she pretended to reach for the books, instead jabbing him with the needle.

Startled, the boy dropped the books, and staggered backward, but before he could make a sound she had bundled him up in her arms and was hurrying out the door. Satisfied that no one had noticed, she buckled the boy into the backseat of her car. Should she be pulled over, she could always explain his heavy sleeping as sickness, whereas an unconscious child in the trunk could not be so easily accounted for. Taking off, careful to follow all road rules, she couldn't wait to get her new little addition home.

~

8:17 P.M.

The couple before him looked destroyed.

Unfortunately, Jonathon knew what they were going through. He remembered when his parents had looked like that. That look had lasted a long time.

Eight-year-old Jimmy Wallander had been reported missing a little over two hours ago. However, his mother hadn't laid eyes on him since around three when she'd picked him up from school and taken him to the library so she could work on a paper for school. She'd recently gone back to study to be a teacher, but between juggling work, a husband, an eight-year-old and an eight-month-old baby, she didn't have a lot of time to complete her assignments, so she'd taken to going to the library after picking up her son from school. She'd settled Jimmy down with a book —apparently, the little boy loved to read and was happy to sit for hours with a favorite book—and gone to work. At six o'clock she had packed up her work and gone to collect her son, ready to go home and cook dinner.

Only her son was nowhere to be found.

No one still at the library remembered seeing the boy walk off with anyone, but given that they had almost a three-hour window where the boy could have been taken, they were organizing tracking down everyone who had been there during that time.

Given that the boy was between the ages of six and eight, and a blue-eyed blond, plus the fact that they knew the killers were in the market for a boy given they already had Katie Logan and they had killed their last two kidnap victims, he and Allina had been given the case. They'd had the couple brought to the station to be interviewed. The father had picked up the baby from daycare and rushed to the library upon hearing his son was missing. Jonathon had thought this neutral location might help; their home was going to be full of distracting memories, as was the library.

He assessed the couple through the window of the conference room they'd set them up in. Heather Wallander had been clutching her baby daughter the entire time. Clutching her so tightly, in fact, that the baby was fussing. Liam Wallander had been downing cup after cup of coffee. To Jonathon's count, he'd already had eight.

"Ready?" Allina popped up beside him.

"Yep."

"Was Clara disappointed you had to cancel your dinner plans?"

"Disappointed, but she understood. She wants these killers caught almost more than anyone else. I said I'd call her tomorrow to reschedule."

Clara had been very sweet on the phone, assuring him she completely understood that if they were to date, sometimes his job was going to require him to have to cancel. She had been devastated, although in a resigned manner, to learn another child had been taken. Guilty, too, which he hadn't liked. None of this was her fault. She was six when she was kidnapped, and her brain had done what it needed to do to protect her, and even if they'd found the original Doll Killers, that might not have stopped Thomas Karl from deciding to replicate the crimes. Clara had also seemed to understand that talking to the parents of the missing boy would be difficult for him even though he hadn't said a word to her, or to anyone else, about his connection to this case.

"When we finish with the parents, I'll swing by your place and pick up your sister-in-law's case files," he told his partner.

She waved him off. "That can wait. It'll be late; you can get them another time."

"No, Allina. Grace has waited long enough for someone to find her. We're partners, and I hope friends, too. I want to do what I can to help you find her." He wasn't going to let Allina brush him off. He understood the torment she and her family were stuck in, torn between wishing Grace was already dead, so she wasn't suffering, and praying she was alive and doing everything in their power to bring her home.

"Okay, thanks," she gave a tight smile. "It's just abduction cases bring it all back up, not that it ever really goes away. And murder cases, part of me always expects the body to be hers."

"I know." He patted her shoulder comfortingly. It was a wonder Allina had managed to stick with the job, given that every day was full of painful reminders of her sister-in-law. He wasn't sure he could do it. As horrible as it had been finding out Dora was dead, it had given him and his family closure. Allina's family was trapped in limbo, unable to move on. "You can't give up hope; Grace is counting on you."

"I know. That's the only thing that gets me through the day. Anyway, this isn't about Grace; it's about Jimmy Wallander and trying to find him before it's too late."

Determinedly, Allina stalked to the door, and Jonathon followed, doubting that anything in the Bennett family had nothing to do with Grace, he suspected she dominated their thoughts, both conscious and subconscious.

Heather and Liam's heads snapped up when they entered the room. "Do you know anything?" Liam asked, standing uncertainly.

"No, not yet; I'm sorry," Jonathon replied, taking a seat at the table.

Liam Wallander remained standing. "But it's them, right? The ones who've been killing kids and leaving them with dolls. They have Jimmy; they're going to do that to him."

"We don't know that." Heather crushed the baby tighter in her arms, and the little girl squawked her protest.

"For goodness sake, Heather, put her down." Liam snapped at his wife as he downed another cup of coffee.

"No." Heather held the child tighter again, and the baby began to wail.

"Stop it! She doesn't like you holding her that tight; give her here." Liam tried to wrestle the baby from his wife's arms.

"No! Don't! Leave her! I need to hold her!" Heather shrieked.

"Mr. and Mrs. Wallander," Jonathon interrupted. He and Allina both moved to physically stop the couple. "I know this is hard, but we need you focused right now. Why don't you put the baby down for a bit? Maybe one of our officers can take her, give her a bottle, and put her to sleep for you," he suggested.

"I can't let her go," Heather cried softly.

Allina kneeled beside the woman. "I know you want to hold on to her, but she's upset. Maybe it would be better if she weren't here while we talk about your son," she gently suggested.

"But she's just a baby; she doesn't know what we're talking about," Heather protested.

"But she knows her mommy and daddy are upset," Allina reminded her.

Reluctantly, Heather allowed Allina to pry the baby from her arms, but her eyes remained glued to the child as Allina took her from the room. Once they were gone, the woman wrapped her arms around herself while Liam poured himself another cup of coffee and drank most of it in one go.

"I know you want to hold her to make sure she's safe, but she'll be fine, and you can get her as soon as we're done talking," Jonathon assured her as he returned to his seat.

"Jimmy was with you, and he wasn't safe," Liam muttered under his breath.

"Are you saying it's my fault?" Heather raged. "How dare you. How *dare* you!" she bounded to her feet and beat her fists on her husband's chest. "Maybe if you were home more often, if you did something to help, then I wouldn't have to drag him along to the library after school to try to get my assignments done. I'm doing this for us so that we can have a better life."

Jonathon wanted to intervene but suspected it wouldn't do any good. Perhaps letting them get out their bottled-up fears and frustrations would help them to focus better.

"A better life? We were doing just fine. I never cared about a better life. I just wanted our family to be happy, and now our son is gone," Liam returned fire.

For a moment, Heather remained frozen in place. Then her tears came in a rush, and she sagged against her husband. "It's my fault," she sobbed. "I should have been watching him. What was wrong with me? It's my fault. It's my fault."

His anger faded, and Liam held her with one arm, patting her awkwardly on the back. He didn't say anything though, and Jonathon suspected that part of him did blame his wife.

Allina reentered the room. "Everything okay in here?"

"Just ask us your questions," Liam muttered, half dragging his wife back to the table and pushing her into a chair.

Once they were all seated, Jonathon began, "Have either of you noticed anyone paying special attention to your family, particularly Jimmy?"

"I haven't," Liam replied.

"Mrs. Wallander?" Jonathon prompted

The woman simply looked at him as though he were speaking a foreign language. She seemed to be quickly sliding into shock.

"Heather, for goodness' sake, answer them. How else are we going to get Jimmy back?" Liam gave his wife a sharp poke in the side.

"No," Heather answered in the merest hint of a whisper.

Jonathon hadn't expected them to answer any differently than they had. All the families of the kidnapped children had said the same thing. None of them had noticed anyone targeting their child. It seemed that the killers simply picked a day and a location and then picked a child who just happened to be there and who fitted their requirements.

"Would Jimmy have spoken to a stranger if one approached him?" Allina asked.

"He knows about strangers, and he knows not to talk to one, but he's eight. If someone approached him, and he didn't see them as a threat, then he might."

Liam seemed to be the designated answerer, which wasn't going to do them any good. He hadn't been at the library; he wouldn't have seen anything. They needed Heather to snap out of her daze long enough to answer some questions. If they could get a handle on how the abductor approached the children and gained their trust, thus allowing them to be removed from a public place without the child putting up a fuss, then it could help them tremendously.

"Mrs. Wallander," Allina pulled her chair closer and clasped the woman's hands in her own. "I know it's tough, but Jimmy needs you to be strong a little longer, okay? We need you to tell us about the people from the library, whatever you can remember about them."

"There were too many," the woman protested dully.

"You don't have to remember everyone, just tell us about the people you do remember. Try to think about who seemed like they fit in, who belonged, and who didn't," Allina encouraged.

"It was after school," Heather began, "so there were a lot of parents with kids."

"Anyone who stood out, maybe a woman who didn't seem to be with a child?" Jonathon asked, aware that with Thomas dead they were most likely looking for his female partner.

Scrunching her eyes closed as she thought, she answered, "Not that I remember, but I wasn't really paying attention. I wanted to get as much work done on my paper as I could before I had to go home and get dinner started. I just settled Jimmy in the children's area—we've been there plenty of times before so he already knew the rules."

"What were the rules, Mrs. Wallander?" Allina asked

"He could talk to other kids, or a parent with a kid, but no one else. He wasn't allowed to leave the children's area unless it was to come directly to me. He knew where I'd be, and he had to ask even if he needed to use the bathroom. Other than that, he was supposed to stay there and read. He *loves* reading; he can do it for hours. Sometimes at home, I have to take his books off him to get him to go and play outdoors. It was the library, I thought he'd be safe," Heather finished helplessly.

Allina dove straight into the next question before the woman had time to wallow, "Other than parents with kids, who else was there?"

"There were some older kids, high school and college age, but all were busy working on assignments, none of them were wandering about."

Thinking that an elderly person might seem harmless enough to a child that they would disobey the never-talk-to-a-stranger rule, Jonathon prodded, "Anyone older? Fifties? Sixties? Seventies, maybe?"

Blue eyes widened. "There *was* an old lady. I remember because she walked so slowly around the whole library, it seemed like she was in pain. I considered getting up and asking her if I could find her book for her so she could sit down and take a break."

That sounded like a genuine possibility. Disguising yourself as an old woman would be the perfect way to scout locations without seeming suspicious—no one suspected the kindly old grandmotherly type. Jonathon wondered if that was how Clara had been lured. Or perhaps, thinking of Clara's insistence that the current crimes were committed by the same couple as the original ones, it *was* one of the original Doll Killers, who would now be elderly.

"Can you give us a description of the woman?" Allina was asking.

"You think it was her?" Heather's jaw went slack with surprise. "But she was just an old lady."

"Would Jimmy have spoken to an old lady if one approached him?" Jonathon asked.

She nodded quickly. "Gray hair, glasses, wearing a dress, I remember thinking that a lot of elderly women always wear a dress even when the weather is so cold—not that there's anything wrong with that. I mean I sometimes wear dresses in the winter myself. It's just that you often see . . ."

Allina quickly cut off the woman's rambling. "Anything else, Mrs. Wallander? Was she tall or short? How old did she appear to be?"

"Shortish, maybe a little under average. I would have thought seventies. That means ... that means ..." Heather Wallander's blue eyes went glassy again, "that it's the same people who were doing this before. When we were kids. They killed almost twenty children back then, and another four now. And they have my baby. They have my baby!" The last was repeated in a hysterical shriek, and she began to sob.

Liam made no move to comfort his wife, so Allina slipped from her chair and went to wrap her arms around the woman. Jonathon could see his family mirrored so closely in the Wallanders. Each parent blaming the other, each parent blaming themselves—that guilt and anger eating away at them until their relationship began to crumble. They may stay together, as his parents had, for the sake of the remaining child, but the love, the joy, the spark between them had been forever extinguished.

His family had all but crumbled under the pressure of Dora's death, but there was still hope for the Wallander family. If they could just find Jimmy and bring him back alive, then this family still had a hope of healing.

CHAPTER
Four

February 10th
1:00 A.M.

"You guys don't have to come in with me. I'm really tired; I'm going to go straight to bed," Clara told her brothers. "Naomi is staying with me, so I'll really be okay."

"Naomi needs sleep, too." Dylan nudged Naomi aside as she fumbled with her keys at the door. "Have you even slept the last few nights?"

"Yes," Naomi shot back defensively, trying to reclaim the keys but Dylan didn't let her.

Unlocking the front door, Dylan said, "You know, even the great Naomi Candella needs more than an hour sleep in three days."

Dylan herded them inside, and Clara was glad that her oldest brother's protective attention was fixed on Naomi at the moment and not on herself. Both of her older brothers had basically adopted Naomi, accepting her as a part of their family, which meant a lot to Clara, and she knew it meant a lot to her sister, too.

"I can spend the night," Davis offered. "Then Naomi can get some sleep."

"Would everyone stop fussing over me, I'm fine. I've gone with less sleep than this before." Naomi stomped off into the kitchen.

Both Davis and Dylan looked amused; neither took Naomi's frustrations personally. They'd known her long enough by now to know that she never gave herself a break. Naomi was like a whirlwind that never stopped.

Following her to the kitchen, Dylan wrapped an arm around Naomi's waist, lifted her off the floor and carried her to the sitting area, where he set her down on one of the couches. "Sit. Rest," he ordered. "Davis will make some tea, then the two of you are going to go to bed. And no arguments, Naomi—you need sleep, and if you won't agree to get any, then I'm going to make you take a sleeping pill."

"Fine," Naomi sighed long-sufferingly.

Clara couldn't help but chuckle; her sister hated being coddled.

"And what are you laughing at?" Dylan turned on her. "You think you look any better than she does? How much sleep have *you* had the last few nights? How many nightmares?"

The reminder of her nightmares sobered her instantly. Her dreams the last couple of nights had been odd, not quite the same as the nightmare that had haunted her sleep right after her abduction. This one kept getting hazy in parts like her mind was trying to unlock the memories it had previously locked away.

"By the look on your face, I'd say the nightmares have been bad." Dylan gentled his voice. "Are you coping okay?"

Was she? She guessed she was coping as well as could be expected, given the circumstances. She hated that another child had been taken, and she felt so guilty that she couldn't give the police anything that might help them figure out who the Doll Killers were. She believed in her heart that it was the same people who had taken her. She didn't know what had made them stop or what had made them start up again, and she didn't care. She just wanted them stopped once and for all.

"Clara?"

"I'm okay," she assured her brother.

"She blames herself because she can't remember what happened," Naomi informed him.

That earned her a frown. "That's ridiculous, Clara. You were six years old. If you could cope with remembering what happened, your brain wouldn't have blocked it out."

She glared at her traitor of a sister. Naomi had just told Dylan that to get the focus off herself. "I'm not a child anymore, though, Dylan," she reminded him.

"Do you want to remember?" Davis asked, bringing over a tray full of cups and a teapot.

"I want to be able to help find the two missing children and stop this," she replied.

"That sounds like a no." Davis handed her a cup and sat beside her, wrapping an arm around her shoulders.

Leaning into him, she was glad that her brothers had insisted on taking her out tonight. She'd been disappointed but understanding when Jonathon had called to cancel. If they were going to try dating, then she was going to have to get used to that and learn not to take it personally. But having the date canceled had left her feeling a little lost. She feared having too much time on her hands, which would leave her mind free to wander into unpleasant territory. But then Dylan and Davis had turned up at her place and taken her and Naomi out for dinner and a movie. She'd enjoyed just chatting and having fun with her siblings like they usually did. Everyone had carefully avoided any talk on the Doll Killers, until now.

"It's not your job to solve this case, Clara," Davis reminded her.

"But they're trying to pin it all on Tommy." Tears were welling up in her eyes and she determinedly held them back. Learning that one of the police officers Tommy shot had died was horrifying. How could her sweet, quiet friend fire a gun into a sea of people? What was he thinking? Why had he stopped taking his medication? Why had he started seeing a psychiatrist again and not told her? Why wouldn't he have told her that he was struggling with depression again? He knew he could trust her, didn't he? So many questions and no chance of getting any answers.

"But if he didn't do it, they'll find that out, honey," Dylan said.

Jonathon had said the same thing to her. And she wanted to believe it; she did. But sometimes it was hard to let go of a notion once it lodged itself in your head.

"All right, drink up, then bedtime," Dylan announced. "I'll stay here tonight."

"No, you should go home to your family," she protested. Her oldest brother had a beautiful wife and an adorable four-year-old son who Clara loved dearly.

"They're fine, they're asleep already, and I told Maria I'd probably stay here tonight. If I don't stay then, Naomi isn't going to sleep, and even if I drug Naomi to make her sleep then you're not going to sleep because subconsciously you need to know that someone is here and awake for you to be able to sleep. So, I'm staying."

"Me too," Davis added. "It'll be like a sleepover," he joked.

Clara was going to protest that she didn't have enough beds for everyone but stopped herself. Maybe it would be a good idea for her brothers to spend the night. Dylan was right—she and Naomi both needed sleep, and they'd both be more likely to get it if the boys stayed. "Naomi can sleep in my room with me, and you two can share the spare room. I'm going to go up; I'm wiped out." She finished her tea.

"I'll come up with you and take a shower." Naomi stood and stretched.

"We'll clean up down here, lock up and be up soon. Sweet dreams, girls," Dylan said.

They split at the top of the stairs; Naomi headed for the bathroom while Clara headed for her room. A giant yawn was just splitting her face in two as she switched on the light. She saw it as soon as she opened her eyes. The yawn froze on her face. The rest of her froze, too.

She heard screaming.

It took her a moment to realize it was coming from her.

"What's wrong?" Naomi appeared beside her, but Clara couldn't answer.

"What is it?" Dylan and Davis came running into the room.

"On the bed," Naomi answered, her gaze following Clara's to the bed. "Get Clara out of here and call the cops."

Davis snatched her up and carried her downstairs. Clara wrapped her arms around his neck and clung to him.

She knew what it was.

It was her doll.

The one the Doll Killers had intended to leave in her lap once they'd killed her and left her on a park bench.

And she knew who'd left it here.

The Doll Killers had been here in her home and left her doll on her bed.

~

2:06 A.M.

Jonathon had no idea if he'd even turned the car engine off as he ran up the path to Clara's front door. All he could think about was Clara. She must be so scared. *He* was so scared. Leaving the doll on her bed had been a message. It was a threat. They were watching her, and he was afraid they were going to take things further.

He hammered on Clara's door. The wait for it to be opened seemed like an eternity. Eventually, it was opened by Naomi, who looked even more tired in person than she'd sounded on the phone when she'd called to tell him about the doll.

"Hey, Jonathon; come on in." She held the door open and then locked it behind him once he'd entered.

"Hi, Naomi," he replied, his eyes roving the room looking for Clara. He found her curled up in the corner of one of the couches, wrapped up in a blanket. She was watching him and her lips curved in a small smile when she saw him looking at her.

As he walked toward her, he was aware of two men in their thirties watching his every move like hawks. Clara's big brothers, he presumed. Naomi had told him on the phone that they were there. While the half-sisters looked like clones, Clara didn't resemble her half-brothers at all. Trying to ignore the half-scrutinizing, half-threatening glares from the two men, he focused instead on Clara. "You doing okay?" he asked as he crouched beside the couch.

"Hanging in there," she replied, stretching a hand out from under her little wooly cocoon to grasp his.

"So you're the cop," one of her brothers noted. To say his voice was icy would be the understatement of the century.

"Dylan," Clara warned.

"That's okay," Jonathon squeezed her hand and stood, holding out his hand to Dylan. Up close, he could see that Clara and her brothers did indeed share a common trait—they all had the same green eyes. "Jonathon Dawson."

Dylan shook his hand in a grip that bordered on crushing. "Dylan Merritt."

"Davis Merritt," the other man said as he, too, shook Jonathon's offered hand.

"Any ideas on how they got in to leave the doll?" he asked.

"Back door," Davis replied. "We didn't notice anything off when we came through the front door, but when we found the doll, little miss diligent over there," he waved a hand at Naomi, "thought to check the back door. It was unlocked."

"Any chance you could have just forgotten to lock it when you left?" Jonathon directed the question at Clara.

"I might have, but Naomi wouldn't."

Now *that* he believed. He didn't think Naomi had forgotten a single thing in her life.

"We should have checked it when we got home," Dylan said self-reprimandingly, "but none of us thought that Clara was in any physical danger."

Fear clawed at him, but he fought it back. The Doll Killers weren't going to get their hands on Clara. Perhaps they didn't even want to. Maybe leaving her doll was just a way of finishing off the old crimes so they could focus on the new spree. "You have a spare bedroom upstairs?" he asked Clara. When she nodded, he continued, "Why don't I take you up and you can get some rest? CSU is going to be here soon, and there's no need for you to watch them work."

"I can take Clara up. She's stressed and scared; she's been having nightmares—it would probably be better for her to have someone she knows and is comfortable with staying with her." Davis both looked and sounded like he was in full-on protective mode.

Jonathon honed in on the nightmare reference—sometimes your subconscious played out things in your dreams that you couldn't face while you were awake. He was leaning toward thinking Clara was right and the original killers were still involved. That made it even more important to find out what Clara remembered—she was their only link left. As soon as he got Clara alone, he was going to find out more about these nightmares.

Now, though, he wanted to play it safe with her brothers; he was serious about finding out if things would work out with Clara, so he needed her brothers on his side. "If you want to go up with your brother, that's fine; I'll hang around down here. I just want to make sure you get some rest." His answer must have impressed both her brothers because he felt them both relax.

"I'll go up with you," Clara said, moving to stand.

He preempted her by scooping her up. She looked tired; there was no need to make her walk up the stairs when he could carry her.

"I can walk," Clara was trying to get her arms free from the blankets she was wrapped up in.

"I know you can, but you're tired and cold and already snuggled in the blankets." He had already started for the stairs. "And someone should make Naomi sleep. I've never seen a person look so exhausted."

Naomi groaned, but the looks exchanged by Davis and Dylan were amused, and Jonathon assumed the topic had already been discussed before he arrived. "We're on it," Dylan noted.

"There're no beds left. Clara's is a crime scene, and she's sleeping in the other bedroom," Naomi protested.

"Sleep down here," Davis told her.

"CSU will be here soon."

"Then we'll ask them to be quiet," Dylan said.

"I can't sleep with you guys watching me," Naomi complained.

"Tough, because we're going to be right here with you," Davis said firmly.

They were still arguing about it as Jonathon reached the top of the stairs. "I take it your sister doesn't like to stop."

"Naomi never stops," Clara confirmed.

Something in her voice had him understanding that something deep motivated Naomi's need to always be on the move. "What's she running from?" he asked quietly, nudging open the half-closed door to the spare bedroom with his foot.

"Herself. So," Clara deliberately brightened her voice, "does you coming here tonight count as our date?"

"Absolutely not." He balanced Clara with one arm and pulled back the covers with the other, then set her down and tucked her in. "I have something much more special planned for our date. Besides, right now you need to get some rest."

Ignoring the part about resting, Clara said, "At least you passed the test with my brothers. They like you, and Naomi likes you, so you're in with my family."

Stretching out on the bed beside her, he was pleased when she snuggled closer and rested her head on his shoulder. "What about your parents?"

"I haven't seen my dad since I turned eighteen, and my mom and I aren't close."

"What about your other sister?"

"Agape? I've only ever spoken to her once. After Naomi and I finally met, we thought it would be great for the three of us to finally get to know each other, being that we're kind of triplets, but when we went to visit her, she didn't want anything to do with us. Lately, Naomi and I have been talking about trying again with her. The first time around we were teenagers, and our moms did have affairs with her dad. I'm sure that we weren't the most popular people in her family when she was growing up; she was just standing up for her mom. But we're older now, and my brothers and sister mean so much to me—I'd really like to know her, too. Even if we're never super close, it would just be nice to think of her as part of my family."

"You're close with your brothers?"

"Yes, very close. Typical kind of big brother, little sister stuff. Sometimes they can be very overprotective, of Naomi too, but we get along well." Clara paused when they heard footsteps on the stairs. "The doll they left; it was supposed to be the one they would leave with me."

"I assume so." He lifted a hand and began to stroke her hair; that had seemed to soothe her in the car the day they'd met, and he hoped it would help again now.

"That proves that it's the same people as before. Not Tommy. He was depressed, but he stopped taking his medication, he must have been suicidal. And his mom, she said that he had feelings for me. That was probably why he carjacked me. Why he fired his gun." She tilted her head to look up at him. "Did you know the officer who died?"

"No, I didn't. Clara, your brother said you've been having nightmares. Have you remembered anything more about the time you were missing or how you escaped?"

She shook her head. "No, but it's like my brain is trying. I want to remember something that will help you; I really do, but I'm scared. I'm scared to know the details of what happened."

"You remember the abduction itself, though," he prodded gently.

She froze, shifted away. "I don't."

"You do," he said firmly. "I know you do. You reacted differently to that when Allina and I were questioning you the other day."

"I don't want to talk about it," she said stiffly, scrunching down in the bed until she was lying flat on her back. "I think I'm going to try and get some sleep now."

"Do you want me to go?"

She sighed deeply, "No, it would be nice if you stayed."

Slipping off his shoes, he climbed under the covers. Clara immediately rolled onto her side and wiggled backward until she was spooned against him. Wrapping an arm loosely around her waist, he brought her closer.

"Can you stay all night?" she asked sleepily.

"I have a meeting at eight, but if you don't mind me showering here in the morning, I can go straight there from here."

"I don't mind." He thought she'd drifted off when she spoke again, her voice sounding half-asleep, "It was an old lady who took me."

An old lady again, just like the one they thought had taken Jimmy

Wallander. So, was it a disguise or a real old lady? Hopefully, Clara's blocked memories held the answers they needed.

~

8:00 A.M.

Allina was the last person to arrive at the morning meeting.

She felt a little stab of jealousy when she spotted her partner looking so calm and relaxed. That didn't seem fair since they'd both had rough nights.

Jonathon had called her when Clara's sister had called him to explain about the doll that had been left on Clara's bed. He'd gone over there and spent the night. Whether he and Clara had just slept or done more than that, she wasn't sure. Nor did she particularly care. Jonathon's private life was his business, and Clara seemed okay. She was glad that she'd told him about Grace. Her sister-in-law could use all the help she could get.

She still remembered when Grace was born. She remembered when Grace said her first word. She remembered Grace's first day of school. She remembered the time Grace fell out of a tree, knocked herself unconscious and spent almost two days in a coma. She remembered helping to teach Grace to drive. She remembered Grace's high school graduation and her college graduation.

And she remembered the last time she had seen her.

It had been almost a month before Grace disappeared. They'd had lunch, done some shopping, and then Allina had dropped her off outside her house. She hadn't even gone inside with her because she'd had to rush off someplace. That was it. Life had been busy for all of them and they hadn't had another chance to catch up. And then Grace was gone.

She remembered that day, too.

With awful crystal-clear clarity.

A delivery man had noticed the broken glass in Grace's front door and called the police. They'd come, and when they'd checked out the house, they'd found a puddle of blood in the kitchen. The blood was tested and turned out, as they'd all expected it would, to be Grace's. There were no witnesses, no leads, and no body ever turned up.

She and her sister, and Grace's brothers, still worked every single lead.

Last night, after Jonathon had picked up Grace's case file, she and her husband had gone to speak with a man who'd witnessed the abduction of a woman who fit Grace's description. They'd hoped it might lead them somewhere, but it hadn't. It looked like the woman had been grabbed by a jealous ex-boyfriend. So, they'd gone home and fallen into bed around two; she'd managed maybe three hours sleep in total, and this morning she was feeling it.

"Ali?"

Jonathon was peering at her in concern, and she realized she was still standing in the doorway. "Sorry," she dropped into the only free seat at the table and looked expectantly at their boss. Heidi knew about Grace, had personally helped her look into numerous leads. So had both the other people in the room. Kane and Tracey Curtis were a happily married Hispanic couple, with no human children but an abundance of fur babies, who also seemed to enjoy working together. Well, not technically together; Kane worked crime scene, and Tracey was a medical examiner, but they often worked the same cases. Three years ago, Kane had gone through Grace's house with a fine-tooth comb, and Tracey still checked the DNA of all unidentified young women who came through the morgue who even vaguely resembled Grace to see if they were her.

It had been Kane who'd collected the doll from Clara's house last night, and now he informed them, "As soon as I finished at Clara Candella's house, I sent pictures to my doll collector friend to find out whatever we could about the doll. This is what she told me: the doll is a twelve-inch French doll from around 1900. Like the others, it has a bisque head and a wood composition body. For those of you who didn't see the doll, she's wearing a blue cotton dress with lace trim and a black sash, cream socks and black leather shoes, and underwear appropriate for the time period. Marks on the doll's neck are F B 3 Paris."

Jonathon cringed at the mention of the marks on the doll. No doubt he was wondering whether Clara bore those marks. Since Ali and Jonathon were partners—and even friends now—she was going to have to try with Clara, even if she didn't like that the woman was deliberately holding back information that might be useful. She reminded herself that Clara was a victim, and in her experience, victims sometimes didn't think logically about things related to their assaults.

"Anything useful on the doll? Fingerprints or something?" Heidi asked.

"Nope, same as all the others, nothing at all on the doll."

Raising a hopeful eyebrow, Heidi repeated, "Nothing on the *doll*?"

"I found a couple of smudgy prints on Clara's back door. I don't know if I'll be able to do anything with them, but it's more than we have so far, so I'll do my best," Kane assured them.

Well, that was progress. Bit by bit, they were starting to move forward. "You find anything else useful, Kane?"

"That was everything from Clara's house."

"Cause of death the same on Lindsey Peters and Kent Mason as all the others?" Jonathon asked the ME.

"Yes, they were given a morphine overdose. At least it would have been painless and quick, given the dosage they were given. They would have fallen asleep; heart rate and breathing would have slowed and then stopped. It was administered intravenously, same as the original murders. From what I saw on these kids now, the IV was inserted well. I only saw one clean incision, no marks from hesitations. I'd say that whoever did it knew what they were doing," Tracey explained.

"What about the kids from twenty years ago?" Heidi asked.

"Obviously, I didn't do any of the autopsies, but the reports indicate again that it was done by someone with experience," Tracey replied.

"Any forensics from the bodies, Kane?"

"I found something on Lindsey," the crime scene tech began slowly.

"Well, what was it?" Heidi snapped, as did the pencil she'd been fiddling with.

"I found a pubic hair in her underwear," Kane told them.

"She was sexually assaulted?" Jonathon asked, rather unnecessarily, but he was clearly wondering if Clara had been, too.

"Yes," Tracey confirmed.

"But none of the other kids were, right?" Jonathon had a tint of desperation in his voice.

"The ones from thirty years ago weren't," Tracey assured him. "Given that they were little kids and they were kept for weeks before they were killed, all of them had the exam done, and none of the original nine girls had been sexually assaulted."

"What about Lottie Hatcher?" Allina asked. This was an unexpected development.

"Undetermined," Tracey replied. "Her exam was inconclusive."

"Did you run a DNA test on the pubic hair?" Allina asked. If they had hard proof that Thomas Karl was involved, they might be able to convince Clara to finally believe it, and then hopefully, she'd be more forthcoming with information.

"Yes," Kane nodded.

"And?" she prompted.

"And it matched Thomas Karl. He was definitely involved; he assaulted Lindsey Peters."

"That's why none of the original children were assaulted. Thomas brought that element to the kidnappings." Jonathon looked livid.

"Any other forensics, Kane?" Heidi asked.

"Nope, that's all from me."

"So we now know for a fact that Thomas was involved, but we still don't know who he's working with. We know he's working with someone because Lindsey and Kent were killed, and Katie and Jimmy were abducted after he was already dead. Given that Clara's doll was left in her house, he obviously has had contact with the pair that kidnapped him and could point to him working with them. Especially since we think an elderly woman took Jimmy Wallander," Allina mused.

"Clara said she was taken by an old woman, too—so it could just be a disguise," Jonathon added.

"She told you about her abduction?" Allina demanded. She didn't like that her partner hadn't informed her of that already.

"No, just that it was an old lady. I'm sorry, Ali, I would have told you sooner only I didn't get a chance. She told me right before we went to sleep, and then you got here just as the meeting was starting," Jonathon soothed.

Acknowledging that he was right, they hadn't had a chance to talk before the meeting; she let go of her irritation. She hadn't been so edgy before Grace's abduction, but living with that stress had worn her down, and these days, she often found herself overreacting. "We know Thomas and the original Doll Killers are involved, but we need to know if Thomas had his own partner. Mrs. Karl mentioned that Thomas had been seeing someone, but she didn't know who it was; however, if there's one person who knows the girlfriend's identity, it's Clara."

"She's not going to take it well when she finds out her friend raped at least one of the little girls. She's already struggling with the idea of him hurting her and shooting at cops." Jonathon looked distressed at the idea of further upsetting Clara.

"No, she's not going to like it," Allina agreed. "But these same people hurt her, and Thomas was working with them. For all we know, he was going to take her to them—I think she wants answers as much as we do."

~

12:23 P.M.

"You want lunch?" Clara asked Naomi. Her sister had been sitting and staring at the TV all morning; only Clara didn't think she'd seen a single thing that had been on.

Naomi shrugged. "I'm not hungry, but if you are, I'll make something."

"You didn't eat breakfast," Clara reminded her.

Another shrug. "I wasn't hungry then, either."

"You didn't sleep last night, did you?"

She bounced to her feet. "I'm fine, Clara. I don't want to hear any more about how much sleep I do or don't get. I don't know why you, Davis, and Dylan are so obsessed with the topic."

She watched as Naomi stalked off to the kitchen and began to rummage through cupboards. She didn't take her sister's outburst personally. They were all on edge, and even the always-in-control Naomi wasn't immune. That the Doll Killers had been here in her home had shaken all of them.

Clara didn't understand why they'd come here. She was no longer a child, so she couldn't imagine that she held any value to the killers. Maybe they thought she had remembered something. She hadn't, her subconscious was dancing around her memories but so far they hadn't come out, either in her dreams or when she was awake. They might never come back.

Still, that Jonathon had come and spent the night was certainly a positive that couldn't be overlooked. Clara dated occasionally, but things usually fizzled out because she didn't know how to have fun, to relax, to find joy in the small things in life, and she spent way too much time in the world of books—eventually the men she dated got bored of that. She hoped it didn't turn out the same way with Jonathon; she liked him, but it was still in the early days. He was attracted to her, she could buy that, she knew she was reasonably pretty, but that wasn't a basis for a real relationship. She wanted someone who understood her; the only problem with that was sometimes she didn't feel like she even understood herself. And if she couldn't understand herself, how could anyone else?

A knock at the door startled her out of her reverie. Somehow she knew that it was going to be Jonathon and his partner. And she didn't have a good feeling about whatever they were going to tell her.

"I'll get the door," Naomi ordered, a hand on her holstered gun. She paused at the door. "Sorry for snapping at you."

"No problem," Clara assured her sister, "we're all tired."

"I'll cook you a really awesome dinner tonight to make it up to you."

Or Naomi could just go to bed early and get some sleep, Clara thought to herself. Maybe she'd call Davis and ask him to come over. Her brother was between girlfriends, so he probably didn't have plans, and Naomi was more likely to rest if she didn't feel like she had to be on guard.

"Hi, Detectives," Naomi said as she opened the door.

"Naomi," Jonathon nodded. "Clara."

His eyes met hers and Clara wanted to go to him, but she held back;

he was here in a professional capacity, not a personal one. Wanting to get whatever horrible thing they had to tell her over and done with, she said, "You have bad news."

"Can we sit?" Jonathon gestured at the table.

"Sure," Clara took a seat at the table, hoping Jonathon might sit beside her, but instead he sat opposite her, Detective Bennett at his side. Naomi brought a tray with cups of coffee, and a plate full of home-baked treats to the table.

"You've been busy." Jonathon looked at the array of chocolate-themed snacks.

"Naomi bakes when she's stressed," Clara replied.

"Of course she does," Jonathon looked mildly amused.

"What's the bad news?" Clara didn't want to let her imagination start conjuring up scenarios.

"Some forensic evidence came up during our investigation," Jonathon began slowly.

"What forensic evidence?"

"A pubic hair was found in Lindsey Peters' underwear," he told her gently.

"She was raped." Clara heard herself say the words, but her voice sounded nothing like her.

"Yes," Detective Bennett confirmed.

"But none of the other children had been raped," she protested. "Right?"

"As far as we know, none of the other children were assaulted," Jonathon nodded.

"As far as you know?" she repeated.

"The medical examiner doing the autopsies thirty years ago checked, and none of the girls showed signs of being sexually assaulted. Lottie Hatcher's examination was inconclusive. But you weren't dead, you escaped, so we don't know if you were assaulted." Jonathon was watching her closely.

"If none of the other children were raped. Then why would I have been any different?"

"I don't know. Is it a possibility?"

"No. I wasn't raped. No one touched me while I was missing," she said firmly.

"I thought you didn't remember what happened while you were missing," Detective Bennett said suspiciously.

"I don't, but I had a sexual assault examination in the hospital after Tommy and I were found. I wasn't raped." She may not remember the weeks she was missing, but she certainly remembered that. It had been a horrible, terrifying, embarrassing, and painful ordeal. "Isn't the report in your files?"

"Yes, but I needed to hear you confirm it," Jonathon acknowledged a little shakily.

The thought of her being sexually assaulted as a six-year-old had upset him, of course. That was natural, who wouldn't be upset by the thought of any child being hurt in that way? What bothered her was wondering if he still would have wanted to go out with her if indeed she had been raped. She didn't understand what had changed with the killers. Why had they started sexually abusing the children?

"Who does the DNA match?" Naomi asked, eyeing the detectives shrewdly.

Her eyes snapped to Jonathon and Detective Bennett. That they had matched the DNA to someone hadn't yet occurred to her, but now that Naomi had brought it up, she realized this was what had been giving her that bad feeling.

"I'm sorry, Clara, I know you don't want to hear this...but the DNA matched Thomas." Jonathon's gaze was anxious as he waited for her reaction.

Clara just stared at him.

She stared at him in silence for so long that at last, he commanded, "Clara, say something."

"Mistake," she murmured.

"What?"

He was frowning at her, and she realized she'd spoken so quietly, no one had heard what she'd said. "It must have been a mistake," she repeated more loudly.

"It wasn't a mistake," Jonathon said gently, but firmly. "Thomas raped that little girl. Possibly Lottie, too. He *was* involved in the recent doll murders."

"No!" she said shrilly. "No! No! No!" She shot to her feet and stormed across the room, dropped onto the couch and pulled her knees up to her chest, burying her face. They were wrong. She was sure they were wrong. She knew Tommy. He wouldn't do any of the things they were accusing him of. But then she hadn't thought he'd pull a gun on her, cut her neck, and put her in danger by making her run from the police. Had Tommy done it? Had he recreated the same crimes that had nearly cost them their lives when they were little children?

A hand rested on her shoulder, and someone sat beside her. She assumed it was her sister, but then Jonathon spoke, "Are you okay?"

She lifted her head, "Are you sure?"

"I'm sure."

Tears filled her eyes. "Why?"

"I can't answer that for you. I wish I could, but the answer to that died with Thomas."

"But I need to know," she begged. How could Tommy do this to her?

"Come here," he put his arms around her and drew her close.

Clara pressed her face into Jonathon's shoulder and let her tears tumble out. She didn't want to believe it; she hadn't wanted to believe it. She'd done everything she could to not believe it, but now it seemed like she had no other choice. Tommy was involved, and she couldn't deny it any longer. "I don't want it to be true," she cried.

"I know you don't, honey. But it *is* true." Jonathon's hand was rubbing her back, and the soothing motion was enough to help slow her tears down before they took on a more hysterical note. Taking her shoulders and sitting her up, he began, "Clara, we have some questions we need to ask you. I know this is tough, but I also know you're strong. You ready?"

Sniffing, she nodded and allowed Jonathon to take her hand and lead her to the table. He set a chocolate-chip cookie on a plate in front of her, and she began to pick it apart. She couldn't eat. Thinking of what her friend had done to that little girl was sickening.

"You were right that the original killers were involved; otherwise, your doll wouldn't have turned up," Detective Bennett began. "We think Thomas probably had a partner of his own. His mother mentioned a woman he'd been dating. Did you know he was dating someone?"

Feeling completely hollow inside, Clara nodded.

"Do you know the woman's name?"

Again, all she could do was nod.

Covering her hands with his, Jonathon coaxed, "Clara, what's her name? I know this has all been a shock to you, but Katie Logan and Jimmy Wallander are almost definitely still alive. If we can find this woman, we might be able to find the children."

She drew in a shuddering breath. Once she said those words, it was like truly admitting that Tommy was guilty. Part of her was still fighting desperately against believing it, but those children were in danger. And if she could help them, then she had to, even if it felt like betraying her friend. At least, she'd thought Tommy was her friend, but obviously, she hadn't known him at all.

"Clara?" Jonathon prompted.

"Sarah Ellis."

~

3:45 P.M.

"Sarah Ellis?" Jonathon asked as they approached the tall brunette who was filling her arms with grocery bags while keeping an eye on three small children who were racing each other up the driveway.

"Yes?" Sarah cast them an apprehensive glance.

"I'm Detective Dawson, and this is Detective Bennett. We need to talk to you."

Apprehension morphed into panic. "Is something wrong? Did something happen to someone? My parents? Are they okay?"

"Everything is fine," he assured her. "We need to ask you a few questions about someone you know."

"Oh, okay." Still wary, she gestured at the trunk full of groceries and the children waiting by the door, "Can I unload the car first and get the children settled?"

"Sure," Jonathon nodded, seeing her interact with her kids would help him to get a read on her. "Here, we'll help," he offered, picking up several of the bags. Allina grabbed the rest, and they followed Sarah to the house.

As soon as the door opened the three children, a girl of about seven, and two little boys who looked about five and three, tumbled inside, rushing into the kitchen. Sarah followed, fixed her kids a snack, then sent them off to watch some after school TV. She unpacked her bags and put a couple of perishables away in the refrigerator. Jonathon watched her carefully. She was calm and comfortable with her children, even though she was clearly nervous about their presence. The children too were completely comfortable with her, no signs that they were afraid of her in any way.

"Do you want a drink? Tea or coffee or water?" Sarah was watching them uncertainly.

"Only if you're having something," Allina replied.

"No." Sarah sat at the table, and they joined her. "What's wrong? Who do you want to talk to me about?"

From her antsy behavior, Jonathon suspected she might already know the answer to her question. "Do you know a Thomas Karl?"

Sarah paled and gulped audibly before nodding.

"How do you know him?"

"We dated," she whispered.

"Dated? Past tense?" Allina asked.

"Yes."

"When did you break up?" Jonathon asked.

"About six months ago."

Six months. This must have been the trigger that started the change in Thomas' behavior. If it were true. Jonathon wasn't getting a psychopathic child killer vibe off the woman, but they needed to know more before they dismissed her as a suspect. "Did he break up with you or did you break up with him?"

"I broke up with him," Sarah replied, chewing on her bottom lip like she was just waiting for them to hit her with a hammer.

"Why?"

"Why are you asking me questions about Tommy?" she countered.

"Are you aware that Thomas was recently killed in a shootout with the police?" Allina asked.

Dumbfounded, Sarah shook her head, and then something that looked like relief flared in her eyes.

"After carjacking a woman," Jonathon added, searching Sarah's face for signs that she was aware of Thomas' violent streak.

"Tommy carjacked someone? And shot at the police?" Sarah repeated, looking like she was sure they must have been making it up.

"After cutting the woman's neck and making her drive from the police for ninety minutes," Jonathon elaborated, pleased that he said it calmly even though thoughts of how terrified Clara must have been left him wanting to hit something.

"Thomas was never violent with you?" Allina asked.

"No, never," she replied adamantly.

"What about with your children?"

"He was great with the children. In fact, he was the first man that I'd dated that I allowed to even meet them. The kids were always important to him; he made that clear from the beginning of our relationship. He wanted us to be a family. I still waited a while before introducing him to them. My husband died when I was pregnant with my youngest; the other two were so young they don't remember their father. I didn't want them to get attached to Thomas if I wasn't serious about him," Sarah explained.

"So you were serious about your relationship with him?" Jonathon clarified.

"I was."

"But something changed because you broke up with him."

"Yes."

Feeling like they were pulling teeth, Jonathon prompted, "Why did you end things then? If you saw a future, and your children liked him, why break up?"

She shifted uncomfortably in her chair. "Tommy is dead, why does it matter now?"

"It matters," he assured her.

"I found out something about him," Sarah began uncomfortably.

"What did you find out?"

"Christina told me something about him," she continued, looking like she'd rather be anywhere but here.

A sinking feeling started in his stomach; Jonathon could guess where this was heading, and a glance at his partner confirmed she was on the same page. "Christina is your daughter?"

She swallowed noticeably, "Yes."

"How old is Christina?"

"She's seven."

"What did your daughter tell you, Mrs. Ellis?" he asked gently.

The woman broke down. Tears filled her brown eyes and quickly flooded out down her cheeks. "She said he'd touched her, made her do things she didn't like, she said it hurt her; she said he'd told her not to tell anyone, that it was their secret. I didn't know. I didn't know that he would do that. He had always been so sweet—he was quiet, shy, but he was always thoughtful and caring. He seemed to love me and my children. I was planning a life with him. I let him around my babies. I left him alone with them. How could I not have seen that something was wrong with him?"

"Some people are good at hiding their true self. And as soon as you found out what was going on you put a stop to it," Jonathon consoled.

Sarah nodded but didn't look convinced.

"Did you file a police report?" he was surprised that this hadn't shown up when they first ran a background check on Thomas Karl.

"No," she wept miserably. "I took her to a doctor and I got her counseling, but I didn't want her to have to go through a trial and relive everything in front of so many people. Is that why you're here? Did he do the same thing to someone else? Do you want to talk to Christina?" Panic filled her face.

As much as he didn't want to, talking to the little girl would confirm her mother's story and help to definitively count Sarah out as Thomas' partner. If Sarah had broken up with him because he molested her daughter, then it seemed extremely unlikely she would then work with him to abduct, abuse, and murder other children. "We may need to ask her a couple of questions," he informed her. "But that's not why we're here."

"Oh." Sarah looked both horrified at the prospect of them talking to her daughter and confused as to what it was they wanted from her. "Thomas is dead, though?"

"Yes."

"Then what do you want from me? Did another child make allegations against him?"

"He assaulted another child, but this little girl turned up dead." He broke the news as gently as he could.

"Tommy killed someone?" Sarah looked shocked.

"What do you know about Thomas' past?" Allina asked.

"He was kidnapped as a little boy by the Doll Killers . . . oh," Sarah paused as she realized what it was they wanted to talk to her about. "Those murders started up again. Are you saying *Tommy* was doing it? It was Clara he carjacked, wasn't it?"

"Do you know Clara?"

"I know of her, but we've never met. Tommy would talk about her a lot; I always thought it was a bit of an unrequited love thing. Tommy didn't have a lot of friends, so I think that's why he never told Clara how he felt about her. He was scared of losing the one really good friend he had."

"How much did he tell you about the abduction?" Since Clara didn't remember anything, maybe Thomas had said something to his ex-girlfriend that could help them find out who the original killers were.

"Not much. He only told me when I broke up with him because of what he did to Christina. He told me like it excused his behavior." Sarah looked disgusted.

That was an interesting development. Jonathon wondered whether it had been the boys who had been sexually abused and not the girls. There was no way to prove that, though. And even if Thomas had been abused while he'd been missing, it did *not* excuse what he'd done to Christina Ellis.

"He said he wanted answers," Sarah continued.

"To what?" Allina asked.

"From when he was missing. He said he wanted to go searching for answers. But I didn't care. I just wanted to get him as far away from me and my daughter as I could." She gave a repulsed shudder.

"Did you know that Thomas had been seeing a psychiatrist, but he then started skipping sessions and stopped taking his medication?"

She paled, "No. If I'd known he was struggling, and that he was supposed to be on medication but wasn't, I wouldn't have left him alone with my kids."

"Did you see him again after you ended things?"

"No. I told him to go, and he did. Then I packed up his things and left them in boxes in the front yard. He came and got them one night, and that was it."

Only that wasn't it.

After being dumped by his girlfriend, Thomas managed to somehow track down the people who abducted him and restarted their crimes.

Because of Thomas, four more children had died, another two were now missing.

At least there was one positive. Thomas had obviously remembered enough from the time he was missing to find the people who had kidnapped him. Which meant that Clara, too, knew enough to find them. They just had to help her remember.

CHAPTER

Five

February 11th
2:29 A.M.

The sound of screaming woke her.

Clara didn't know who was screaming, but the sound echoed in the dark.

Disoriented, she couldn't quite figure out where she was or why someone was yelling.

She jumped when arms wrapped around her, unsure of whether she should fight back.

"Shh, Clara. You were just dreaming."

The voice calmed her almost immediately.

Sinking into the arms that held her, Clara focused on clearing her mind. It had to be the early hours of the morning, and she was in her bed. She'd thought that after finding that doll on her bed, she'd never want to sleep in it again. But tonight she'd been tired and craved her soft mattress, her feather pillows, her favorite quilt, so she'd fought off the last dregs of nerves, climbed under the covers, and promptly fallen asleep. It was pitch black outside, but Clara didn't like to sleep with her curtains drawn, so moonlight streamed into the room. In it, she could make out Jonathon's concerned face watching her.

Noticing her looking at him, he asked, "You okay?"

Nodding, she closed her eyes and rested her head on Jonathon's shoulder. She took long, slow, deep breaths to calm her ragged breathing. Just a dream. That was all. Just another nightmare.

"Want to talk about it?" His hands and his voice both seemed to possess magical powers when it came to calming her. His hand smoothed her hair; his voice was soothing but not patronizing.

"No." What was Jonathon doing here anyway? He hadn't been here when she'd gone to bed. Without lifting her head, she opened her eyes again and peered up at him, "Where's Naomi?"

"I sent your sister home to rest. I think she's had even less sleep than you have the last few days. She was starting to look like she'd collapse if she didn't sleep soon."

Agreeing completely with his assessment of Naomi, she thought it was sweet of him to care enough about her sister to worry. She'd gone to bed early, but she'd thought her brother was going to come and spend the night so Naomi could get some rest. "Is Davis here?"

"Your brother and I arrived here at the same time; we agreed he would take Naomi home and I'd stay here with you."

"How did Naomi like that idea?"

"She protested a little," he smiled.

"A little?"

"Okay, more than a little," he chuckled.

She garnered up enough courage to ask what she wanted to know. "What did Sarah Ellis say about Tommy?"

Since she was still in Jonathon's arms, she felt him stiffen. "Are you sure you want to know?"

"Yes," she answered immediately—she needed to understand what had made Tommy change so dramatically from the shy, sweet person she'd always known into a child-murdering monster.

"Sarah broke up with him six months ago," Jonathon began.

"Six months ago is when I stopped hearing from him," she inserted.

"His mom, too."

"Why did they break up?"

"Because Sarah's seven-year-old daughter told her that Thomas had been sexually abusing her," he said in a rush.

"What?" she shoved at his arms that encircled her and bounded off her bed.

"I'm sorry, Clara; I know this is hard for you to hear. When Sarah ended things, she said that Thomas told her he had been abused as a child during the time you two were missing. He said he wanted answers, and he obviously knew enough to find the Doll Killers."

"Which means I must too, only I can't remember." Taking a leaf out of Naomi's book, she paced the bedroom, struggling to come to terms with everything she'd learned about Tommy the last few days. Her mind was on overload. How had she not seen that he was so unbalanced?

"Come lie down," Jonathon patted the mattress.

For the first time, she realized that Jonathon was wearing only a pair of sweatpants. For a moment, all she could do was stare at his sculpted chest and hope she wasn't drooling. It had been a while since she'd had sex—not since her last serious relationship broke up almost eighteen months ago. But she didn't just jump into bed with someone she hadn't even known a week, no matter how good-looking they were. Sleeping in Jonathon's arms last night had been comforting, made her feel safe, but she hadn't wanted anything more. Now, however, given the emotional turmoil and stress of the last few days, she was tempted to throw out her no-sex-with-someone-you're-not-in-a-committed-relationship-with rule.

He looked at her with an amused expression. "Relax. I'm not asking you for sex. I was just going to offer a massage, to help you relax."

"Oh," was all she could manage as her cheeks heated in embarrassed.

"Not that I don't want to, of course," Jonathon continued cheerfully, his brown eyes twinkling merrily, obviously enjoying watching her squirm. "And we will. But not like this, not when you're scared and suffering. I don't want you to wind up regretting it. When we do, it should be perfect. So, come, lie down, and I'll give you a massage."

She smiled despite the nervous fluttering butterflies that had taken up residence in her stomach.

"Take off your nightgown," he instructed as she rejoined him on the bed.

Clara did as he asked, glad that she'd kept on the simple white cotton camisole and panties under her pajamas because without them she feared she'd almost definitely end up breaking her own rules. Tossing the pink and green plaid flannel nightgown on the floor, she stretched out on her stomach as Jonathon indicated.

He started with her feet, paying attention to each toe, then the ball of her foot, the arch, and then up her legs. His strong hands worked magic on her taut muscles. Bit by bit, her body liquefied as she relaxed more and more with each stroking movement of his hands. By the time he reached her back, she wasn't sure she could have strung together a cohesive thought if her life depended on it. If he'd asked her right now to make love to him, the answer would have been a resounding yes.

"You're so tense," he murmured as he moved on to her shoulders.

And then she tensed completely as his hands brushed the back of her neck. He froze too and she knew he'd felt it.

Immediately, she rolled over and scooted up onto her bottom; her knees came to her chest, and she wrapped her arms around them, instinctively forming her own little protective shield. She didn't like anyone to see it. She hated knowing that it was there.

"You have one, too, I wasn't sure," Jonathon said softly.

The Doll Killers had branded her. Left the mark of a doll on the back of her neck. At first, it had hurt a lot, and due to an infection, it had taken a long time to heal. The pain hadn't bothered her—it was that people would see it, know what had happened to her. Ever since she made sure that she wore her hair long enough to cover her neck, and she never, ever put it up, it *always* hung down her back covering her neck from prying eyes. Over time the burn had faded, gone from bright red to a purply color, and now it was the same color as the rest of her skin. It was barely noticeable unless you touched it. Then the raised scar was obvious.

"It's nothing to be ashamed of, Clara."

Ignoring her body language, which clearly shouted *stay away*, he moved to sit beside her, curled an arm around her stiff shoulders, and urged her head to lean against his broad chest. After resisting for a moment, she relaxed a fraction and snuggled closer.

"You feel guilty; that's what's holding back your memories," his fingers began to play with her hair.

"I was just a kid, I didn't do anything wrong," she protested.

"You walked away from your mother that day, even though you knew you weren't supposed to speak to strangers."

It felt like he was fishing for answers, so she could simply say nothing. Instead, she said, "Sometimes kids know the right thing to do, but when they're put in that situation they still don't do it."

"Why did you walk away, honey?" he asked gently.

What broke her down and pushed her into answering was how gentle he was with her. He'd meant it when he'd said he wanted sex; she'd felt it, both physically and emotionally. But he'd held back because he knew she wasn't ready; he was right when he'd said that she would have wound up regretting it if they slept together tonight. Instead, he'd made helping her relax his priority, setting aside his needs to focus on hers. "Because of my mom," she answered softly.

"You two weren't close? Even back then?"

She and her mother had *never* been close. "She blamed me for ruining her marriage."

"She was the one who chose to cheat on her husband," he reminded her.

"I know, but if she hadn't gotten pregnant, she might not have had to tell her husband and then her family wouldn't have been broken up."

"You know none of that is your fault, right?" he frowned down at her.

"I know. But still, my mom getting pregnant with me broke up her marriage. Apparently, the divorce was messy. He wanted custody of my brothers, and he wanted the house because it had been his before the marriage. He got the house, and we moved to a much smaller place. He had my brothers every second weekend. Whenever he came to the house to pick them up it was like he couldn't even stand to be near me—he could barely be civil." She paused before continuing; she hadn't told anyone what she was about to say next—even Naomi. "I found out later that my mom wanted to give me to my father. She thought it would save her marriage. Apparently, my father was happy enough to take me; only his wife said no."

Slipping an arm under her knees, he pulled her sideways, so she sat on his lap. "I'm sorry, honey. That must have been tough to deal with growing up."

"My brothers were great, though, and then when I was older, I met Naomi. I'm not close with my mother, but I still have a really great family." She wondered about Jonathon's family; she really didn't know anything about him. So far, because of the case, the focus of their fledgling relationship had been all about her.

"So, you walked away on purpose that day?" he carefully guided the conversation back around to her abduction.

"Yes, at least, at first," she admitted tiredly. She was feeling drained now, empty, she just wanted all of this over, and if telling Jonathon what happened that day helped, then she'd do it. "I was angry because my mom wouldn't let me have friends over for a sleepover. I thought it was unfair because my brothers always had friends over. We were doing the weekly grocery shopping. I hated going to the supermarket; it was so boring. The boys were talking sports, my mom wasn't paying attention, there was an old lady outside, and she had a puppy. I wanted my mom to be scared and worried when she couldn't find me; I was so angry with her. So I went outside to see the puppy." Clara paused to shake her head at her stupidity, "It all seems so stupid now, I was such an easy mark, I fell for such a simple trick."

"You were six," Jonathon reprimanded sternly.

"I deliberately walked away from my mother, straight to a stranger, even though I knew better," she repeated.

"So you felt guilty, blamed yourself," he added.

"Some children are snatched from their beds in the middle of the night. I walked right into my kidnapper's arms."

"Which doesn't make it your fault. Like you said, sometimes kids know the right thing to do, but it doesn't mean they do it. What happened next?"

"I asked if I could pet the lady's dog and she said yes. There was a man there too—an old man—who asked if I liked dogs, and I said I did but my mother wouldn't let me have one. Then something sharp pricked my arm, and I felt really sleepy, and that's it. That's the last thing I remember clearly."

"Except for feeling cold and hungry?"

"Right, and it's always dark in my dream, but I think the room was actually light."

"Your memories are there, Clara. Would you be willing to try hypnosis to see if we can unlock them?"

"We? You'll go with me?"

"Of course," he said it like that was a ridiculous question.

For years, she had debated wanting to remember versus being happy she didn't. Now she was at a point where she wanted to know, maybe even needed to know. It was daunting. What Tommy remembered had driven him to rape and murder, but she was ready to face it.

"I'm going to try to set it up for tomorrow."

She almost balked at the idea of it being so soon, but better to get it over and done with. Katie and Jimmy still stood a chance at being found alive, and she wanted to help make that happen.

"Now, we sleep." Jonathon lay down, taking her with him so that she lay on top of him. Staring into her eyes, he cupped her cheek; his thumb caressed her lips, then his hand moved to her neck. Instinctively she tensed, but he whispered, "I don't care about the scar. I'm falling for you, Clara."

Clara stared back into his eyes. He looked so handsome in the moonlight. "I'm falling for you too."

"Good," he smiled.

Then his lips were on hers, and he was kissing her, softly and sweetly, but her pulse skyrocketed. Sooner than she would have, he ended the kiss, then slid her off him. Resting her hand on his stomach and her head on his chest, Clara promptly fell into a dreamless sleep.

9:12 A.M.

"I can't believe you got an appointment this quickly," Clara mumbled as he led her up the steps and into the office building's lobby.

"It's in Katie and Jimmy's—and *your*—best interests to get this done as quickly as possible." Jonathon took her hand and entwined their fingers.

"I know, but we only talked about it a few hours ago and already you found someone to see me."

"She's a friend of Allina's; she rearranged her schedule to fit you in."

She looked up at him with large, frightened eyes. "What if I'm not ready?"

"Do you want to back out?"

"No, but I'm scared."

He was pleased with her admission. Not that he wanted her to be scared, but it was nice to know she trusted him enough to open up to him. "It's okay to be scared, Clara," he assured her. "But I'll be right there with you."

"Holding my hand?"

"If that's what you want."

That seemed to settle her, and she pushed the elevator button.

"You look beautiful." He turned her to face him as they waited for the lift. She was dressed in a simple pair of jeans, a white coat, and a sweater in a shade of green that perfectly matched her eyes.

"Thank you," her cheeks turned a bright pinky red.

"Are you going to get embarrassed every time I compliment you?" he chuckled. She was very endearing when she was self-conscious.

"Probably," she laughed, a real laugh—the first he'd heard. He liked the sound, liked even more that he'd brought it about, and vowed to make her laugh more often.

The ding of the lift had her sobering, and she pulled her hand free from his and walked into the elevator. He hated to see her so serious again so quickly, but the reason for them being here was a serious one.

"What floor?" she asked absently.

"Fourth," he pressed the button and reclaimed her hand.

She stared at their joined hands and then looked up at him. "What if I don't remember anything helpful?"

"You remember what you remember; there's no pressure, Clara. You're not responsible for solving this case."

They lapsed into silence, and when the lift reached the fourth floor, he led her out and down the hall to Dr. Linda Chan's consulting rooms.

The psychologist and qualified hypnotist was a friend and colleague of Allina's husband's brother. When he'd called his partner around six this morning to tell her that Clara had agreed to try hypnosis, Allina had immediately called her brother-in-law to ask for a recommendation. He'd promptly called her back to say a friend of his would clear her schedule and they could bring Clara in first thing this morning.

"We're here," he told Clara as they stopped in front of a door and he wrapped on it with his knuckles. She just nodded. Jonathon didn't like seeing her so quiet and withdrawn, but she'd had a lot thrown at her in such a short amount of time that it was no wonder she was struggling to process it all.

"Morning, Jon. Clara," Allina greeted them as she opened the door.

"Morning, Ali. Thank your brother-in-law for setting this up so quickly." He had to tug Clara into the room behind him; she seemed to have zoned out.

She roused herself with a shake. "Detective Bennett," Clara nodded formally.

"Since Jonathon spent the night at your house again, I'm assuming you two are dating?"

He glanced at Clara for confirmation; he didn't want to pressure her or make any assumptions. She glanced back at him and nodded.

"Then I guess it's Allina. Dr. Chan is just finishing up a phone . . ."

"All done," a petite Asian breezed into the room. "You must be Jonathon and Clara." She shot them a warm smile.

"Nice to meet you, Dr. Chan." He shook her outstretched hand. "Thanks so much for rearranging your day for this." Clara just stood there, nervousness rolling off her in waves.

Dr. Chan noticed that and got immediately down to business. "Okay, Clara, come and take a seat. Have you ever been hypnotized?"

"No." Clara's hand tightened around his as they followed Dr. Chan through into a small sitting room.

"Allina filled me in on the background of the case, but I'd like for you to tell me the specific things you remember so we can move on from there."

Clara sat in the recliner Dr. Chan indicated, but her fearful eyes remained glued to him, and she refused to release her grip on his hand.

Taking note of that, Dr. Chan pulled up a chair for him so he could sit beside Clara, then spread a blanket over her and took a seat in the armchair beside the recliner.

"I remember that we were in an attic; it was cold, and I was hungry," Clara said.

"Do you remember the abduction itself?"

"Yes."

"What's the last thing you remember clearly?"

"I was petting a dog, and complaining that my mom wouldn't let me have one." Clara's hand reflexively squeezed his as she battled her guilt. "Then I fell asleep."

"Okay, I want you to relax now. I know this is a stressful situation, but if this is going to work, then you need to want it to work. Do you, Clara?"

"Yes."

"Good. Now a little bit about hypnosis: It's like being in a heavily meditative state. You'll be able to hear what's happening around you, but I'll instruct you that any sounds just help to make you relax further. I want you to just focus on my voice. Now we may or may not make progress today. Since this is your first time, you might find it difficult to relax sufficiently. And even if you do, that's no guarantee that you're going to remember anything. If we don't make any progress today, we'll keep working at it. Hypnosis is a skill, and like any other skill, you get better at it the more you do it. It's also important that you're prepared for what you might remember. Sometimes with some distance, traumatic memories that your brain had blocked as a survival mechanism can come back. Are you okay with that?"

"They're already starting to come back. In my dreams. Only I can't see them properly. It's like they're there, only all foggy and unclear," Clara admitted.

"Well, hopefully, today we can help to make them clearer. I'm going to talk you through some relaxation techniques, and then I'm going to lead you back to what you do remember, and we'll see how we go from there. Do you have any questions before we begin?"

"Am I going to remember everything I tell you? I mean when I wake up again?" Clara asked.

"Yes, you are."

Clara absorbed this, looking distinctly disturbed. "You don't have to do this, Clara," Jonathon told her. "If you're not ready, that's okay."

"No, I want to do it. Katie and Jimmy are still alive. Tommy knew how to find our kidnappers, so I must, too."

"Okay then, are you ready?"

Drawing in a long, deep breath, she replied, "Ready."

"All right, I want you to close your eyes and let yourself relax. If it helps, you can picture yourself someplace that is calming—otherwise, just clear your mind. I'm going to count down from ten, and I want you to imagine relaxing each part of your body, starting with your head, and working down to your feet." Dr. Chan's voice had become calm and soothing. "Ten, nine, eight, seven, six, five, four, three, two, one."

Clara's hand had gone limp in his, and Jonathon assumed she'd gone under.

"Clara, can you hear me?" Dr. Chan asked.

"Yes," her voice was heavy, kind of sleepy.

"Clara, you're walking down a long hall," Dr. Chan instructed. "On either side of you are doors. I want you to find the door with the number six on it. When you open that door, you're going to be six years old again. Have you found the door, Clara?"

"Yes."

"Did you walk through it?"

"Yes."

"Where are you?"

"The supermarket, there's an old lady with a dog. I'm petting the dog. Then I'm asleep."

"Now you've woken up, Clara. Where are you?"

Clara's forehead crinkled, and Jonathon thought she wasn't going to remember, but then she spoke. "I'm in an attic."

"Is it light or dark?"

"Light. Too light." Clara's closed eyes squinted.

"What does the attic look like?"

"The walls are white. There are no windows, but someone painted some on the walls. The furniture is all made of wood, and it's small, like the things at school when we play house. There's a kitchen and a bathroom, a bedroom and a lounge room. The floor is cold, but there are some colorful rugs in the lounge room."

"A dollhouse," he murmured to Allina, who nodded her agreement. It made sense if the killers wanted the children to be dolls, they would make them live in a doll's house.

"You said you're cold, Clara. What are you wearing?"

"A blue and white dress."

"That's what her doll was wearing," Jonathon interjected quietly to the doctor. But it hadn't been what she'd been wearing when she'd escaped. At some point, the killers must have changed her into her doll's clothes and then back out of them again. "Ask her if the back of her neck hurts."

"Clara, does your neck hurt?"

"No, I'm just cold."

"Clara, where are you when you wake up?"

"I'm in bed, but it's not a comfortable bed, not like my bed at home, it's hard."

"Is anyone there with you?"

"A little boy. Tommy. He's in the lounge room watching the TV. It's not a real TV, just a wooden box with a picture painted on it. My throat feels dry, and I want a drink of water, but the sink in the kitchen is just pretend."

"Do you feel anything else? Does anything else hurt, Clara?"

"Just when I talk."

"What happens when you talk, Clara?"

"It hurts."

"Hurts how?"

"Like a zap."

Jonathon would bet anything that the Doll Killers had used a shock collar, like the kind people used to try to train their dog to stop barking, to keep the children quiet.

"All the time when you talk or just sometimes?"

"If I talk quietly, it doesn't hurt, but if I talk loud—if I try to call for help then it does."

"Does the same thing happen to Tommy?"

"Yes."

"Is there something on your neck?"

Clara's hand moved to her neck. "Yes."

"Can you hear anything, Clara?"

"No. Just Tommy. He's always crying."

"Can you smell anything?"

Wrinkling up her nose, she murmured, unsure, "Doctor things?"

"'Doctor things'?" Dr. Chan repeated. "Can you be more specific, Clara?"

She shrugged. "It smells like a doctor's office."

"While you and Tommy are in the attic, do you see anyone else?"

Clara shivered, and Jonathon wanted to wrap his arms around her in reassurance and comfort. Instead, since he didn't want to disturb her, he simply kept hold of her hand.

"Clara?" Dr. Chan prompted. "Do you see anyone else while you're there?"

"*They* come," she whispered, her voice losing the monotone and becoming very childlike.

"Who are *they*, Clara?"

"The man and the woman. They weren't really old. They were just pretending."

"What do they look like, Clara?"

"The lady has a big red mark on her face. The man, he's sick, he doesn't have any hair."

"What do they do when they come to the attic?"

Shaking her head, Clara whimpered.

"It's okay, Clara. You're safe now. What do they do when they come?"

"They play with us; they say we're dolls. I'm so hungry, but they only give us this yucky tasting drink."

"What else, Clara?" Dr. Chan pushed, sensing, as Jonathon had, that she was holding something back.

"Sometimes they take their clothes off, and they do stuff," Clara's voice trembled.

"Do they ever touch you or Tommy?" Dr. Chan asked carefully.

Shaking her head, a single tear leaked out of one of her closed eyes and rolled down her cheek. Jonathon found himself letting out a relieved breath. Although the doctor's report from after Clara was found had stated that she hadn't been sexually assaulted, and Clara herself had denied being molested, hearing her confirm it now that she remembered some of those missing weeks helped him to believe it.

Leaving that for the moment, Dr. Chan veered the conversation in a different direction. "Clara, I want you to remember how you and Tommy got away."

"I . . . The door . . . It was open. We ran. Down the stairs. There were toys everywhere. Then we were outside, and we were walking and walking. I was so tired."

"Toys everywhere?" the doctor repeated.

"Like a toy shop," Clara added.

"Who opened the door, Clara?"

She became agitated. "I don't know. It was just open."

To Jonathon and Allina Dr. Chan offered, "It's understandable not all her memories are going to come back in one go. Unless you really want me to, I'd rather not push her anymore today. She's done remarkably well."

"We have enough for now," Jonathon replied. "Ali?"

"Just ask her if she ever saw the dolls while she was there," Allina suggested.

The doctor nodded. "Clara, while you were in the attic, did you see any dolls?"

Pulling her hand free from his, she began to twist them in her lap. She squirmed. "One day they brought them. They made us lie down on the bed on our stomachs. They moved my hair out of the way. They put something hot on my neck. It burned." Growing panicky, her hands batted at her neck, her face crumpled in pain like she was physically reliving the experience. "It hurts. It hurts," she cried.

"Wake her up. Now," Jonathon ordered. Clara's distress had his heart thumping a million miles a minute.

"It's okay, Clara," Dr. Chan's voice remained calm and controlled. "It's time to wake up now, okay? As we did before, I'm going to count to ten, and I want you to imagine each part of your body waking up, starting with your toes and moving up to your head. One, two, three, four, five, six, seven, eight, nine, ten."

When the doctor reached ten, Clara's eyes blinked open, still full of tears, and when Jonathon put his arms around her, she wrapped hers so tightly around his neck he could hardly move. "It's okay, Clara," he soothed. "You did great. Really great. I'm so proud of you." Clara cried in his arms for several minutes, and when her tears were spent, she rested heavily against him.

"Clara, over the next few days, you might have more memories start to return to you. I'm going to give you my number; you can call me any time you need to, day or night," Dr. Chan told her. "I recorded this session, Clara—are you happy for me to give a copy to Jonathon and Allina?" Clara nodded. "Ali, how about we go into my office, and I'll get you a copy."

Once they were alone, Jonathon sat Clara up so he could see her better. "Why don't I call Naomi, have her drive you to Thomas' funeral instead of you taking a cab," he suggested, not liking the idea of Clara being alone when she looked so emotionally drained.

Blinking slowly, Clara's eyes cleared, and she gave him a small smile. "I really need to go on my own. I'm so confused about Tommy; I need some time to figure things out in my head, reconcile the two sides of someone I considered a close friend. The funeral is only going to be me and Mrs. Karl anyway."

Brushing a stray lock of hair off her still wet cheek, his fingers lingered on her soft skin. "Don't go getting all embarrassed on me, but I think you're amazing."

She leaned forward to rest her forehead on his. "I think you're kind of amazing, too."

"Perfect," he whispered, his lips hovering just above hers, "I was hoping you did."

~

1:32 P.M.

"Come on, Katie," Jimmy pleaded. "Help me."

"What's the use?"

"There has to be a way out," he insisted.

"We've already checked out the whole place," Katie protested.

Katie had given up. She just sat there, curled up in a ball, in the corner of the attic. Jimmy couldn't give up. He wouldn't—he'd find a way out of here.

Jimmy knew he'd been stupid to fall for the old lady's trick. Of course, she didn't have a grandson. He should have known better than to talk to a stranger. How many times had his mother cautioned him about it? And teachers at school, too—they were always talking about how to be safe.

And what had he done?

He'd gone and ignored it all and look where that had gotten him.

Trapped in some weird dollhouse room.

At least that was what it reminded him of. A doll's house. The furniture was all small, kid-size, and all wooden. Just like the kind of stuff he'd played with in preschool whenever they played house. It looked old too; there were dents and bumps all over everything.

Jimmy wasn't sure how long he'd been here. There were no real windows, just ones that someone had painted on the walls, so he couldn't tell when it was daytime and when it was nighttime. It felt like months had passed since he'd first woken up, but it probably wasn't more than a day or two.

Were his parents looking for him? He thought they would be. His mom must have been so scared when she finished working on her paper for school and came to get him, only to find he wasn't there. Jimmy hated knowing that she must be frightened and worried wondering who had taken him and where he was. Were his parents fighting about it? They fought a lot. Because his dad lost his temper a lot. He never hit them, but he yelled all the time, especially when he was stressed.

Jimmy was a take charge kind of kid. He could be bossy, which was why he didn't have a lot of friends at school—but he was also smart and confident, which was why the kids always liked working with him on school projects. He was also used to being treated like an adult; his dad didn't like to baby him and given that his mom had diabetes, he sometimes had to act like an adult. One time his mom's sugar levels had dropped so low that she had a seizure. He had called an ambulance, did what he could for his mom, and taken care of his baby sister until help arrived. He'd been scared, but he'd done what needed to be done. If he'd been able to cope with that, then he could cope with this, too.

"Come on, Katie," he urged. "Do you want to still be here when they come back?"

Repulsed, she shuddered and shook her head.

Neither of them wanted to see the man and woman again.

They were creepy. They were old, about the same age as his grandparents. The lady had a big, red mark on her face, and the man was sick. When they came, they did bad stuff. Grown-up stuff that shouldn't be done in front of children. Jimmy knew it was sex, even though he wasn't quite sure what exactly sex was. He was scared that one day they were going to do those things to him and Katie, and he didn't want to wait around to find out if he was right. He wanted to go home. Now. And he was determined to find a way out of here, and Katie was going to help him.

Taking hold of her hand, he tried to pull her to her feet. Katie had been here longer than him, but she hadn't done anything about finding a way to escape. When he'd first woken up in here, she'd been in this same corner, curled up in a ball, just like she was now. In fact, other than when the man and woman came and played with them, pretending they were dolls, or when Katie had to use the toilet—the real one, over in the far corner—she hadn't moved from this spot at all.

"Let's go, Katie. We can find a way out of here, I know we can. Don't you want to go home?"

Katie sniffed and nodded.

"Then come on, we can do it," he encouraged.

"What do you want me to do? You already made us check all the walls."

Despite her obvious pessimistic attitude, Jimmy wasn't giving up. He would *never* give up. He would never stop looking for a way out of here. "We check everything again, just like before. The floors, the walls, the door, and the ceiling if we can reach it."

He expected Katie to protest. Instead, she just stood, brushed at her teary eyes, and started tapping on the closest wall.

Jimmy dragged the wooden table over to another wall, then the four wooden chairs that went with it. Maybe if he stacked them all on top of the table, he'd be able to reach the ceiling.

There had to be a way out of here.

There had to be.

He just had to find it.

~

2:12 P.M.

"They're checking the walls again."

"I know, I think it's sweet," she smiled at the screen. Watching the two children circling the room was adorable. Katie and Jimmy were going to make the two best dolls so far. In fact, she thought they might be so perfect that it was going to be hard to part with them. Extremely hard.

But hers was not to judge.

She simply did what was right.

Instead of constantly slamming her, the public should be praising her. Bowing down to her even. Rushing to follow suit and save all the poor children of the world. So much pain, so much unhappiness, so much disappointment.

But not for her dolls.

All they knew was peace and tranquility.

Sometimes she wished she could join them. Wished that someone had done this for her when she was but a small a girl.

Even now, could it be done?

She wasn't sure. She hoped, she hardly dared to, but she couldn't help it.

She had even started making some plans to make it happen. They'd gotten derailed a bit when Tommy had gone and gotten himself killed, but she could recover, rebuild—she'd already formulated a new strategy as to how. It had to work. She would not accept any other outcome. She couldn't; she had too much to lose.

"Where has your mind wandered to, my dear?"

Her eyes filled with tears as she looked at him.

He was the love of her life.

She couldn't live without him. And yet if she couldn't find a way to transform them into everlasting dolls, then she'd have to.

"Do not cry, my sweet one." His hand cupped her cheeks and brushed away her tears. That only made her cry harder, and he took her hands and tugged her down onto his lap.

She wrapped her arms around him and clung. Sobbing so violently her chest ached. Why was life so unfair? Why was the universe going to take the man she loved away from her?

"It will be all right, darling," he soothed, patting her back.

"No, it won't," she wept into his shoulder.

"It will," he assured her.

"No, you're dying, you're going to leave me."

"Not yet, my love, not yet."

"But soon." She didn't want to be comforted right now. She wanted to feel the full force of her emotions so that she was sufficiently motivated to find a solution. She hadn't told him yet; she didn't want to get his hopes up in case it didn't work out.

"Sweet one, I have beaten the odds twice before," he reminded her.

That was true of course. When he was a child, he had beaten acute lymphocytic leukemia. Then thirty-four years ago, he was again diagnosed with cancer, this time in one of the bones of his left leg. It was then when they thought that he wouldn't survive when the doctors had given him only months to live, that they decided to think about how they would create something that would live on after his death. Because of the lifesaving treatment he'd undergone as a child, he was sterile. Living on through children was, therefore, out of the question.

So, the idea of creating immortal dolls had been born.

After each set of dolls was created, his doctors gave him a little longer to live.

And then a miracle.

His cancer was gone. After a ten-year battle with the disease, it was gone. Those eighteen sweet, beautiful little dolls that they'd made together had saved him. There had been no need to go after Tommy and Clara when the children escaped. No need to take any more children.

They had achieved their goal. They would live on forever through their dolls, and with the cancer gone, they could now enjoy their lives together.

But then that horrible beast had returned. Her beloved was now riddled with the disease. And given that they were now in their seventies, neither had much hope that he would beat it again. But then Tommy had turned up on their doorstep, and it seemed like a sign. A reminder of how they could remain together forever...

As dolls.

Once they were transformed into dolls, then nothing would ever be able to separate them. And Tommy was just the person to make the transformation. But first, he had needed to learn the craft. And each pair of dolls that were created bought her husband some time.

However, that time was almost up.

Soon he would die.

"I hate to see you sad, my love," he crooned in her ear. "Especially when we have our next two precious little ones waiting for us. I still have time. Time to enjoy with you. Let us go up, see if the time of planting is upon us."

He was so smart—if it weren't for him, she would never have known how to turn a child into a doll. But he had discovered the secret. Through the magic of making love while the doll children were there, they could capture their spirit, the seed would be planted, and when the time was right, the dolls would be born with blood. Since she was past the age now where the time of blood came, they had had to improvise these last two times, but soon they would have a remedy for that.

He was right. They had a little longer left together, surely enough time for her to teach another pair how to create dolls so that she and her husband could become immortal together.

∼

5:19 P.M.

. . .

"I'm just pulling into the cemetery now," Jonathon assured Naomi, who had called him to see if he knew where Clara was when she didn't come home after Thomas Karl's funeral.

"Maybe I should head down there." Naomi's anxious voice came through the phone.

"No, I can handle it. I'll bring her back there, but maybe you could give us a little privacy," he suggested. He wanted some alone time with Clara, but at the cemetery in the rain wasn't his idea of the ideal location.

"Are you sure? I mean, not that you want privacy, but that you don't need me?"

"I'm sure."

"You'll call me if you need anything?"

"Yes. Naomi, stop worrying."

"Text me when you find her," Naomi ordered, then hung up.

Smiling despite himself as he dropped his phone onto the center console of his car, he liked Clara's tornado of a sister. Following the directions he'd been given, he drove through the cemetery's winding roads until he reached the area where Thomas had been buried earlier this afternoon.

It didn't take him long to spot Clara. She was standing beside a fresh plot, seemingly oblivious to the rain pouring down on her. It was peaceful here—or would have been if it wasn't raining; there were lots of large trees and garden beds that in the spring, he suspected, would be a blazing display of color. Parking under a tree, he typed a quick text to Naomi, threw on his jacket and grabbed an umbrella, before hurrying to Clara.

She didn't acknowledge him as he approached. Her gaze was fixed, almost unblinkingly, on the headstone.

"Clara?"

She didn't move, not even when he stood close and held the umbrella so it covered them both. When he put a hand on her shoulder, she turned slowly toward him. She looked dazed, her glazed green eyes reminiscent of the first time he'd met her.

"What are you doing?" he asked.

"Doing?" she echoed.

"You're standing here in the torrential rain."

"Rain?" she repeated.

"You're soaked," he pointed out the obvious but wanted to snap her out of her haze.

"Soaked?"

"Come on, Clara," he gave her a one-handed shake.

His shake seemed to clear away some of the cobwebs, and her eyes focused a little. "Jonathon? What are you doing here?"

"Looking for you. Naomi was worried when you didn't come home after the funeral."

She returned her eyes to the headstone. "I needed some time to think," she whispered.

"You've had enough time to think; you're going to catch your death of cold out here. Let me take you home."

Clara didn't protest as he put an arm around her shoulders and guided her back to his car. He bundled her into the passenger seat, then grabbed a blanket from his trunk and draped it around her. She sighed and sank farther into the seat, resting her head on the window when he closed the door, and by the time he slid into his seat, her eyes had closed. Her breathing evened out, and she dozed during the twenty-minute drive back to her house.

"Clara," he roused her as he parked in her driveway

Blinking sleepily, she still looked lost but no longer appeared disoriented.

"Feeling better?"

"I feel empty." Her lips were tinted with blue, and she was shivering, "And cold. Maybe standing in the rain wasn't the best idea," she joked lamely.

He was encouraged by her attitude; she was struggling but hanging in there. "Come on, let's get you inside and out of these wet clothes."

Jonathon helped her from the car and steered her up the path and inside, where Clara just stood, staring helplessly around her house. Taking charge, he put the kettle on, led Clara into the laundry room where he stripped off her soaking clothes with clinical detachment, wrapped her in a blanket, threw her clothes into the washing machine, and then maneuvered her back into the living room. Sitting her down on the couch, he went to the kitchen and made her a steaming cup of tea and brought it back to her.

Her teary green eyes looked up at him, then dropped to stare at the golden-brown liquid in her mug. "If I'd been sexually assaulted as a child, would you still want to go out with me?"

Frowning, he sat beside her, encircling his arms around her and holding her close, both because he wanted to and because he thought it would help to warm her. "Why would you ask me that?"

She shrugged fitfully. "I don't know. We don't even know each other, and my past—it's a lot to take on. And I can't pretend it's not going to be an issue, everything is so fresh right now, it's like reliving it. And if you'd rather not get involved in all of that, I totally understand, but it might be better for you to walk away now before feelings develop further. And . . ."

"Shh," Jonathon took the mug of tea from her hands and set it on the coffee table. "The feelings are already there, Clara. You know that. You feel it, too. And I don't want to walk away." Taking a deep breath, he decided it was confession time. "There's something you should know."

"What?" Clara stiffened.

He scooped her up so he could cradle her on his lap. "Relax, it's nothing for you to worry about, I'd just prefer that you keep what I'm about to tell you between us for now."

"Why?" she looked confused.

"You'll understand when I tell you. I have a vested interest in the Doll Killer case," he admitted. "No, don't tense up. I said a vested interest in the case, not you. I'm not trying to get close to you to solve this case. When I first saw you, I felt a spark of something ignite, and I didn't know your name or anything about you." Clara relaxed, and he continued, "But this case, it's important to me. To my family."

Horror and understanding lit Clara's face. "A brother or sister?" she asked.

"Sister."

"How old was she?"

"She was six, the same age as you were when you were taken."

"What was her name?"

"Her name was Dora."

"You should have told me sooner; I would have tried harder to remember," her voice was full of self-reproach.

"You would have put more pressure on yourself, and that probably would have hampered your memories. Besides, no one knows—not Allina, not my boss, no one. Dawson is a common enough surname that no one thought to connect me to Dora Dawson. And when we divided up the old case files to read through them, I made sure that I got hers, so Allina didn't read my statement from the day my sister disappeared. I don't want anyone to find out; I don't want to get taken off this case. My mother is dying, and I want to give her closure. I want this case solved, so we know who killed Dora, then my mom can have peace of mind before she passes away."

"I'm so sorry, Jonathon. I wish you'd told me earlier. I understand why you didn't, but I really would have tried harder to remember if I'd known how much it meant to you."

"Dora and a little boy named Dominick were the last two children killed. Next were you and Thomas and you two escaped. If they had seen you first, then . . ." he broke off as he realized what he'd just implied.

"Then I would have died, and your sister would have been the one to escape," Clara finished woodenly.

"I'm sorry, Clara. I didn't mean it the way it sounded," he implored.

"That's okay," she wriggled backward off his lap.

Tears were swimming in her eyes, and he hated that he'd caused her pain when she was already struggling to come to terms with so much. He needed to get better at thinking before he spoke. He hadn't dated much since his divorce, and his ex hadn't been one who'd gotten offended easily. "No, it's not okay, I hurt you. I didn't mean to. I'm glad you're alive, Clara. I wouldn't ever wish anything to change that; I just wish my sister had survived, too. Forgive me?"

"Really, it's fine. Don't worry about it. I understand."

Clara said it in such a way that made it sound that she believed what he'd said to be what she deserved. He didn't like that. "What I said was thoughtless, and it came out wrong. If you weren't alive, then I couldn't do this." Jonathon pressed his lips to her, pleased when after a moment she responded, tilting her head up and deepening the kiss. He could have kissed her all night, could have done a lot of things with her and to her all night, but he wanted to know why she thought it was okay that anyone, whether it had been what they meant or not, wished her dead. When he pulled away, Clara sighed—a half-content, half-sad sigh—and closed her eyes. Cupping her cheek in his hand, still damp from her wet hair, he asked, "What's wrong, Clara?"

"Sometimes I think it would have been better for one of the other little girls to have lived instead of me."

"Why would you think that?"

"Because I feel like I'm wasting my life. I just go through the motions. I feel like in those six weeks I lost the ability to feel joy. It's like I'm numb." Fresh tears filled her eyes, and she brushed at them. "I don't want to cry again. It makes me feel weak."

He wasn't sure where to start with that. "Well first off, you are *not* weak. Anyone who goes through something so traumatic in childhood and then goes on to lead a perfectly normal, productive life, is the very definition of strong. And you can learn to have fun." Clara said that she no longer got joy out of life, but she had a job she loved. She was close with her family, and she had a beautifully whimsical home—he suspected it was more that she didn't allow herself to enjoy things. "Maybe you've put so much energy into convincing everyone, convincing yourself, that you can lead a normal life despite what happened, that you haven't had anything left for just being silly and spontaneous. But I can help you with that," he grinned. In his first marriage, it had been all about fun and craziness, and while that wasn't all he wanted, it was certainly an important part of keeping the magic alive.

"Okay," Clara smiled back, lifting a hand to cover his. "Can you stay?"

"I'm sorry, honey; I'd love to, but I have to work. I told Allina I'd only be an hour, and I've already been way longer. I could come back later, though? Spend the night again?" he asked, hoping she'd say yes. He loved sleeping with Clara curled up against him.

"I'd love that," she smiled. "Where's Naomi?"

"Upstairs—at least I assume she is. I asked her to give us some privacy. I better be going. I'll see you later."

"I'll miss you." Most traces of pain and confusion were gone from her face; now she just looked tired.

"I'll miss you, too."

Unable to resist one more kiss, as his lips met hers, he knew he was falling hard and fast for Clara Candella.

CHAPTER
Six

February 12th
12:04 A.M.

It had been a long day. A long, emotionally upheaving day that had left her exhausted. And yet as tired as she was, she couldn't fall asleep. Clara had been lying in bed for hours now, tossing and turning, getting too hot and then too cold, trying to will her mind to relax enough to turn off and let her sleep.

Snippets of memories from the missing six weeks had been trickling into her mind all day ever since the session with the hypnotist this morning. That had been a truly terrifying experience. To put herself in a stranger's hands and let the woman pull out of her the memories her brain had deemed scary enough to block out for her own good had been daunting enough, but to do nothing and know that those children's deaths might have been preventable would have left her eaten alive by guilt.

As horrible as the memories of the cold, the hunger, the pain, the fear every time the man and the woman entered the attic had been, it was the memories of her time with Tommy that were the most unsettling.

They'd talked to each other, played games, encouraged each other, comforted each other—they'd been each other's lifeline. Clara didn't think she would have survived if it hadn't been for Tommy. He'd been there for her after they'd returned home and to their regular lives, too. She'd never seen him be violent; she'd never seen him touch a child inappropriately or even hint that it was something he thought about. She'd known that he battled depression at times, but nothing to suggest he was capable of such horrible crimes. Never in her wildest dreams would Clara have seen him as anything other than the quiet, shy, sweet guy she'd always known.

And yet he wasn't any of those things.

He was a cold-hearted, vicious, child rapist, and killer.

Trying to reconcile that was making her head hurt.

At the funeral service, she'd sat quietly, listening to Mrs. Karl talk on and on about all her happy memories with Tommy. When the woman had asked her if she'd like to speak, she'd had to say that she wasn't up to recounting memories. How could she stand there and say nice things about someone she clearly hadn't known at all?

After the minister had spoken and the casket had been lowered into the ground, Mrs. Karl had invited her to spend the afternoon together, but again she had declined. Instead, she had stood at Tommy's grave trying to make sense out of the nonsensical and understand what had made Tommy change. She had been trying so hard to comprehend it that she hadn't even registered the rain.

If Jonathon hadn't come and found her, she would probably still be standing there.

Jonathon.

Maybe that was why she was having trouble sleeping—subconsciously she was waiting for him to arrive. After only two nights, she'd grown accustomed to falling asleep in his arms. Talking with him yesterday had given her hope, that Jonathon might hold the key to helping her learn how to enjoy life again.

That he'd trusted her with the secret that his sister was also a victim of the Doll Killers was also important to her. Sure, it had hurt her when she'd thought he was implying that he wished he could trade her life for his sister's, but she believed him when he'd said that wasn't what he'd meant. Now she just wanted to remember everything she could about the time she'd been missing so she could help him bring peace to his dying mother by solving this case.

She gave up on sleep for the moment. Maybe she'd go and see if there was any sign of Jonathon. She crept quietly out of her room, not wanting to wake Naomi who was asleep in the spare room. Downstairs she looked out the front windows but didn't see Jonathon's car. It was a beautiful night, though—clear sky, full of merrily twinkling stars, and a huge full moon.

Since she was up, she may as well have something to eat. There was a lot to choose from thanks to Naomi's baking binge. Choosing a cupcake that Naomi had made rainbow colored by coloring and layering the mixture before putting them in the oven, she put the kettle on to boil, then realized the clothes Jonathon had put in the washing machine earlier were still there. She'd forgotten about them until just now, but now that she had remembered them she may as well throw them in the dryer.

Clara was just opening the laundry room door when someone grabbed her.

At first, she thought it was Jonathon, but why would he grab her without saying something? Maybe he didn't want to wake Naomi?

No.

It wasn't Jonathon whose hand clamped painfully on her shoulder.

Someone was here in her house.

She knew instinctively that it was the Doll Killers. They had come back to reclaim her. They'd already reclaimed Tommy—she was all that was left now.

These people were *not* taking her again.

Yanking her arm free, she stumbled backward, almost losing her footing and bumping against the door, sending it banging into the wall.

Before she could recover, something sharp scraped down her cheek. As her hands sprung reflexively to her face, someone grabbed her arms and jerked her forward.

Clara was opening her mouth to scream when a voice spoke.

"Step away from her, put the knife down, and put your hands on your head."

Naomi was here.

She was safe.

Taking a deep, steadying breath, Clara ordered herself to calm down. The Doll Killers weren't going to get her again. Her sister wouldn't let that happen; as long as Naomi was here, she was okay.

"Call the cops, Clara," Naomi ordered.

The woman who had attacked her released her grip on Clara's shoulders but still stood between her and her sister, blocking her path.

"I said, step away from her." Naomi came to physically move the woman.

Clara saw the glint of metal too late to yell a warning.

When Naomi was within striking distance, the woman whirled, plunging the knife downward. It connected with Naomi's shoulder, and she yelped in pain.

Lunging for her sister, who was swaying unsteadily, Clara felt something pierce her arm.

It was a needle.

She'd just been injected with something.

Not one to go down without a fight, Naomi swung a fist at the woman, catching her on the side of the head. Woozy from the blood loss from her heavily bleeding shoulder, both Naomi and the woman staggered. The other woman was old, at least in her seventies, and even injured Naomi managed to get in a couple more blows.

Then another figure emerged, slamming something into Naomi's head.

Her sister crumpled immediately.

Feeling woozy herself from whatever she'd just been injected with, Clara made a move for Naomi's gun, which had clattered to the floor when Naomi had been stabbed.

Her legs refused to cooperate.

Refused to even hold her up.

She fell to her knees.

The world was spinning around her, the sensation sickening.

Her vision was beginning to gray, but Clara clung to consciousness; if she passed out, then both she and Naomi were as good as dead.

She tried to crawl on all fours to the gun.

She didn't move at all.

Her arms wobbled.

The next thing she knew she was lying flat on her stomach.

She tried to drag herself.

She couldn't.

The world was fading around her.

Two sets of shoes appeared before her.

Voices bumbled above her.

The world turned black.

12:53 A.M.

Jonathon knew as soon as he stepped inside the house that something wasn't right.

He'd wanted to get here earlier, but he and Allina had been busy running owners of toy shops from thirty years ago to see if anyone matched the description Clara had given them during her hypnotherapy session. Then he'd had some questions about Allina's sister-in-law's case.

By the time they'd talked that through, it had been around eleven and he'd thought he better pop home. So, he'd brought in the mail, taken a shower, packed a few clothes, then headed to Clara's house.

Now he wished he'd come straight here.

His gaze was drawn to the back door, which stood partially open.

He snapped immediately into cop mode. With his gun in hand, he carefully scanned the large room, looking for anything out of place.

Sitting area was clear.

The dining area was clear.

His heart all but stopped as he visually searched the kitchen. There was a plate with an untouched cupcake sitting next to a mug. The door to the laundry room was open. A body lay on the floor.

A blonde-haired body.

Barely able to breathe, he ran to it. It was facedown. Grasping a shoulder, he rolled the body over.

Simultaneously, he was both relieved and terrified.

It was Naomi. If she was lying unconscious in the kitchen, then that didn't bode well for Clara. Jonathon suspected that Naomi would gladly give her life without a second thought if it meant protecting her sister.

His hand that had grasped Naomi's left shoulder was covered in blood from a deep wound. Blood also streaked her face from a nasty looking cut just under the hairline on her right temple.

He confirmed she was alive by pressing his fingertips to her throat, where he felt her pulse fluttering. Yanking out his phone, he called for backup and an ambulance.

Torn, he wanted to go and check the rest of the house for Clara, and yet at the same time he had to do something to try and staunch the flow of blood, or he was afraid Naomi was going to bleed to death.

Gun still in hand, he darted into the laundry room. After confirming it was empty, he grabbed a couple of towels and returned to Naomi's side. Jonathon knelt beside her and pressed one of the towels to her shoulder.

A small moan escaped from Naomi's lips.

"Naomi?" he whispered urgently, keeping his voice quiet in case anyone was still here. "It's Jonathon, can you hear me?"

"Mmm," she groaned.

"Naomi, open your eyes," he instructed.

Her eyelashes fluttered on her pale cheeks and then her eyes struggled open, unfocused as they looked up at him.

"Naomi, I have to go check the rest of the house, and you're bleeding pretty badly, so I need you to try and keep pressure on your wound until I get back to you." He spoke slowly; she had a head injury, so she might be struggling to understand him. Taking her right hand, he lifted it and pushed it down on the towel. As soon as he released it, her hand slid limply down her body. "Come on, Naomi," he urged.

Blinking as though trying to get her eyes to focus, she whispered, "Jonathon?"

He let out a relieved breath, "Yes."

"Wh . . . what happened?" her voice was faint, blood loss already affecting her.

"You were stabbed; just keep pressure on this for a moment," he tossed aside the old towel, now saturated with blood, got a fresh one and returned her hand to her shoulder. "You got it?"

"Yeah."

"Good girl, I'll be back as soon as I can," he assured her.

Jonathon didn't like the idea of leaving Naomi alone and injured, but he didn't have a choice—Clara could be here, also injured. Or worse. He dared not think the word in case that would somehow make it happen. Clara was not dead. None of the other options were much better. She was either injured enough that she hadn't heard him downstairs or had been unable to get to him. Or she wasn't here.

That the Doll Killers—for there was no doubt in his mind they were who had been in her house tonight—had taken her was a genuine possibility. It was also a terrifying possibility.

Upstairs, everything was quiet.

He checked Clara's room first, then the spare bedroom, then the bathroom.

There was no sign of Clara. No signs of a struggle up here either. The beds were mussed from the girls' sleep, but nothing else in any of the rooms was out of place. There was no blood, either. Which meant that all the action had taken place downstairs.

Clara was gone.

They had her.

That he had no idea what they had planned for her was leaving him struggling for control. He assumed they planned to kill her at some point, but maybe they had something else in store for her first. Somehow they had convinced Thomas Karl to recreate their crimes; perhaps they thought they could get the other survivor to do the same.

Battling fear for Clara, he dashed down the stairs and back to Naomi, flicking on the lights as he went. Her eyes were closed, the towel had fallen from her shoulder to the floor, and her right hand was now resting on her stomach. She'd passed out again.

Blood was pooling around her and soaked through his pants as he knelt at her side. Jonathon was extremely concerned about her. If help didn't arrive soon then he was scared she was going to bleed to death, and he didn't want to have to tell Clara when he found her—*when*, not if—that her sister was dead.

"Come on, Naomi, hang in there." He pressed another towel firmly against her shoulder.

Naomi whimpered in pain, and her eyes opened slowly. Her breathing was labored now, too fast and too shallow, her skin was cold and clammy, she was pale and her lips were tinted with blue. She'd lost too much blood, she was going into hypovolemic shock.

"Naomi, look at me." Her eyes moved to meet his. "You have to hold on, okay? Help will be here soon."

"It hurts," she cried.

"I know it does," he soothed. "I'm just going to grab a blanket; I need to keep you warm. You're in shock. Here, hold this again," he took her icy hand and put it on the towel.

So long as he had something to concentrate on to keep him focused, he could keep his panic at bay. Retrieving a blanket from the sitting area, he was just spreading it over Naomi when he heard footsteps. He hadn't heard or seen any lights or sirens, so he didn't think it was either backup or the ambulance. He wondered whether it could be the Doll Killers returned for some reason, maybe to make sure Naomi was dead.

Blocking Naomi as best he could while keeping pressure on her wound, he had his gun pointed at the door when the doorknob rattled. He tensed. If it was the Doll Killers, he'd have to resist the urge to shoot them on the spot for everything they'd done to Clara, Dora, and all those other children. But if they had Clara now, then he needed them alive to find her.

The door opened, and the breath he hadn't realized he was holding rushed out in a whoosh of relief. "I need help here, now."

Dylan and Davis Merritt turned toward him. Their eyes grew wide when they caught sight of the blood-soaked body behind him.

"What happened? Who is that?" Dylan demanded

"It's Naomi."

Both men's faces drained of color as they came closer, leaving them as pale as Naomi herself. Dylan recovered quicker than his younger brother. "Where's Clara?"

Jonathon met the man's green eyes, so like Clara's eyes. "Gone."

Shock and terror flooded their faces, but Dylan immediately bottled it up and knelt beside Naomi. "How bad is she?"

"She was hit over the head and stabbed in the left shoulder; she's already lost a lot of blood. A *lot* of blood," he repeated.

"Conscious?" Dylan took another towel and Jonathon removed the blood-drenched one he'd been using. That was three towels soaked through now.

"In and out."

"Naomi?" Dylan's voice was very gentle as he brushed away a lock of hair from her blood-streaked cheek. "Come on, honey, open your eyes for me."

She complied, her lids sluggishly lifting, her pain-dulled eyes darted around before settling on Clara's brother. "Dylan?"

"Right here, sweetheart."

"So tired," she murmured.

"I know, honey, but you stay with me, all right?"

"Bang . . . downstairs . . . knife . . . Clara . . . tried . . ." she mumbled incoherently. "Where's Clara?"

Jonathon didn't want her to know her sister was missing right now. Given her condition, he didn't want to upset her. He was going to tell Dylan that, but the other man was apparently on the same page. "An ambulance will be here any minute now, help is coming, you just need to hold on a little while longer." Despite the fear in his eyes, Dylan was able to keep his voice perfectly soothing and comforting, which was helping to keep Naomi calm.

Dylan pressed the towel more firmly against Naomi's wound, causing her to whimper in pain. "It hurts."

"I know. I'm sorry, honey, but I have to keep pressure on this."

"I need to close my eyes now," Naomi's voice was so weak, barely more than a tiny hint of sound.

"No, you don't," Dylan said firmly. "You need to keep looking at me, keep talking to me. You're a fighter, Naomi, you can do this."

"I'm sorry." A single tear made its way down her cheek, mixing with the blood and leaving a watery red trail in its wake. "I don't feel so good." Her eyes drooped closed.

"Naomi?" Dylan carefully jostled her, but she didn't stir.

Dylan looked ready to fly into a full-blown panic attack. Davis was still standing frozen in place. And fear over where Clara was and what was happening to her was about to tear him apart.

Then he heard the sirens.

Help was almost here.

Help for Naomi and help to find Clara.

Jonathon prayed for strength for Clara to stay strong until he found her.

~

3:24 A.M.

Her head was pounding. Worse than when she got stress headaches. Her stomach felt queasy, too. It felt like she had the flu, only her mind was practically screaming at her that she wasn't sick.

She'd been drugged.

The first thing that hit her was a deep, dark, fear for her sister.

Clara remembered watching the knife gouge into her sister's shoulder.

Then someone had hit Naomi over the head, knocking her out.

The last she'd seen of her sister, Naomi was lying unconscious on the kitchen floor.

What had they done with her?

Was Naomi dead?

Had she bled out?

With her mind occupied by thoughts of her sister, Clara didn't even give her situation a second thought. If the Doll Killers had killed Naomi to get to her, then she would never forgive herself.

Surprised, Clara realized that she didn't doubt that she would get home alive. She knew that Jonathon would stop at nothing to find her. And it seemed she trusted implicitly that he would rescue her.

She prayed he had gotten to her house in time to save her sister. It had already been after midnight when she'd gone downstairs to wait for him. Surely he couldn't have been that much farther away. He must have gotten there shortly after she was taken. Naomi couldn't have bled out that quickly.

Clara wanted to believe that, and yet she hadn't seen how badly Naomi was injured. Her sister could have been dead before the Doll Killers ever left the house. Or she could have died all alone and scared. Or maybe she never even woke up again after she'd been hit in the head. She might have died without ever realizing what was going on.

No.

No. Naomi wasn't dead. She couldn't be.

And yet, Clara knew she could be. Her sister had risked her life to try and help her. Even after she'd been stabbed, Naomi had continued to try and fight off their attackers. And that might very well have cost her sister her life.

Working herself into knots over Naomi wasn't going to help her right now. Clara forced herself to take slow, deep breaths. She had to keep calm. If she didn't keep calm, then she wasn't going to be alive when Jonathon found her.

She drew in a long breath, holding it, counting to five and then letting it out...she repeated that several times.

In and out. In and out.

When she felt sufficiently calm, Clara took stock of her body. Starting with her toes, and working her way up, she mentally searched for injuries. Finding none, she willed her eyes to open.

She was scared of what she would see.

Clara suspected what she was going to see when she opened her eyes was the place that had haunted her dreams for the last twenty-three years. A place that, while it had only just become clear to her when she was hypnotized, was as familiar as her own home. She might not have known the specifics of what it looked like, but she knew what it felt like. It felt like fear.

She quickly assessed her current situation. She was sitting in a chair. It felt like her ankles were taped to the legs of the chair, and her wrists to the arms. There was tape over her mouth, too. She wasn't usually claustrophobic, but the feeling of being restrained was eating at her; bubbling inside her until she thought she was going to explode.

She forced herself to breathe slowly again. In and out through her nose until she felt like she could think again.

Just like panicking over Naomi wasn't going to help, so panicking about her own situation wasn't going to help. She could do this. She could keep herself calm, alive, and in one piece until Jonathon and the police found her. She'd survived this once before, and she could most definitely do it again.

First thing's first, she needed to get her bearings. And to do that, she was going to have to make herself open her eyes. Surely, she could manage that. She'd give herself a countdown. That was what she always did when she was in the shower, standing under the delightfully hot stream of water when she didn't want to get out. She'd count backward from ten and then when she reached zero, just turn off the tap. She'd try the same thing now, only this time when she reached zero she'd open her eyes.

Ten.

Nine.

Eight.

Seven.

Six.

Five.

Four.

Three.

Two.

One.

Zero.

Open.

As soon as Clara opened her eyes, she immediately scrunched them shut again in protest to the glare. She went slower this time, inching them open just a little, giving them time to adjust to the bright light after being closed for so long.

Once she'd gotten them open all the way, her heart sunk.

A tiny part of her had been hoping she was wrong, and she wasn't going to find herself back in this room.

It was like being thrown back in time twenty-three years. She suddenly felt like a scared, helpless six-year-old all over again.

She reminded herself that she wasn't. She wasn't a little girl anymore, and she wasn't helpless. The Doll Killers were older now; they had to be in their late sixties or early seventies. She was a strong, healthy, twenty-nine-year-old. At her house, they'd caught her by surprise, and then drugged her. Now all she had to do was bide her time, and then when an opportunity presented itself, she'd grab it.

Besides, Jonathon knew that the Doll Killers kept their victims in a toy shop—that should make it a lot easier for him to find her.

However, as she looked more closely at the room, her optimism dipped.

The room looked the same; only it wasn't.

There were subtle differences to the room she'd seen so clearly in her mind just a day ago. The furniture was the same as she remembered. There was the bed, the dressing table and stool and wardrobe. There was the kitchen sink, table and chairs, and fridge. There was the bath, toilet, and sink. There was the TV, couches, and lamps. None of it was real, it was all wooden play furniture, but it was all just as she recalled. There was even the same picture painted on the pretend TV.

But the room itself was different somehow.

Smaller, maybe? Although she knew that might just be her mind playing tricks on her, when she was smaller the room would have seemed bigger. And the painted windows on the wall looked different, too. The ones she remembered had a park painted as the view, but these showed a beach scene. The toilet, the real one, was in the far right corner of the room; but as she remembered it, it should be in the far left corner.

This was *not* the same room she'd been held captive in before.

She didn't know what that meant, but she did know that it didn't bode well for Jonathon finding her. He would be looking for her in a toy shop, but now she could be anywhere.

The children, she thought suddenly.

Katie Logan and Jimmy Wallander—they should be here somewhere.

Scanning the room, Clara couldn't see them anywhere. Were they dead already? They shouldn't be; they'd only been missing a few days, and the Doll Killers usually kept their victims for at least a month before killing them. But the killers had already changed several parts of their MO. They'd included Tommy; they'd raped Lindsey Peters and possibly Lottie Hatcher, they were using a different location, and maybe they'd decided to keep the children for a shorter amount of time before killing them.

Then her breath caught as she heard something behind her.

The Doll Killers were coming.

～

10:03 A.M.

Jonathon strode down the hospital hallway. "How is she?"

"She's going to be okay," Davis replied, scrubbing his hands down his face. "Knife nicked an artery. She lost a lot of blood, and they had to give her two transfusions. We all have the same blood type, so Dylan and I both donated. For a while, they couldn't get her to stabilize, and they weren't sure she was going to make it, but she made it through surgery, and she's stable now. They moved her out of ICU about an hour ago."

"Long-term prognosis?" Jonathon asked. He'd been so busy at Clara's house, he hadn't had a chance to call and get an update on Naomi. He'd assumed she was doing all right because he'd told Davis and Dylan, who had both accompanied Naomi in the ambulance, to call if anything happened to her and he hadn't heard anything from either of them.

"She's going to need a lot of physical therapy to get back full movement in her shoulder and strength in her arm," Davis explained.

"She awake?"

"Dylan's in with her right now; she's supposed to be sleeping, but you know Naomi."

Jonathon had only known her a few days, but he could already guess that keeping her still and quiet in a hospital bed was going to be a nearly impossible feat.

"She's already talking about going home," Davis continued. "At the moment, she's still too weak to do anything about it, but give her a couple more hours, and she's likely to be attempting to drive herself home."

"Does she know about Clara?" he asked quietly. Every time he thought about Clara, he nearly had a heart attack. His mind would conjure up images of her alone, hurt, scared, and it was all he could do to hold it together.

"Yes. As soon as she woke up from surgery, she was asking about her. We had to tell her."

From the look on Davis' face, it didn't look like that had gone down too well. "I need to talk to her, find out what she saw."

"Do you know anything yet?" Davis asked, his green eyes so full of fear and desperation that Jonathon could barely stand to look at them.

"No, nothing yet. We're assuming it's the Doll Killers, and we're doing everything we can to identify them," he assured Clara's brother. "Have you told your mother what's going on? And Naomi's family?"

"Dylan called Naomi's family while she was in surgery. He called our mom too but she, uh," Davis paused, anger flaring on his face, "She said that she's too busy to come but that we can call her if they find Clara."

Anger flared on his own face. What was wrong with the woman? Her only daughter was in the hands of a pair of serial killers, and she was too busy to come? "What about their dad? Naomi and Clara both spent time with him as kids, right? Wouldn't he want to be here for them?"

"As far as I know, neither of the girls has had much to do with him since they graduated high school, but Dylan tried to call him, he didn't get any answer. Let's go see if Naomi is awake."

Jonathon followed Davis into a nearby hospital room. The blinds were drawn, making the room dim. Dylan stood as the door opened, taking a step toward them and holding a finger to his lips. He needn't have bothered trying to keep them quiet—Naomi was obviously awake, as her head lifted from the pillows as they entered. Her shoulder was heavily bandaged, her arm in a sling to help protect it. Bruises peeked out from underneath a white, square bandage on her temple, spreading down most of the right side of her face.

"Did you find Clara?" Naomi asked, her voice faint and hoarse.

"No, not yet," he told her.

She struggled to push herself into a sitting position. "What time is it? How many hours has she been missing?"

"Stop." Dylan put a hand on her good shoulder to try to keep her still. "Stop. Would you please stop moving," he said when she continued her struggle. "I'll elevate the bed, just stay still."

Naomi stopped and sunk back against the mattress, but whether she'd deliberately done as Dylan asked or she'd simply run out of strength, Jonathon wasn't sure. Dylan fiddled with the bed's controls and raised it, so Naomi was semi-reclined.

"It's ten o'clock; she's been gone about nine hours," Jonathon answered as he pulled a chair up beside her bed.

"Nine hours?" Naomi echoed, looking crestfallen.

"I know you must be feeling awful, but I need to ask you some questions. Are you up to it?" he asked, even though he knew what her answer would be.

"Of course," Naomi nodded emphatically. She was clearly in pain, but her brown eyes were sharp.

"Just try to keep it brief, she's supposed to be resting," Dylan cautioned.

"Don't speak for me, Dylan," Naomi snapped. "I'm not a baby. If it's too much, I can tell him to stop myself."

"But you won't," Dylan muttered and resumed his seat, he glared at Naomi but took her hand and held it tenderly.

"What made you go downstairs? Did you and Clara go down together, or did something make you go down?" Jonathon tried to be as clinical as possible. Clara needed him focused, not a blubbering mess.

"I was still in bed, and I thought Clara was, too. When I heard something—a crash—I went down to check it out and there was a woman holding on to Clara."

"What did the woman look like?"

"She was old; I'd guess seventies."

"Did you see her face?"

"Not well. Her back was to me." Naomi's legs moved restlessly under the covers like she needed to be moving. Dylan looked like he was ready to lie on top of her if necessary to keep her in the bed, should she try to get up.

"Then how do you know she was old?"

"She had gray hair, and I saw her a little when we fought."

"Tell me how you fought."

"I had my gun; I told her to let go of Clara. She did, but she wouldn't move out of the way. I went to physically move her, I was going to cuff her and then call you, but she had a knife. She cut me. Then she tried to go for Clara again. I hit her in the head, then we scuffled."

"Can you give me anything more specific about her appearance?"

"No. I'm sorry. Usually, I'd have taken notice of everything so I could give a detailed description, but I didn't. I'm sorry." Naomi looked devastated that she had failed them.

"You'd been stabbed," Dylan reminded her. "You were bleeding badly. If Jonathon hadn't gotten there when he did you would have bled to death."

Naomi shrugged dismissively. She looked so agitated that Jonathon was tempted to stop the interview here and come back when Naomi was stronger. Instead, he forged on, "Is there anything else you can give me?"

"While I was fighting with the woman I heard footsteps behind me. I didn't see the person, but right before they hit me over the head I heard him say something. I think he said Ruth."

A name. That was extremely helpful. They already knew that at some point the couple had owned a toy shop, and they knew that twenty-three years ago the man had been sick. Now they had a name to go with it. "That's great, Naomi. You did great."

But Naomi was not to be appeased. "It's my fault," her eyes had gone dull, from shock and pain. "I was tired. Because I hadn't gotten much sleep this past week. Everyone kept telling me to sleep, but I thought I was okay, I thought I didn't need it. If I hadn't been so tired, I would have seen that the woman had a knife. Then she never would have stabbed me, and I wouldn't have been woozy and gotten knocked out, and Clara wouldn't have been taken," she finished miserably.

"Naomi, there were two of them and only one of you. And you kept fighting back even after you'd been stabbed," Dylan reminded her.

"It's all my fault," Naomi intoned numbly.

"No, it's my fault," Jonathon contradicted. "I was supposed to be there earlier, but I got busy at work, then stopped by my house and got distracted. If I'd been there just a little earlier, then none of this would have happened."

"You're both being ridiculous," Davis snapped. "Clara is missing because of *them*. Because of those killers. They're responsible for all of this. All those children they killed, Clara almost dying, Naomi almost dying—that is on them. Not either of you."

Jonathon disagreed but didn't bother arguing. What good was guilt going to do Clara? None at all. And the only thing that mattered right now was getting her back alive. Anything that didn't help him achieve that was useless. Including his guilt.

"Naomi?" Dylan had stood up and was leaning over the bed. Naomi had fallen silent, her eyes were blank, she was shaking, and her face had gone even whiter than it had already been. "Davis, go get her doctor. She needs painkillers and a sedative."

"She hasn't taken anything for the pain?" Jonathon was surprised, and impressed, that she had been able to focus at all when between her head and her shoulder she must be in agony.

"She refused," Dylan brushed affectionately at the hair on her forehead. It was clear both Clara's brothers thought of Naomi as another sister.

"No sedative," Naomi murmured, making a vain attempt at getting out of the bed.

Dylan held her easily in place. "Sorry, Naomi, right now I overrule you," Dylan informed her.

"Not fair," she pouted.

"It *is* fair because I care about you."

"I have to help."

Naomi said it so desperately that Jonathon took her good hand. "Naomi, you have helped," he assured her. "You gave me a name, and that's going to help me find your sister and bring her home."

≈

12:19 P.M.

It had taken Clara ages to convince them to trust her. Even now they were still on edge. Still unsure. Still scared.

The noises she had heard earlier weren't the Doll Killers—it was the two children, Katie and Jimmy. Unsure who she was and why she was there and what she might do to them, the children had hidden behind the chair she was bound to.

When she'd heard their scuffling noises and then not seen anyone she had wondered if it was the children, but tied up she hadn't been able to turn around, and with her mouth taped she couldn't talk to them, reassure them that she was a victim, too. Clara had tried grunting and mumbling through the tape, but the children had refused to budge. Then she'd tried to turn the chair around, convinced that if she could make eye contact with the children she would be able to assure them that she was not a threat.

In the end, her efforts to try and move the chair had resulted in her sending it tumbling to the floor. She had landed painfully on her left shoulder and head. She hadn't caused herself any serious damage, but now she was stuck in an awkward position on her side. From this position, though, she could finally see Katie and Jimmy. They looked so small, so scared, and their little faces were tearstained. While she didn't know what they'd been wearing when they were taken, she guessed it wasn't what they had on now. Jimmy was wearing what looked like a brown, knitted, one-piece suit with checked trim and a matching hat, and Katie was wearing a pink and white cotton, short-sleeved dress.

The hypnosis had been like turning on a tap; once the memories had started to come back they hadn't stopped. They continued to trickle back into her consciousness. As she'd laid there, looking at the children in their doll costumes, memories of herself dressed in a blue and white dress came flooding back. They'd put the clothes on her and Tommy shortly before they'd branded them with their doll's marks.

Clara remembered being told to lie down on the floor. The man had sat on her back, the weight of him crushing her poor little chest and making it almost impossible for her to breathe. His legs had pinned her arms to her side, so she couldn't fight back even if she wanted to. And by that point, she was too scared to fight back. The man had pushed her hair up over her head, exposing her bare neck, then he'd kept one hand on her head, the other between her shoulder blades to keep her still.

And then the pain had come.

The red-hot poker had pressed into her flesh, forever scarring her.

Memories of the excruciating pain had brought tears to her eyes, and she'd had to fight them off for fear of suffocating if she cried and got her nose all stuffed up. Her tears had helped to edge the children closer toward trusting her, and after a few more muffled begs for them to help, they had finally exchanged glances and whispers and then Jimmy had crawled carefully to her and pulled the tape from her mouth.

As soon as the tape was off, she had taken several deep breaths, although she'd been able to breathe through her nose with the tape on it hadn't seemed like enough, and she had relished being able to open her mouth wide and breathe deeply. After that, she'd immediately asked the children if they were okay.

Still scared, they hadn't answered. Just stared at her.

They were still just sitting there on the floor staring at her.

"My name is Clara," she told them. "You two must be Jimmy and Katie."

Their blue eyes widened when she used their names.

"The police are looking for you, that's how I know your names," she explained. "Do you know who brought you here?"

Again, the little boy and girl exchanged glances but wouldn't talk.

"Do they talk about dolls a lot?"

Another shared look. Then Jimmy nodded slowly.

"It's a man and a woman, isn't it?"

Jimmy nodded again.

"Is the man sick?"

Both children nodded this time.

The man had been sick back when she was a child, too—and yet here he was still alive twenty-three years later. He must have recovered from whatever was wrong with him back then. Perhaps that was why the killings had started up again. Perhaps they thought that killing children somehow brought about healing.

"Do you know them?" a soft voice asked. Jimmy was looking at her quizzically.

"A long time ago, a *very* long time ago, they took me, too. Me and a little boy called Tommy," she explained.

"Why?" Jimmy crept a little closer. Katie stayed where she was.

"I don't know, honey, but they hurt a lot of kids."

"Are they going to hurt us, too?"

Now was not the time for sugarcoating things, she needed Jimmy and Katie's help if they were all going to get out of this alive. "Yes, I think they are," she replied, hoping the kids could handle it.

Katie started to cry, but Jimmy wiggled closer. "Hurt us or kill us?"

"Kill us," she clarified.

He nodded soberly. "I thought so. When I heard them talking about dolls, I remembered my mom and dad watching the news. The lady on the news was talking about kids who had been killed and left with dolls. Is that what they're going to do to us?"

"Yes, it is." Clara admired the child's spunk. He was holding it together better than most adults would be under the same circumstances. The eight year old's calm was helping her to remain calm herself.

"How old were you when they took you?"

"I was six."

"Why didn't they kill you?"

"Tommy and I escaped."

Blue eyes lit up. "How?"

"I don't know, I can't remember. All I know is the door opened, and we ran." She wished the hypnotist had worked harder to draw that memory out of her. At the time, the specifics of how she and Tommy had gotten free hadn't seemed all that important; it wasn't going to help them find the Doll Killers. But if she'd known she was going to end up trapped in a replica room, then she would have stayed in Dr. Chan's office until the woman had helped her unlock those memories. Hindsight, she grumbled to herself. "Are you two hurt?"

"No, we're okay," Jimmy answered for both him and Katie.

"Are you sure? They didn't do anything to your neck?"

"I'm sure," Jimmy said firmly.

"Okay, good." At least the children would be spared the physical scars of this ordeal if she could get them out of here soon.

"How are we going to get out of here?" Jimmy was all business.

"Have you checked to see if there's a way out?" She and Tommy had checked the attic they'd been kept in several times in the six weeks they'd spent there. In the first few days, searching for a way to escape had been pretty much all they'd done. Over time they'd stopped, given up, accepted that they were trapped.

"Yes." He said it like it was so obvious that asking him about it was a waste of both of their time.

Smiling at the boy, she decided she liked Jimmy Wallander. "I need you to try to find something sharp to cut through the tape." She gestured with her head at her bound wrists and ankles.

Immediately, Jimmy jumped up and started working on that task. With Jimmy occupied, Clara turned her attention to Katie. The little girl looked petrified; she was crying quietly, her skin was very pale, and her eyes almost deadened with shock. Clara was extremely concerned about the child.

"Come here, honey." She wished she had her arms free so she could hold the little girl and comfort her properly.

Katie shrank farther back, wrapping a blanket tighter around herself like a shield.

The blanket reminded her for the first time that she was cold. She was still dressed in the yoga pants and tank top she'd gone to bed in. This attic was cold, just like the one she remembered from her childhood. Ignoring the cold—she couldn't do anything about it anyway—she tried to hold her head in a position that didn't make her neck ache, and called again to Katie, "Come on, honey, come here. You can trust me, Katie. I'm going to do whatever I can to make sure you get home to your family."

"Promise?" The girl's voice was so soft she had to strain to hear it.

"That I'll do everything in my power to get you home? Of course."

"No," Katie shook her head, her blonde braids flying from side to side. "Do you promise we'll go home?"

Her heart was breaking for all of them. How much she wished that she had the power to make that promise. "I can't promise you that, sweetheart. But if I can make it happen, I will. Come here, baby."

Giving in, Katie crept over, curling up against Clara's chest and pressing her face against Clara's neck. "I want to go home," the girl cried.

"Me too, baby." She twisted her head so she could kiss Katie's wet cheek.

"I want my mommy."

While she didn't want her mother, Clara empathized with the child's need to be in the arms of someone who made her feel safe. For her, it was Jonathon's arms she longed to be in.

"I'm scared." Katie tried to get closer.

"Me too, honey; me too."

～

3:40 P.M.

Clara had been gone for well over twelve hours now.

That fact haunted him.

Jonathon knew it was plenty of time for the Doll Killers to enact whatever they had planned for her. He was terrified that she was already dead. Every time a phone rang, or an email or a text came through, he found himself holding his breath, expecting it to be news that Clara's body had been found.

"Let's get started." Heidi was pacing up and down the conference room.

"Wait," he exhaled slowly and prepared to just get it over with and say it. "I know I should have said something sooner, but my sister was one of the Doll Killers' victims."

"I already knew that," his boss nodded calmly.

"Me too," his partner agreed.

"But—but . . ." he stammered.

"Neither of us are stupid," Heidi reminded him. "But at first it wasn't apparent if we were after the original perpetrators or copycats.

When it became clear that the killers from thirty years ago were involved, you seemed to be holding it together. Allina said it wasn't affecting your ability to work the case, so I saw no reason to remove you from it."

"Oh," was all he could manage.

"Although, I was hoping you'd have come clean before now," Heidi sounded slightly disappointed.

Jonathon could feel his cheeks tint pink in embarrassment and he thought of Clara. "I'm sorry, I should have, but I thought you'd take me off the case. My mother is dying, and I want her to know who killed her daughter so she can die in peace. I'm sorry," he repeated.

"Apology accepted, but next time, trust me. I may be your boss, but it's my job to oversee things—not to tell you what you can and can't handle. So, was Thomas Karl working with a partner?" Heidi asked.

"No, it doesn't look like it," Allina answered. "We checked into Sarah Ellis, Thomas' old girlfriend, even though it didn't seem likely that she'd be involved, given her daughter's accusations against Thomas. She and her children had been out of the state for a month spending time with her grandmother, who'd been ill. They only returned on the ninth; that's the day after Lindsey and Kent's bodies were found, and Katie Logan was abducted. Plenty of people remember Sarah and her children from the grandmother's nursing home—apparently the kids were quite a hit with the residents. Thomas died on the seventh; Sarah Ellis was out of town—that means someone else committed the crimes."

"The original killers?"

"Seems logical since Clara's doll was delivered to her house," Allina nodded.

"How do we know that it is the doll that was going to be left with her?"

"The scars on her neck match the markings on the doll," Allina explained.

Jonathon couldn't help but flinch at that, remembering how sensitive Clara was about her scars. If—*when*—he got her back, what other scars would she bear? He was trying to remain positive, refusing to accept Clara's death as a possibility, but doubt was starting to creep into his mind. What possible reason could the doll killers have for keeping her alive? To them, she couldn't be more than a loose end that needed to be tied up.

"The original killers would be old now. Are we sure they would be up to doing all of this?"

"They're going after children," Allina reminded their boss, "and according to Clara, they drug the children. Even in their late sixties or early seventies that should be fairly easily accomplished."

"But they went after Clara," Heidi pointed out. "And she's not a small child; she's a healthy, strong adult."

"That was definitely a risk. And I don't think they anticipated anyone else being there with her. But Naomi said that it was an old woman who stabbed her," Allina replied.

"How is Naomi Candella?"

"Jonathon?" Allina prompted.

"Apparently, it was touch and go for a while, but she's stable now, and she should make a full recovery, with extensive physical therapy. Clara's brothers are still with her, and she's already driving them crazy insisting that she's ready to go home. She was very lucky to survive the attack." Now if Clara could be just as lucky, everything would be okay.

"She wasn't lucky," Allina contradicted. "You saved her life. If you hadn't gotten there when you did, then she would have bled out, and we wouldn't have known what she'd heard."

"What she heard?" Heidi paused in her frenetic pacing and raised a hopeful eyebrow.

"She told Jonathon that before she was knocked unconscious, she heard the man call the woman Ruth," Allina answered.

"So we have a name," Heidi looked delighted. "That should help narrow things down."

"We've been working through what Clara told us under hypnosis," Allina explained. "She said that the man of the couple was sick. She also told us that when she and Thomas were escaping, they were in a toy shop. We started going through toy shops from thirty years ago, searching for any that were owned by a couple, one of whom was ill enough that a child would notice. We didn't find any. Until Naomi gave us the name."

"And now?" Heidi prompted.

"And now I think I might have identified them," Allina smiled brightly, her blue eyes sparkling.

"Ruth Lincoln, aged seventy-two, married to Job Lincoln. When the killings began thirty-three years ago, Job was suffering from bone cancer; he ended up losing one of his legs to the disease. Then apparently ten years later he went into remission. His cancer was just gone," Jonathon explained.

"We're assuming that's why the murders stopped," Allina added. "I guess Ruth and Job associated the murders with his cancer, and once the cancer was gone, there was no need to keep abducting and murdering children."

"And then six months ago, his cancer returned," he continued.

"So they started up the crimes again," Heidi mused.

"Seems like a logical conclusion," Jonathon nodded.

"So, the Lincolns owned a toy shop thirty years ago?" Heidi finally took a seat at the table.

"No," Allina replied.

"Then why are we looking at them as suspects?" their boss looked confused.

"*They* didn't own a toy shop, but Ruth's parents did," his partner smiled. "In fact, they didn't just own a toy shop; they owned the shop and museum that the original investigators on the case consulted with."

Heidi was surprised. "So they were involved in the original case?"

"No, neither Ruth nor Job ever talked with the police. Being experts in toys, including antique dolls, the parents were checked into—but there was no apparent need to look into the family. Especially since Ruth and Job weren't involved in any aspect of the business, and were supposedly occupied dealing with Job's health issues."

"They had access to the toy shop, though," Jonathon took over his partner's narrative. "And it was a big building, lots of the rooms weren't used because the parents wanted to expand the museum side of the business, but they'd had health issues of their own and hadn't gotten around to it."

"Have you checked out the attic? Was it as Clara described it?"

"Building burned down almost ten years ago," he replied.

"So do we know where the Lincolns are now? Let's bring them in for questioning immediately," Heidi demanded.

"We haven't been able to track them down yet. Job's doctors said that when they got the news that his cancer had returned and was terminal, they decided to do some traveling," Allina explained.

"Convenient way to disappear for a while, so no one is looking for them while they resume their killing spree," Heidi noted. "Any family?"

"None living," he answered. "We're looking into major websites that specialize in antiques. If we can find where they're getting the dolls from, we might be able to find an address. Or," Jonathon added dismally, "the dolls may be leftovers from Ruth's parents' collection."

"Speaking of the parents," Heidi looked thoughtful, "wouldn't they have noticed their daughter and son-in-law smuggling abducted children into their place of business? And okay, the place may have had empty rooms, but wouldn't they have heard the children calling for help?"

"Could have brought the kids in at night," Allina shrugged. "Maybe they soundproofed the attic, or maybe they threatened the children into keeping quiet. Clara mentioned under hypnosis that she wasn't able to talk loudly because she'd get a zap, so it's also a strong possibility that they used a shock collar."

"I was thinking," he began slowly, "Clara couldn't remember how she and Tommy escaped, just that the door was open. What if it was one of Ruth's parents? They went up to the attic for some reason; maybe they heard something, or maybe they just wanted to store something up there. Maybe that was who opened the door."

"Why do you think it was one of her parents and not the children themselves that somehow got it open?" Heidi looked curious.

"Not long after Clara and Thomas were found, Ruth's parents died in a car accident. Their car crashed into a tree on a quiet country road. Weather that day was nice, the car wasn't found to have any mechanical faults, and the driver, Ruth's father, had no drugs or alcohol in his system."

"You're thinking suicide?" Allina asked.

"Could have been driver fatigue," Heidi suggested.

"Could have been," he agreed, knowing it wasn't. "But what if it was suicide? If they found out what their daughter was doing, that their own child had killed eighteen innocent children, would have killed another two and who knows how many others if they hadn't stumbled upon the attic. It would have been a terrible choice. Turn in your only child to the police or let them keep murdering kids. Maybe they couldn't bring themselves to turn her in, but they couldn't live with letting her keep killing, and guilt ate at them until they had no choice but to end it however they could."

Jonathon wondered where his own guilt would leave him if he didn't get Clara back alive.

~

5:18 P.M.

"Almost there," Clara encouraged.

Jimmy had been working at sawing through the tape at her right wrist for what had to be a solid hour or more. She wasn't sure exactly since she wasn't wearing a watch, but progress was slow. The little boy had found a screw coming loose from one of the small chairs at the table. With nothing but his hands, it had taken him a while to work it all the way free. His small hands also made work slow cutting through the tape, and he had to stop often because of cramps. Add to that that he kept slipping and cutting her with the sharp end of the screw and he was going even slower. Clara didn't mind the scratches; she barely felt the pain, all she cared about was getting free. Once Jimmy got her right hand undone she could do the rest herself and probably get all three other limbs free in about a tenth of the time.

While Jimmy worked on cutting the tape, Katie was curled up in a ball on her lap. The children had managed to get her chair upright again, and ever since, Katie had been sitting in her lap, arms wrapped tightly around her neck.

"Got it," Jimmy declared triumphantly, a smile breaking out on his face. When he smiled, he was a beautiful little boy. Clara could see why the killers had chosen him.

"Great job," she smiled back at him. "Here, give me the screw, I can do the others, you just rest now," she told Jimmy, who sank to the floor with a weary sigh. "Honey, I need you to hop down for a moment," she told Katie.

Whimpering, Katie shook her head and snuggled closer. "I'm scared."

"I know, sweetheart, but I need to get out of this chair, so I can find a way for us to get out of here." Clara also thought she stood a pretty good chance at taking the couple when they came back. They were old, and this time she was going to be ready for them. But if they returned while she was still stuck in this chair, then none of them stood a chance. "Just for a minute, honey. Sit there with Jimmy, and as soon as I cut through all this tape then I can hold you again, okay?"

Reluctantly, Katie slid off her lap, sitting as close as to Jimmy as she could. With her hand free and no time to lose, Clara began to saw at the tape on her left wrist. The screw wasn't a good tool; it was too small, and not sharp enough to cut easily through the layers of duct tape that wound around and around her arm. Still, she didn't give up, working steadily away and she was about halfway when she heard footsteps.

"No," she wailed.

They were coming.

And she wasn't free yet.

She'd been so close.

So close to getting free.

So close to standing a real chance at getting herself and the children home.

And now it was ruined.

Frantically, she gouged at the tape with the screw in desperation to break through it, to get free, even though she knew it was pointless—the door handle was already jiggling. There was no way she could get the duct tape off her wrist and both ankles before the door opened.

"Go, hide," she hissed to the children.

"They're coming back," fresh tears brewed in Katie's eyes.

"Yes, go, now," she commanded.

"You didn't get free." Jimmy had bounded to his feet.

"No, I didn't. Take Katie and the screw and hide, maybe you can use it as a weapon." She tried to give it to him, but he shook his head.

"You should keep it, you have one hand free, maybe you can use it." Then he took Katie's arm, pulled her to her feet and ran to the other side of the room, hiding them both behind the wooden kitchen sink.

Giving up on trying to get free, instead Clara put her arm back in place, the screw clutched in her fist and hoped that they wouldn't notice the tape had been disturbed until she had a chance to use it to her advantage. The screw wasn't big enough to cause any serious damage, but perhaps there was something she could do with it.

"Clara, have you gotten acquainted with the children?"

Almost against her will, Clara's head turned in the direction of the voice. An old woman stood there. She didn't recognize her at all. If she had walked into her in the street, Clara would not have suspected that this was the woman who had abducted her and held her captive in an attic for six weeks. She would have sworn she had never met the woman before in her life.

Until she looked in her eyes.

Those blue eyes were hauntingly familiar.

As she stared at them, the face slowly morphed. Became younger. The wrinkles smoothed into the clear white skin, the red mark on the woman's face was obviously a birthmark, the hair was gray now but back then it had been a dirty blonde.

"Long time, no see." The woman smiled.

All she could do was stare at the woman in shock, feeling every bit as terrified and helpless as she had twenty-three years ago. Biting on her lip, she fought the fear. The painful sting as her teeth broke through the skin snapped her out of her scared daze. She wasn't a frightened little girl anymore. She was an adult. And her every instinct screamed at her that attempting to talk her way out of this was her only option. Even if she couldn't convince them to let her go, and she suspected she could not, she could at least keep herself alive until Jonathon found her.

Forcing herself to sound calm and in control, Clara asked, "What's your name?"

The old lady raised a surprised eyebrow.

"You know my name, but you never told me yours, not once in all those weeks I spent with you," she explained.

"Ruth. Ruth Lincoln. And this is my husband, Job," she stepped sideways, and Clara saw a man in a wheelchair. Maybe it was because she saw him second after the woman had already triggered her memories, but she recognized him immediately. He was bald, just like he had been back then, and thin—too thin. In her memories he was sick, and it seemed he still was.

"We're so glad to have you here with us again, my dear," Job rolled his wheelchair closer.

Her bravado waned a little; they had planned and executed her abduction so perfectly. They obviously had something specific in mind for her. "Why am I here?"

"To join us," Ruth replied. "Us and the children. Jimmy, Katie, come here. Now," she added sternly when the children didn't comply.

"No," Clara called to the children. "Stay where you are. Why do you need me here with you?"

"So you can witness their transformation," Ruth answered as though it were obvious.

"Their transformation into dolls?" Is that why Ruth and Job had done all of this? Because they thought they were literally transforming the children into dolls?

"They are lucky," Ruth strode towards Jimmy and Katie's hiding place.

"Please, leave them alone," she begged as the old woman grasped both children's arms and began to drag them out.

"You are lucky, too, my dear." Job caught her by surprise. She'd been distracted by Ruth and hadn't noticed him rolling over to her. She went to swing her free arm at him, but he already had the duct tape ready to go and promptly re-secured her wrist to the chair's arm. "You don't understand yet, but you will. You're going to help us. You're going to enter immortality just as we did. You are our chosen one." He reached out a withered old hand and stroked her hair, and Clara shrank away from him, repulsed.

"You must be initiated." Ruth's eyes were not like her husband's; they were cold and calculating. "You will kill the children."

"You mean make them into dolls?"

"No. The time of blood hasn't come." Job's smile was borderline insane. "They cannot transform yet, but we are willing to sacrifice one. The girl."

Katie squawked and tried to flinch away from Ruth, but the old woman was surprisingly strong.

"I'm not going to kill her." Clara was not going to do that under *any* circumstances.

"Do not worry, dear; we can find plenty of others who can make the transition." Job gave her a smile she thought was intended to be soothing. "Once you learn how, you will be able to help many become eternal."

"No," she shook her head violently. "I won't hurt her. I won't. And there is nothing you can do to make me." The calm she'd been clinging to was rapidly evaporating. Job was crazy and Ruth was evil—a terrifying combination. Jonathon was coming, but she had no idea how long it would take him to find her. It seemed like the Lincolns intended to keep her alive for a while at least, but not the children. If she didn't kill Katie, would they?

"You will." Ruth released the children and moved out of sight, returning moments later with a red-hot poker.

Clara knew what that meant and her body convulsed in fear.

"You need to take on their marks, to properly understand, to make them part of you," Job explained somewhat apologetically.

"No, please," she begged, trying to pull her arm away as Ruth held the branding iron so close she could feel the heat pouring off it. Of course, she was powerless to move her arm as it was still firmly secured in place by duct tape.

"Their marks will bring you enlightenment," Job assured her.

Although she promised herself she wouldn't, Clara couldn't help but scream as the glowing iron burned her flesh.

∽

9:52 P.M.

. . .

It was quiet up here.

And not a good kind of quiet. It was too quiet. Eerily quiet.

It was like Clara's house was crying out for her. Missing her. He certainly was. Now that work was done for the day, all his fears about Clara had nothing to hold them back.

Jonathon had been afraid that his fears would overwhelm him, so he'd offered to come back to Clara's house and clean it. Naomi's blood was all over the kitchen floor. Of course, there were people who specialized in that sort of cleanup, but he'd needed something to do, something that would keep him occupied for as long as possible, and it had taken him at least an hour to scrub the blood from the floor and kitchen counters.

It also had the bonus of giving him an excuse to spend time at Clara's house.

He felt closer to her here since it was pretty much the only place where they'd spent time together. He liked being surrounded by her things; her home was such an embodiment of her that it almost felt like a part of her was still here.

Right now, he was sitting on her bed. He loved her bedroom; each of the walls was painted a different color—pink, purple, green, and blue —all pastels. The colors reminded him of flowers—beautiful and delicate, yet strong. Just like Clara. Like the downstairs, the furniture up here was also a mishmash of different wood types. The dresser was a pale yellowy brown, the wardrobe a medium brown, and the bed was a dark wood canopy bed, with an intricately carved headboard. The bed had dainty white lace curtains, tied with satin ribbon around the bedposts, and was spread with a colorful patchwork quilt that looked like it was homemade. Jonathon wondered whether Clara had made it herself.

There were so many things he didn't know about her. Sure, they'd talked about some major stuff because of the case, and he was glad that Clara had trusted him enough to open up to him about her guilt over deliberately walking away from her mother, but he wanted to know *everything* about her. Even the smallest most incidental of things. He wanted to know her favorite color, her favorite food, her favorite movie, her favorite music, her favorite season, her favorite holiday destination— he wanted to know it all.

That he might never get a chance to find those things out was a very scary, and yet unfortunately very real, possibility.

He picked up her pillow and held it to his chest. He could smell her on it. Slipping off his shoes he climbed under the covers, desperate to feel as close to Clara as was possible. The whole bed held her scent, a delicious mix of vanilla perfume and apple shampoo.

Jonathon remembered lying in her bed, just forty-eight hours ago, with her curled up in his arms. His attraction to her was strong. He'd wanted more than simply holding her, but she hadn't been ready, and when they made love for the first time, he wanted it to be perfect. Now part of him wished that their bodies had been joined that night; he might never get another opportunity. And yet, even as he wished it he knew he wouldn't have changed anything. He would never do anything to hurt Clara, and if they'd had sex that night, then she would have wound up hurt.

Closing his eyes, he concentrated, tried to focus on Clara, tried to connect somehow with her. He needed to know that she was okay, that she was still alive, that she was holding it together, that she knew he would come for her.

He needed her to know that he would find her.

And he would find her.

He couldn't accept anything less.

He *would* find her.

He would.

But a tiny flicker of unwanted doubt sprouted in his mind. What if he found her too late and she was already dead?

CHAPTER
Seven

February 13th
2:20 A.M.

"Let's go try again," Ruth begged her husband.

It felt like time was running out. Like if she didn't accomplish her goals soon, then she never would. They needed someone to take over. Someone to keep creating dolls, someone to help her and Job become dolls. She had thought that person would be Tommy, but now that he was dead, there was only one other choice. Clara Candella.

The woman was the answer to her prayers. The answer to *their* prayers. The only one who could make sure that she and Job were together forever.

Only she wouldn't cooperate.

Ruth had already given her the marks of four of the children, but it hadn't been enough. She wouldn't do it. She wouldn't kill Katie Logan. If she didn't, then she'd never learn. And she *had* to learn. Clara had to know what to do, how to transform a living person into a doll. If she didn't, she wouldn't be able to save her and Job. They didn't have long.

Job didn't have long. He was fading. She was losing him. She wouldn't—she wouldn't lose him. She wouldn't let it happen. Clara just needed more of a push. She needed more of the marks to help her understand. Maybe she needed all twenty-two.

"Be patient, my dear," Job took her hand in his and brought it to his lips, kissing her palm. "She has only been with us a few hours; it will take some time."

But she couldn't be patient. They didn't have much time left. She could feel it in her bones. "Maybe she just needs all the facts. We didn't explain everything to her. Maybe if we did, she would understand better."

Job's blue eyes turned serious. "Why are you in such a rush? What are you afraid of, my love?"

She couldn't help it; tears welled in her eyes. Ruth didn't want to cry in front of Job; it always worried him when she did. He hated for her to be sad, he had spent his whole life trying to make her happy. And he did make her happy. That was why she was crying now. She couldn't imagine her life without him. She didn't want a life without him. From the moment they had met, she had known he was hers—her soul mate, her other half.

They had met in their late teens. Two lost, lonely souls wandering through life unsure of who they were and what the future held for them. Their connection had been immediate. They'd both felt it. Back then, both of them had been battling suicidal thoughts. Ruth had thought that her life was worth nothing, that *she* was worth nothing, and then there was Job. A handsome, smart, sensitive man who made her feel, for the first time in her life, that she was wanted. She hadn't realized that anyone else was like her, that there were other people who hated themselves, too—but Job had revealed his own deep, dark depression that left him feeling that death was a better option than living. Together they had healed. Together they had grown. Together they were one.

"I'm afraid of losing you," she wept.

Drawing her closer, down onto his lap, his arms engulfing her in the warm hugs that had comforted her so many times before. Grabbing his face, she pulled it down to meet hers. Her mouth found his, hungry, starving, for him. They may be in the seventies now, but their love was still as passionate as when they'd met over fifty years ago.

Job's hands reached for her blouse buttons, but Ruth stopped him. "You don't want to?" he asked.

"Oh, I want to, but not here."

"Upstairs?"

"She should see. Clara. How it works. So she understands."

"But, sweetheart, the time of blood can't come through you anymore."

"But it can come through her." Ruth prepared herself to make the ultimate sacrifice for the greater good.

"You want me to join with her to help the children pass on?" Job looked surprised.

"Yes, but not yet, not until she understands, not until she's ready to do what needs to be done. Maybe it would help her to know that it's painless. That we make sure of that. That it's just a journey from one existence to another. To a better existence," she added. "Please, let's try again. It can't hurt. She's had some time to calm down, to think about what we told her. Please."

His face softened into the smile she loved so much. When she looked at her husband, she still saw the man she'd met at nineteen; she didn't see the toll the years and his illnesses had taken on him. "Whatever makes you happy, my dear."

Pleased, she stood, took his wheelchair handles and pushed him to the bottom of the stairs. Using the handrail, Job managed to slowly make his way up the stairs. With his health in decline again, he was struggling to get about without the wheelchair. He had a prosthetic leg, but he didn't like to wear it; he said it irritated the sensitive skin where his leg ended halfway down his thigh. They kept another wheelchair on the second floor, and getting up to the attic was easy because they'd been able to install a ramp.

Ruth was tingling with excitement as she pushed her husband up the ramp and unlocked the attic door. She was so close; they'd make Clara understand. Of course, they would. Why wouldn't they? Tommy had come to understand. Clara would, too. After all, she *was* one of the chosen ones.

All three heads snapped toward her when she opened the door.

Katie was curled up in Clara's lap, and Jimmy stood, standing protectively between her and Job, and the girls.

"Let the children go, please." Clara's voice was weak, her eyes hazy with pain.

"The children aren't going anywhere." Ruth pushed Job inside and relocked the door, dropping the key into her bra where the children wouldn't be able to get it.

"Jimmy, take Katie and go over to the far side of the room," Clara instructed.

"No," the eight-year-old shook his head defiantly.

"Jimmy, now," Clara repeated firmly.

Reluctantly the child obeyed, grabbing hold of Katie's arm, dragging her off Clara's lap. The little girl cried out in protest, and then they ran to the other side of the attic. He grabbed the wooden bed and stood it up on its side, then pulled Katie behind it, as though it were a shield that would protect them.

"The police are looking for you, they're getting closer," Clara spoke, diverting her attention away from the children. "They know that Tommy knew enough to find you, and they know everything I remembered. They will find you."

"They haven't yet," Ruth contradicted.

"Because they didn't know what I knew, I couldn't remember, and Tommy never said anything. But they *will* find you," Clara's green eyes shot daggers.

"How would they find us?" She was more amused than annoyed. "We aren't using the same place as when you and Tommy stayed with us."

"I know, but they'll find out who you are, and then they'll know where you're hiding out."

"*You* didn't even know our names," Ruth reminded her, chuckling.

"Please, just let us go," Clara begged.

"I can't." As the gravity of her situation and the enormity of her need settled on her, Ruth sobered.

"Why?"

"Because we need you, my dear," Job replied when Ruth found her emotions had clogged her throat and she couldn't speak.

"You need me? You mean to kill the children? Because you want me to help you turn them into dolls? Why can't you do it yourself? Isn't that what you've been doing all these years? So why do you need my help all of a sudden? I don't understand." Clara looked like she was quickly getting overwhelmed.

"No, dear." Job wheeled himself over next to Clara's chair. "It's us. We need you to turn *us* into dolls, but first, you must learn the process."

"Turn you into dolls?" Clara looked incredulous. "That isn't even possible. You two are insane. You haven't been turning children into dolls; you've just been killing them."

"Poor child." Job shook his head. "You don't yet understand, but you will. We will help you. Ruth," he turned to her, "you were right, we must try again; we must keep trying until she understands."

"What? No," Clara protested, beginning to jerk her body in a panic, knowing what was coming and attempting to flee.

"You don't have another little weapon on you this time, do you, Clara?" her hand subconsciously moved to the small scratch on her arm where Clara had gouged at her with a screw. The younger woman's hands were curled into fists, and Ruth had to pry them open to check that they were empty.

When she was satisfied that Clara posed no threat, she retrieved her keys and unlocked a small cupboard built into one of the walls, depositing the keys in her pocket. In the cupboard was a small electric hot plate and all of their specially crafted brands; each one had been lovingly handmade by Job himself. One was there for each child—from the first two down to the ones that would soon mark Jimmy and Katie. Ruth had kept the hot plate on, anticipating taking another go at Clara soon after the first. She set about heating the fifth child's brand, virtually oblivious to Clara's begged pleas.

With the brand red hot, she put another on to heat and returned to Clara, whose skin had gone so white Ruth wondered whether she was about to pass out.

"Please don't, please." Tears streamed down Clara's pale face.

"Are you ready to kill the girl?" Ruth asked, holding the branding tool mere millimeters above Clara's flesh so she could feel the full force of the heat, anticipate what it would feel like when it scorched her flesh. Ruth knew what it felt like, too, for she and Job also bore the marks of all the children who they'd transformed into dolls.

"No," Clara sobbed. "I'd rather you burn me a million times than hurt her."

Clara clamped down on her bottom lip to keep from screaming as the brand made contact with her skin. Ruth could see the small dots of blood on her lip.

"I'm sorry, dear." Job always hated inflicting pain; he was such a sensitive, good-hearted soul. "But you must bear their marks, just as we do." He had removed his shirt to show Clara the brands that covered his back, arms, and chest.

"Please, not again," Clara begged as Ruth returned with another brand.

Just as she was about to lower the poker, she was rammed from behind. Stumbling, she fell, landing hard on her knees. The poker and the keys both went flying.

"Stay away from her," Jimmy Wallander screamed, his small fists swinging.

Irritated, she swatted the boy away as though he were no more consequential than a fly, which he wasn't. Jimmy fell, bumping his head on the side of the chair, and lay still.

Angry now, Ruth recollected the branding tool and pressed it to Clara's arm, enjoying the woman's moans of pains.

Then she got another and another. She was feeding off the moans, that grew to screams, and then dropped to moans once more.

Nothing was going to stop her from getting what she wanted.

Nothing.

Not some stupid woman, not some bratty kid, not sickness, not death.

Nothing.

∾

4:11 A.M.

. . .

The smell of burning flesh assaulted her nostrils, rousing her.

For a long moment, Clara couldn't remember where she was or what had happened to her to make her feel so awful.

Unfortunately, it all came slowly trickling back.

The Doll Killers had taken her again. Locked her up in another attic along with two little children. And then they burned her repeatedly.

She must have ended up passing out from the pain.

Thankfully, Job and Ruth appeared to be gone now. She couldn't hear them, she couldn't see them, and she couldn't sense them.

Clara remembered at least ten brands, in addition to the four they'd given her earlier.

The feel of the metal scorching her skin and the agonizing pain that accompanied it was forever seared into her brain. The scars, too, would be with her forever. Unlike the one on the back of her neck, the ones that marred her arms would not be so easy to hide. Glancing down, she saw that her tank top had been removed, leaving her in just her bra and yoga pants. The skin on her stomach was also covered in bright red welts. They'd branded her there, too.

Her burns were blistering and extremely painful and left her feeling an odd mix of too hot and too cold. She felt woozy, too, but she'd have to fight through it until the feeling passed. She had to think of a way to get the children out.

Jimmy.

Panic suddenly brushed away her pain. The little boy had tried to come running to her rescue. He'd attacked Ruth Lincoln, tried to fight her off, and the old woman had hit him. For an old lady in her seventies, Ruth was surprisingly strong, and the blow she'd given the child had been enough to send him flying. As he'd fallen, he'd hit his head on the chair and been knocked unconscious. Clara couldn't remember seeing him wake up.

She looked around the room.

Her panic grew with each passing second.

She couldn't see Jimmy anywhere. Katie either.

Had they taken him? Had they killed him already, him and Katie?

She'd failed.

She could hardly believe it, but it was true. She'd failed. The children were dead. She hadn't been able to save them.

If she couldn't save them, how was she going to save herself?

The simple facts were, she couldn't.

She was tied up, injured, and groggy from the pain—she didn't stand a chance at getting away. Talking her way out also didn't seem like a viable option. Ruth and Job didn't want to hear a word she had to say. They were convinced that they could get her to agree to help them change children into dolls and then change them into dolls. They weren't going to let her go. Not ever.

Jonathon.

She knew he was looking for her.

She knew he would *keep* looking for her.

Forever.

But he didn't know the Doll Killers' names. How would he be able to find where they were hiding out?

It was hopeless.

Completely and utterly hopeless.

She began to cry. She couldn't help it. She didn't want to die like this, alone and scared. She wanted to go home. She wanted her family, and she wanted Jonathon.

Clara was sobbing now. Huge, violent sobs that ripped out of her chest. She was crying so hard she could barely breathe, but she didn't care. Jonathon would never find her in time. Even if he could manage to find the identities of the Doll Killers, and where they were keeping her, she'd be dead before he ever made it here. When Ruth realized she was never going to give them what they wanted, they'd kill her. She'd never go home. She was going to die here. And if she was going to die here, then she may as well just get it over with.

"Clara?"

The voice startled her. She'd thought no one else was here.

"Clara?"

She tried to see through the lake of tears in her eyes. She could just make out a small face, with blue eyes framed by blond hair, before her.

"Are you okay?"

Struggling to rein in her weeping, she hiccupped out a few more sobs, then drew in several deep breaths. She was borderline hyperventilating and totally out of control. She needed to get it together. She had to hold on and keep the faith; Jonathon would never give up on her, so she couldn't give up on him either.

"Clara? Are you okay?"

The tears in her eyes cleared enough that she could finally see properly. It was Jimmy with Katie right behind him. His face was bruised and bloody, but he was okay. Alive. She had to calm herself, she didn't want to scare the children more than they already were. "Are you okay?"

"You thought we were dead," Jimmy muttered.

"I saw Ruth knock you over, you were unconscious, and then when I woke up, I couldn't see either of you. I was afraid the worst had happened," she admitted, still battling to get her breathing back to normal. "Jimmy, are you all right?"

"My head hurts," he admitted. "But I'm okay."

She searched his eyes to see if he was telling her the truth. There was pain in his eyes, but they looked focused. "Dizzy?"

"No."

"Nauseous?"

"No."

"How long were you unconscious?"

Shrugging, he responded, "Not long I think. When I woke up, the lady was burning you over and over again. I was scared, so I just laid there and pretended that I wasn't awake."

"That was smart, Jimmy." Not that she'd have expected anything else from the boy. "Katie, you doing okay?"

The little girl was crying again, her cheeks wet and her eyes red and puffy, but she nodded. Katie was holding it together as best as she could.

"All right then, we need to decide what our next move is . . ." Clara broke off as she looked down at her wrists. The duct tape on her right wrist must have been burned by the branding tools because it was black and charred and half-ripped. Her stomach dropped in relief, and her eyes fell closed, her head resting against the back of the chair. This was the break they'd needed. But they had to work quickly. "Jimmy, do you see this?"

His eyes lightened, and he nodded. Producing something from his pocket, he stated, "I found this. She dropped them when I tackled her. She picked them up again, but this one must have come off the chain."

The key glimmered as it caught the light.

Salvation.

"Quick, Jimmy," she urged.

With the tape already weakened from heat, it didn't take long for him to saw his way through it. The sense of relief Clara felt when it came away was almost overwhelming. Taking the key, she went to work on her other wrist. There was no time to waste. The key was bigger and sharper than the screw had been and soon she had her left wrist free, too. Ripping the remaining tape from her skin, she barely felt the sting of all the hairs being ripped out. Instead, she went straight to work on her ankles. She thought of nothing else, heard nothing else, saw nothing else as she was completely consumed by her task.

At last, she was rewarded with success.

The tape came free. She ripped it from her ankles, and then desperate to relish her hard-fought freedom, she pushed to her feet. Weak and light-headed, she swayed, but Jimmy's hands grabbed her and steadied her. It didn't take her long to get herself together.

She knew what she had to do.

She had to get the children out.

Dragging them with her to the door, she had little hope the key that had been left behind was the right one, but she tried it none the less. As expected, the door didn't open. But hope was flowing through her now—nothing was going to make her give up.

Something long and thin—that was what she needed. Naomi had once taught her how to pick a lock; she wasn't sure she remembered everything, but surely she could recall enough to get the door open.

Her hair was loose, hanging down her back as it always was, but Katie's hair was in braids. "Katie, are there any pins in your hair?"

The child just looked at her.

Not bothering to wait for the little girl to process her question, Clara ran her hands through the child's hair and was rewarded with two pins. Her hands were shaking now, with fear, with excitement, with adrenalin. Pushing everything else aside, she focused every ounce of her concentration on the lock. She worked the pins this way and that until she was rewarded with a click. Naomi was going to *love* that her lock-picking techniques had stuck.

"You did it," Jimmy looked at her in awe.

Taking each child by the hand, she dragged them down the stairs. Katie stumbled, but Clara didn't stop—they didn't have time to stop. Ruth and Job could reappear at any second. Jimmy kept pace with her as they darted down a hallway and then down another staircase.

A door.

Clara spotted a door.

"Come on," she urged Katie, but the child was in shock and continued to stumble.

Then Clara heard a noise.

Footsteps.

Someone was coming.

Fear quickly wiped out the hope. They were going to get caught *this close* to freedom. She couldn't allow the children to be hurt. Placing Katie's hand in Jimmy's, she commanded, "Don't stop. Not for anything," and gave them a shove in the direction of the exit.

Jimmy hesitated, turned to look at her, not wanting to leave her alone.

"Go," she ordered.

She could fight off Ruth and Job. They were elderly, and Job had only one leg and was ill, virtually confined to a wheelchair. The children were safe; she could catch up to them later.

She spun in circles, scanning the room, searching for anything she could use as a weapon. Her eyes settled on something, and she was taking a step toward it when something hit her in the back, knocking the air from her lungs.

"Sorry, Clara. They're replaceable, but you aren't."

Something slammed into her head, and she dropped.

∼

5:31 A.M.

. . .

Katie ran.

She had no choice.

Jimmy was running, and he still clutched her wrist, dragging her along with him.

She didn't want to run. She was so tired. All she wanted to do was curl up somewhere and cry. Katie hadn't known it was possible to cry so much, but it was pretty much all she'd done since the horrible lady from the bank had taken her.

She had woken up on the uncomfortable little bed in that horrible room that reminded her of her dollhouse at home. She hadn't understood. Why was she there? Why had that woman taken her?

Until Jimmy showed up, the thought of trying to find a way to escape had never even occurred to her. There was no way out. She was going to die there. Every time the old lady and the old man came, she thought they were going to do it. But they never did. They just played at pretending she was a doll, and then did . . . stuff . . .

Stuff she didn't want to think about. She didn't want to think about any of it. She didn't want to think at all.

That was why she cried. When she cried, she didn't have to think— she could just feel. Feel every ounce of her fear and terror and panic.

It wasn't herself she was worried about.

She hadn't cried for herself.

It was her brother.

The nasty old lady hadn't brought him to the attic, so she must have killed him.

What else could she have done with Kevin?

The lady, Ruth, had given her a shot of something to make her sleep like the doctors at the hospital the time she had her tonsils taken out. With Katie asleep, Ruth wouldn't have been able to take Kevin back to the bank. That would have looked too suspicious.

She must have killed him.

Her brother was dead.

Because of her.

Because she'd been busy worrying about her own problems. Her own *stupid* problems. Who cared about her friends from school? Who cared that Jasmine and Kelly didn't want to play with her? Who cared that she had to be Missy's partner? Who cared if the kids at school teased her? That meant nothing to her now. Nothing. She had as good as murdered her own baby brother.

Her mother was going to be so mad at her.

Probably didn't even want her back.

"Katie," Jimmy sounded exasperated.

Her mom always sounded exasperated, too. She never seemed to be able to make her mother happy, and that was before. Now, when her mother found out what she'd done, that she was responsible for Kevin's death, she would hate her.

"Katie, don't slow down," Jimmy urged, pulling on her arm.

But Katie wasn't going to run another step.

She wanted the old couple to find her. To take her away. To kill her. She didn't deserve to live.

"No," she whispered, sinking to the ground right where she was. She wasn't moving another foot.

He kneeled in front of her, scanning the area around them. "We haven't gone far enough. We have to keep moving. They could be coming."

Katie hoped they were. Hoped they weren't far away. Hoped they killed her soon.

"Come on." Jimmy yanked her to her feet, tried to pull her forward, but she resisted.

"I don't want to."

Shaking her, Jimmy's voice became more commanding, "You have to. Clara stayed so that we could get away. We have to go find help before they hurt her."

That stirred Katie a little. She liked Clara. The woman had been comforting and kind, and she'd felt safer around her. Maybe she should keep going, for Clara. But then again, only one of them needed to get help. Jimmy could go on without her. He could find someone to help Clara. He didn't need her. No one needed her.

"Katie," Jimmy sounded angry now. "Let's go!"

"Go without me." She could feel more tears coming on. "Just leave me and go."

"No, I'm not leaving you, Katie!" Jimmy said fiercely.

He hauled her to her feet and began to run again, towing her along with him. Too tired, too numb to protest, Katie allowed him to guide her.

She didn't know how long they ran. It felt like forever.

It was dark, but she liked the dark—she felt like darkness was inside her and when she was in the dark she blended in. It didn't make her feel so out of place.

Suddenly, Jimmy froze. Not expecting him to stop so suddenly, Katie crashed into him, and both of them sprawled onto the ground.

"I hear footsteps," he whispered. Not remaining still for long, he reclaimed his hold on her and pulled her into a nearby alley. "Shh," he cautioned.

Katie thought she was being quiet. But it seemed she was wrong, because Jimmy clamped a hand over her mouth.

Footsteps.

Coming closer.

She could feel Jimmy tense and ready himself to spring if a threat presented itself.

It was *them*.

Katie was sure of it. They were going to take her and Jimmy back to the doll room and kill them.

"Hello?" a voice called. A voice she hadn't heard before. It wasn't them.

Jimmy relaxed, released her and jumped to his feet, throwing himself at the shadowy figure that stood at the end of the alley. "Help us, please, we need help. You have to call the police. They have to find her. They have to find Clara before it's too late."

"Whoa, young man. We'll get you help, just calm down."

"Please, you have to hurry," Jimmy begged.

"Let's get you in the car and then we'll call for help."

"No, wait, Katie," Jimmy tugged his hand free of the man's grip and came toward her.

A moment later she was bathed in bright, white light. She tried to shrink away from it. She didn't like the light. She wanted the dark back. She could hide in the dark, but she couldn't hide in the light.

"Hello there, little lady." A man knelt in front of her, his smile was warm, his manner comfortable and easy. He felt safe, but she no longer trusted her instincts. Sensing her fear, he reached out a hand, held it in front of her, "It's okay, little one; you're safe now. We'll get you and your friend in my car, warm you up, get you something to eat and call your parents so you can go home."

Home. That should comfort her, but it didn't. Bursting into tears, she threw herself into the man's arms. She wasn't sure she wanted to go home. She felt so alone, so lost; she didn't know what to do to make those feelings go away.

~

6:44 A.M.

The sky was just beginning to lighten, transforming from the inky black of night to the dull gray of a winter day.

Jonathon's heart had almost stopped when Allina called him earlier. Her phone call had roused him from a deep and dreamless sleep, and for a moment, when he'd awakened in Clara's bed he had expected to find her slumbering in his arms. His partner had prefaced the conversation with a warning not to panic and to keep listening to her until she was finished. Of course, as soon as she said not to panic, the first thing he did was indeed panic. Allina had told him that Katie Logan and Jimmy Wallander had been found, but that there were no signs of Clara.

Clara had been gone for over twenty-four hours now.

That terrified him deep down inside. It made it feel like something was eating at him, each second that Clara was gone, another piece of him was gone. That Clara hadn't been with the children when they were found terrified him even more. Did that mean that the Doll Killers had murdered her? Did it mean that Clara had sacrificed herself to save the children? Did it mean that Clara had gotten away too, but she was lying somewhere, injured?

He hated that he didn't know the answers to any of those questions.

"Paramedics are finishing up with the kids; then we can talk to them." Allina appeared beside him.

Clinging to patience, Jonathon questioned, "What about the guy who found them?"

"Waiting for us over there." Allina pointed to a guy in his twenties, with long, messy hair, dressed in sweats, lounging against the wall of a shop. The man wasn't dressed for the icy morning. Snow was forecast for later in the day, and the temperature was dropping in preparation, but the man didn't appear fazed by the cold.

"Name?" he asked his partner, already heading for the young man.

"Aaron Lloyd."

"Mr. Lloyd," Jonathon stretched out his hand, and the man shook it firmly. "Detective Dawson, and my partner, Detective Bennett. How did you find the children?"

"Was driving out to the park, I go every morning to jog with my dog. I saw two little figures in my headlights, thought it was odd that two children would be out wandering the streets, all on their own so early in the morning, so I pulled over to check it out," Aaron explained.

"Did you see anyone else?"

"No, just the children. They were running, I pulled over, was catching up to them, they must have heard me and panicked because they darted down that alley," he pointed across the street. "They were hiding. I couldn't see them, so I called out. Then the boy, Jimmy, he just came running at me, telling me they needed help, and that we needed to find someone named Clara before it was too late. I figured Clara was their mom, well maybe a stepmother or foster mother or something."

At the mention of Clara's name, his blood turned to ice. The only thing that thawed it a little was the knowledge that at least as recently as an hour or so ago, Clara had still been alive. Whether or not she still was, he had no way of knowing. "Did they say anything else about Clara?"

"No, I told the little boy to calm down, that we'd go to my car and call for help, but he said to wait and went running back to where he'd been hiding. I'd thought I'd seen two kids from my car but when only the little boy came over to me I thought I must have seen wrong, but no there were two of them. The little girl was a mess. Pale as a ghost, shaking, petrified, then she just burst into tears and threw herself into my arms. That was pretty much it. I bundled both of them into my car, turned the heat up high, and called you guys. The little girl, she took right to my dog, Bingo, clung to him—it seemed to calm her, so I let her take him with her when the paramedics wanted to check her out." Aaron pointed to a nearby ambulance.

"Did they say anything else?"

"Nope. Both of them were exhausted. The boy fell asleep as soon as I'd called the cops, and the girl just sat there and held Bingo."

His patience had pretty much-reached breaking point; he was ready to talk to the children. Now. "Thank you, Mr. Lloyd; if we have further questions, we'll be in touch. I'll have an officer bring Bingo over to you."

Dismissing the young man, Jonathon strode to the ambulance the children had insisted on sharing. Or rather that Jimmy had insisted on sharing. Katie still wasn't saying anything. When he climbed in the back of the ambulance, both children turned to look warily at him. They were sitting side by side on the gurney, the dog lying across Katie's lap. Their faces were thin and drawn, both were dwarfed by the blankets they were swaddled in, and both children looked as frail as newborn babies.

"Hey, kids." He tried to keep his voice calm and gentle and take his time with them. Scaring them by losing control wasn't going to get him answers, so he clung to control with every bit of strength he possessed because finding Clara depended on getting those answers. "Your parents are on their way here," he assured them. Predictably, Jimmy looked enormously relieved, but Katie became more agitated. "We're going to go wait for them in the café over there. You guys can have hot chocolates and anything else you want. But the dog has to go back to his owner."

Katie immediately clutched the dog tighter, but Jimmy stood and let one of the paramedics lift him down from the ambulance.

"Katie, honey, I know you like the dog, but your mom's going to be here soon." He held out his hand to her, but she shrank away from it. Something about seeing her mother scared her, but there were no indications that her mother had been abusive in any way, which meant Katie's fears were rooted elsewhere. Taking the dog's collar, he guided Bingo down to the ground, and an officer took hold of him. "You don't want to go home, honey?"

She shook her head fiercely.

"Why not, sweetheart?"

Instead of replying, the little girl flew at him. Her small, thin arms entwined around his neck, and her little, wet face pressed against his cheek.

"Why don't you want to go home, honey?"

"I killed him," she whispered.

"Killed who?" Had she somehow managed to kill one of the Doll Killers? Maybe she thought her family would be angry with her about it?

"My brother. I was supposed to be watching him at the bank, but I wasn't. I was thinking about my friends from school, and I didn't notice that the lady took him, then I couldn't find him, and I ran outside. He was with an old lady, and I thought I wasn't going to get into trouble, but then I saw that Kevin's knees weren't dirty, so he didn't go outside on his own. I knew the lady took him on purpose but it was too late, she made me go to sleep, and then she killed my brother, and it's all my fault." The words tumbled quickly from the girl's mouth, broken by sobs.

Rubbing the child's back, he murmured, "No, honey, your brother isn't dead. He was found outside the bank. He's okay. He's not dead," he repeated in case she couldn't hear through her weeping.

Abruptly, the girl grew quiet. She pulled back her head to look at him, her eyes shining with tears. "Kevin isn't dead?"

"No, sweetheart," he assured her.

"I thought my mom would be so mad at me."

"She's not. She's been very scared and worried about you; she can't wait to see you."

Katie laid her head on his shoulder and rested heavily against him. Climbing out of the ambulance, he carried her to the café where Jimmy was already wolfing into a large chocolate walnut brownie. Setting her down at the table where Allina and Jimmy were already seated, he brought Katie a hot drink and chocolate chip cookie. She took both and hungrily began devouring the cookie.

After letting the children relax for a moment, he began questioning them. Some things could wait until later, but there were other things he needed to know right now. "Jimmy, Katie, do you know who took you?"

Both children nodded. "It was an old man and an old lady," Jimmy replied. "Their names were Ruth and Job."

That was confirmation that they had accurately identified the killers. "You told the man who found you that someone named Clara needed help."

"Clara helped us escape, but we heard someone coming, and she told us to run," Jimmy explained.

Jonathon both hated and enormously respected her for that. She had put herself in danger to ensure the children could get to safety. "Do you know where they were keeping you?"

"A house, with a big garden . . ."

"A *really* big garden," Katie inserted.

"It wasn't that far away, I don't think," Jimmy looked unsure. "We ran for a long time, but it didn't take us too long to get back to where there were lots of houses and shops."

"It was a holiday place," Katie added. "I saw a sign. It said holiday cottages."

Looking at Allina, they both announced at the same time, "Hyatt's Holiday Cottages." There were twelve cottages as part of the estate, located on the city outskirts, known for its beautiful gardens and equestrian facilities.

"Was there anything on your neck that stopped you from talking loudly?" Jonathon asked, thinking of the shock collars.

"No," Katie replied.

Then that meant the house was remote enough that Job and Ruth knew no one would hear their victims' cries for help. "How many stories was the house?"

"Three, we went down two lots of stairs, only the first one was a ramp," Jimmy explained.

"You have to find her; you have to find Clara," Katie begged.

"They wanted her to kill us but she wouldn't, so they hurt her," Jimmy explained.

Jonathon tried his best not to lose it at that revelation, He hated the thought of anyone laying their hands on Clara. They needed to find her—as soon as possible. For now, they had what they needed from the children. It was only a fifteen-minute drive to the Hyatt

Estate. He and Allina could go there now and start searching the cottages. Jonathon was about to tell the kids they'd see them later when Katie's blue eyes suddenly darted to the door. They all followed her gaze and Jimmy beamed, bounced to his feet, and ran to his parents. Heather and Liam Wallander embraced their son, both freely shedding tears of joy.

Katie's parents stood there, too, but the little girl didn't move toward them. Instead, she shot him a glance, seeking reassurances that her parents weren't angry with her. Then a toddler cooed and stepped out from behind the Logans. Kevin, Jonathon presumed. At the sight of the little boy, Katie flew from her seat, flinging her arms around her brother. Her mother picked up both children, hugging them tightly and showering Katie with kisses. Her father wrapped his arms around all three, and the family just stood there holding one another.

Jonathon prayed that soon he'd have a similar reunion with Clara.

~

7:19 A.M.

Job was tired.

He tried to hide it from Ruth because it upset her so. She couldn't imagine life without him, and he couldn't imagine life without her either. He had faced death twice. He knew what it was to believe he was dying, but it had never been death itself that had scared him, only that death meant separation from the woman he loved.

In a quest to create something that would last forever, he had come up with the idea of making beautiful living dolls. Since he and Ruth were unable to bear offspring, this had seemed like the best of both worlds, taking flawed, imperfect children and transforming them into something so much better.

Dolls were perfect.

When they'd started, he had never dreamed that making the dolls would save his life. And yet it had—until recently, at least. But now he was old, his cancer had returned, and his body couldn't survive another round of illness, so Ruth had devised a way for them to beat this disease once more.

Once they were dolls themselves there would be no more sickness, no more pain, and nothing would ever be able to separate them. They would live together forever.

But Job knew that time was running out. Each day he felt a little worse, a little weaker, a little closer to death. He tried not to let it show; he tried to keep positive and optimistic. He didn't want Ruth to know that the end was near.

The last thing in the world Job wanted to do was cause distress to his beloved. His love for her was all-consuming. She was the best thing that had ever happened to him. He couldn't wait to spend eternity with her.

And it all rested on the woman in front of him.

Clara Candella. She had grown into a beautiful, smart, strong woman. He remembered her as a little girl, the time she'd spent with them—she had been one of his favorites. And now she was going to do for him what he'd intended to do for her. It might take some time, but she would understand eventually.

"You're awake, aren't you?" he asked.

Slowly, her blonde head lifted. Her green eyes were dulled by pain but still managed to shoot arrows of anger and defiance at him. After finding her by the front door, Ruth had knocked her down, and they'd administered another sedative. Once she was safely unconscious, they had tied her to one of his wheelchairs while Ruth got the room ready for her. Clara would be staying with them for quite some time, and he wanted her to be as comfortable as possible.

"I'm sorry. I know this is hard for you, and you don't understand yet." Job wanted to offer whatever comfort he could. He hated to see anyone suffering, even if it was necessary and for a good cause. He hadn't been the one to mark the children or administer the morphine to put them to sleep so their souls could move on. Now, even though he knew they were only doing what had to be done, he didn't like knowing that it caused Clara pain.

"I *don't* understand," Clara said. "Why do you think you have to turn the children into dolls?"

"To give them a better life."

"But you're killing them," Clara protested.

"No, dear, they are reborn into the dolls, where nothing bad can ever touch them again," he explained.

"Did something bad happen to you when you were a kid?" she asked quietly.

Job didn't like to think about that. He didn't like to think about his childhood at all.

"Job? What happened to you when you were a kid?"

Maybe he should tell her the story, even though it would cause him pain. Perhaps if she understood that, then she would be closer to understanding the rest. "I had a twin sister," he began. "Her name was Joy. She was such a beautiful little girl. She had hair like sunshine and eyes as endlessly blue as a summer sky. She was every bit as sweet as she was pretty. She brought joy to everyone who crossed her path."

"And you?"

"I was sick. I had leukemia. I was in and out of the hospital. I was nauseous a lot from chemotherapy. I didn't eat much; I was too thin, gaunt, ugly."

"I'm sure that's not true," Clara protested.

"It was true. My parents said it all the time. I was a burden. My treatments cost a lot of money, and it wasted a lot of their time taking me to and from hospitals and doctor appointments. It took away from the time they could have spent with my sister. They didn't love us the same; Joy was the light, I was the dark. She was good and sweet and beautiful—everything that I wasn't."

"What happened to her?"

"She fell." Pain stabbed his chest as he talked about it. "We were playing in our tree house. She fell. She and her doll. She broke her neck when she landed. Died instantly. But her doll, it survived intact. It was just lying there beside her in a pool of Joy's blood. Then as I looked down at them, it smiled at me. Joy's soul, it went into the doll, because she was such a good little girl, and she deserved to live on forever. I still have the doll. My parents didn't realize I took it. But I had to. She was my sister, my twin; her soul should stay with me."

"How old were you?"

"Seven. We were seven. You see," he implored, "that's why we do this. We're helping those children live forever, just like Joy. Through blood she was born again, this time immortal. Do you understand? There are other beautiful children like Joy; we are helping them take the same path so that they don't suffer pain." Job so badly wanted Clara to understand. And not just so she could save him and Ruth, but so she could save herself, too.

"What about Ruth? Did she go through something terrible as a child, as well?"

"Why don't you ask her?" He gestured behind her where Ruth was standing, having entered the room halfway through his recollections of his sister's death.

Twisting as best as she could in her seat, she prompted, "Ruth?"

"I was an only child. My parents owned a huge toy shop—they specialized in dolls. They had hundreds, maybe even thousands. They would restore antique dolls, too, and they had a small toy museum. The dolls, I was never allowed to touch them, but they were so beautiful." His wife's face went dreamy and then hard. Job didn't like it when she looked liked that. So cold, so harsh, so unloving. That was not the real Ruth, not the Ruth he knew.

"You loved the dolls," Clara said it as a statement, not a question. The love for dolls was written all over Ruth's face and in her voice.

"They were so pretty, beautiful, gorgeous, nothing like me." The darkness in Ruth's face grew till it was as dark as a thunderstorm. "At school, all the children teased me, called me ugly, because of this," Ruth's fingers traced the bright red birthmark on her face. "My parents thought I was ugly, too. They never said it out loud, but I could tell. They were always taking me to doctors to try and find ways to get the birthmark to fade. They didn't want an ugly daughter; they wanted a beautiful one, beautiful like the dolls. *I* wanted to be beautiful like the dolls," she finished wistfully. No matter how many times he told his wife she was just as gorgeous as any doll, she struggled to believe it.

"Do you understand yet?" he implored. "We aren't killing children; we're saving them, giving them something better. I'm dying, and Ruth and I, we want to be together for eternity. We need you to help us. We want to show you how it works so you can save us. Please, Clara; please say you'll help us."

~

7:44 A.M.

"I won't kill anyone," Clara replied. "It doesn't matter how many children you kidnap and bring here, it doesn't matter how long you keep me here, it doesn't matter how many times you burn me or hurt me, I'm *never* going to kill anyone. Including you."

At her declaration, Job looked disappointed; Ruth, on the other hand, looked furious.

"Why won't you help us?" Ruth raged, storming over and slamming her fist into Clara's jaw.

The blow made her head snap back and pain pulse through her face. Clara ignored it. If she let herself think about it, her whole body throbbed. There were still remnants of the drugs used to knock her out in her system, and she hadn't eaten or had anything to drink since being brought here. Concentrating required effort, but she knew if she didn't put the effort in she'd never get out of here. That Jimmy and Katie had gotten safely away gave her the strength she needed to keep fighting.

"Ruth," Job soothed, wheeling to her and taking her hand, kissing the reddening knuckles. "She will come around, just give her time. Remember how long it took Tommy to understand."

"Tommy?"

Smirking smugly, Ruth said, "That's right, your precious friend came to understand what we were doing. He kidnapped four children, helped us transform them into dolls."

Knowing she wasn't going to get any real answers from Ruth—the woman was too angry—she turned her attention to Job. He seemed unbalanced but the least violent and volatile of the two. "Please, Tommy was my friend, and he's dead now. I need to know why he helped you."

Releasing his wife, he wheeled closer. "Because he realized that what we were doing was saving lives."

"He came to you six months ago?"

"Yes, dear. He said he'd broken up with his girlfriend, that he wanted to see if we were still alive and that he wanted to turn us in to the police."

She was more confused now than ever. If Tommy had intended to turn in the Doll Killers, then why had he ended up working with them? And if Tommy had known all along who the killers were, then why hadn't he done something about it? Why hadn't he told the cops? "Then, why didn't he? Why didn't he turn you in?"

"We were very persuasive," Job replied.

"Very persuasive? What does that mean?" The need to understand her friend was going to wind up driving her crazy.

"It means, we kept him here, locked in a basement for three months until he was finally convinced that helping us was going to save lives," Ruth snapped.

"You brainwashed him?" That possibility was distinctly comforting. It meant that Tommy hadn't willingly decided to kidnap, rape, and murder small children.

"We didn't need to brainwash him, dear. It was a sign when he turned up the day after I found out my cancer had returned. Over time he simply learned that what we were telling him was true. He listened to us. We showed him pictures of the past children whose lives we transformed. He saw photos of them before and then pictures of their dolls. He came to see their souls had moved—traveled to the dolls. He was intrigued. He wanted to learn how to do the same thing. He said there was a little girl whose life he wanted to save."

Clara wondered if that had been Christina Ellis. No matter how much she wanted to believe that this couple had turned her sweet, kind, gentle, Tommy into a monster, she knew it wasn't entirely true. No one had forced him to sexually assault his girlfriend's seven-year-old daughter. He'd done that all on his own. Just like he'd chosen to let the Doll Killers walk free all these years. "Why did Tommy rape the little girls? You and Ruth never did that before. You never laid a hand on me that way when I was here."

Job flinched, and she realized he hadn't liked what Tommy had done. "It was a necessity, I'm afraid. Ruth is older now. She is past the time of blood, and a child cannot pass over without blood."

Because there'd been blood when his sister died. In his mind, the blood and the doll had related to Joy's death. She assumed the time of blood he was referring to was a woman's menstrual cycle. Why they'd jumped to that she had no idea, nor did she care, it didn't matter. All that mattered was finding a way home. "Whose idea was it? To rape the girls? Yours or his?"

"It was his," Job answered softly.

"No!" she cried. She'd been expecting the answer, but it still hurt like a physical blow. She really hadn't ever known Tommy Karl.

"Yes," Ruth snarled. "Tommy stared at the girls' pictures for hours. *Hours*. That was pretty much all he did. He just sat in his room and thought about them. After three months, he was practically begging us to find another pair of children, that he was ready to help us turn them into dolls."

"No!" she protested again. She didn't want to hear this. If she could press her hands to her ears, she would have. She'd wanted answers, and now she had them, but she wasn't sure she wanted them anymore.

"Enough chitchat time." Ruth stalked over, took the handles of the wheelchair she was bound to and began to push her through the house; then she stopped at the door in the kitchen.

Clara assumed it led to a basement, which must be where they intended to keep her locked away while they attempted to brainwash her. That they intended to keep her alive and imprisoned indefinitely was good news. That gave Jonathon more time to find her. And now that he had Jimmy and Katie, hopefully, he had enough to figure out her location.

Producing a knife, for a split-second Clara feared that Ruth had changed her mind and was about to kill her here and now, but then the old woman moved the knife to the tape that once again bound her to the chair. "You make one stupid move, and he shoots you," Ruth warned.

She eyed Job, who held a gun trained on her with shaky hands. "Please don't make me kill you, dear."

Trusting that Jonathon would be coming for her, Clara simply stood once Ruth had cut off all the tape. There was no point in getting herself shot and risk dying, either from blood loss or infection, when hopefully she'd be found anytime now. Ruth then took possession of the gun and gestured for her to head down into the basement. The space down here was large. Half of it was made into a room blocked from the rest of the attic by a wall of metal poles. Inside the room was a bed, a table and chairs, a sofa, a bookcase, a toilet, and a sink.

"Inside," Ruth nudged her with the gun.

Fighting her instincts to run, to fight back, to do something, Clara instead walked into the cage. Ruth closed and locked the door behind her.

"You will end up doing what we want, Clara. I won't accept another outcome. Because if you don't, Job will die, and I won't live without him. So, you *will* learn how to transform us into dolls."

Then Ruth was gone, and Clara was left alone, praying that Jonathon would find her and she wasn't going to die in here.

~

8:59 A.M.

In the interest of saving time, he and Allina had split the twelve cottages on the Hyatt Estate and Jonathon had already checked out all six of his. Each of the properties were isolated enough that screams for help wouldn't carry from one cottage to the next. The whole estate was thirty-five acres, approximately one house every three acres, plenty of space for guests to feel like they were all alone in the beautiful forest where they could enjoy the peace and quiet.

Four of the cottages he'd checked had been empty; none showed any signs that an elderly couple and three kidnap victims had recently inhabited them. Given that Job and Ruth Lincoln had created a child-sized dollhouse in the attic, and that the children had escaped only a couple of hours ago, there was no way that the attic could have been cleared out and the walls repainted already. If the Doll Killers had been hiding out in any of those cottages, then there would have been signs of it. Of the two that had been occupied, one was by a young couple on their honeymoon, the other by a young family with two toddlers. Neither fit the descriptions of the Doll Killers, and both had allowed him to check out the cottages, which had turned up no hints of recent prisoners.

Despair was quickly raining down upon him.

Allina hadn't called to say that she'd found anything, and he hadn't found anything, but Clara had to be here somewhere. Katie had said that they had run past a sign that said holiday cottages and the Hyatt Estate was the only place close enough that the children could have come from. Clara was here somewhere; he knew it—he just didn't know where.

Perhaps there were other buildings here. There were stables, but that would have been too public, and the kids had said that they were kept on the third floor. The stables might have had a loft, but that was it; they wouldn't have had multiple stories. Since the place was known for its gardens, there might be greenhouses or something, but again they would be single story, and the children hadn't mentioned plants or flowers. They said they'd been in a house.

What other buildings could be here?

Then it hit him.

The house. The main house. The Reebs, who had taken over the Hyatt Estate about a year ago, lived on site.

That had to be it.

It was the only house left.

He consulted the map that he'd downloaded on the drive here. The main house was only a half-mile from where he was right now. Yanking out his phone, he turned the car engine back on and started to drive. "Ali, I think they're at the main house," he said without preamble as soon as his partner answered her phone.

"I'm right up the other end of the property, wait for me."

"I can't. Clara is in danger every second she spends with those people. Hurry." Hanging up and throwing the phone onto the passenger seat, he turned down a long driveway that led to the main house. As he drove, he saw the sign that Katie had mentioned. Convinced he was in the right place, he left his car where it was, got out his gun, and went the rest of the distance on foot, hoping not to alert

Job and Ruth Lincoln of his presence. He didn't want them to panic and do something to Clara.

Reaching the front door, he put a hand on the brass handle and turned, praying that it wouldn't be locked. It wasn't, and he eased the door open and stepped inside. The house was elegantly and simply decorated. The walls were all painted white giving the house a bright and airy feel. The floorboards looked old, probably original from when the farmhouse was built about two hundred years ago. The décor was modern, lots of white and glass, and a few paintings dotted the walls along with a couple of framed photographs.

Working his way down the central hallway, he cleared the lounge room on the left, the dining room on the right, and the huge kitchen at the back. Back in the hall, he headed slowly up the stairs to the second floor. Up here, there were three bedrooms and a bathroom. More white walls and floorboards, the bedrooms contained only beds and night-stands, with mirrored built-in wardrobes and floaty white curtains at the windows. A lone wheelchair sat in the largest of the bedrooms, further convincing him that he was in the right place. All four rooms were unoccupied, so he headed for the final staircase. As the children had told him, it had been converted into a ramp by laying several long, smooth pieces of wood over the steps.

Expecting to find the door at the top locked, as he assumed that Clara was still being held inside, he was surprised when instead it swung open at his touch.

The room was empty.

Well not empty, but Clara wasn't in it.

It was set up just like she had told them, just as he had pictured it in his mind—a child-sized dollhouse. It was creepy.

A chair sat off to one side, torn bits of duct tape on the floor around it.

Clara had been here, but where was she now?

Had they fled with her when they realized the children were gone?

If they had, how would he ever find them?

Jonathon was about to call Allina and tell her that the Doll Killers had been here, but they were gone now when he remembered a door in the kitchen. There had been two doors; one had led back outside to a decked patio; the other door probably led to a basement. And a basement would be the perfect place to keep a prisoner, especially if they wanted Clara to kill the children they abducted. They probably thought keeping her away from them would prevent her from bonding with them and make it more likely that she'd do what they wanted.

Flying back downstairs, a light was on in the basement as he slowly edged open the door. Gun out in front, he resisted the urge to barrel down the steps; instead, he took his time, until he saw her.

Clara was lying on a bed. She was inside a large cage. The rest of the basement was empty.

At the sound of him clattering down the stairs, her head snapped up.

At the sight of him, she scrambled to her feet and stumbled a little unsteadily to the bars.

Jonathon froze as he looked at her. She was pale, her eyes red-rimmed and puffy, and a bruise was forming on her jaw. There was a long scratch on one cheek, her left shoulder was badly bruised, and most of her exposed skin was red and blistered. An anger so strong it nearly knocked him off his feet rushed through him. He'd never experienced something so powerful before. He'd known that the Lincolns had hurt her—Katie and Jimmy had told him that they had—but seeing it made it seem so much more real.

"You came," she smiled up at him.

"Baby." He reached for her, took her face in his hands, his thumb brushed gently over the darkening bruise. "Are you all right?" He searched her eyes, seeking the truth and not the platitude he was sure she was going to offer.

"I'm okay now you're here." Her hands stretched through the bars and took hold of his face, bringing it down to meet hers. Their lips touched, and he felt some of his anger float away as relief took its place. She was alive. That was what mattered.

He kissed her as long and as hard as he could. When he had to stop to draw a breath, he reluctantly pulled away. His fingers dropped to her arms, tracing around the fresh brands. "How badly do they hurt? And don't lie to me," he cautioned.

Her composure cracked a little; her eyes grew watery, and her bottom lip wobbled. "They hurt a lot."

He gave her another quick kiss. "Then let's get you out of here and to a hospital to get checked out."

"My sister—is Naomi okay?" Clara asked as he began to search the room for the keys.

"She lost a lot of blood, but she's going to be okay."

"You saved her, didn't you?"

"She was lucky I turned up when I did," he acknowledged.

"Thank you."

She said it so seriously, he paused to look at her. "It would have been luckier if I'd turned up earlier so that your sister didn't get stabbed and you didn't get kidnapped."

"No," Clara shook her head. "They just would have come after me another time. They wanted me here, Jonathon. They think that I can learn how to turn people into dolls so I can do it to them because Job is dying. Jimmy and Katie, did they get away?" she was breathing hard now, getting panicky. "Did you find them?"

"We found them," he soothed. "We found them. Try to keep yourself calm; you just need to hold it together a little longer."

"Yeah, okay." Clara took several long deep breaths. "I'm glad you found them. I was scared that Ruth and Job had gone after them once they knocked me out."

"Both of them are fine; they're with their families," he assured her. "Bingo."

"What?"

"Found the keys," he grinned. Now he could get Clara out of the cage and someplace safe. Allina was already on her way; then they just had to wait for the Lincolns to turn back up here and arrest them.

"Jonathon."

Clara said the word at the exact moment he heard the gun cocking.

"I don't think you're going to need the keys."

He weighed his options. He still had his gun. He could attempt to shoot before they shot first, but he didn't want to risk Clara getting caught in the crossfire. Allina would be here soon. Perhaps it would be better to play along until then.

"Toss the keys on the floor."

He did as he was instructed

"Now walk over to the cage."

Again, he did as directed.

"This has all worked out so perfectly, my dear one," a new voice spoke. "Now she has a partner and we don't even need to go looking for one."

That seemed to spark something in Clara. "Tommy didn't have a partner. When he carjacked me, he said he had to show me something. Was he going to bring me to you? Was I supposed to be his partner?"

Wanting to hear the answer to that, Jonathon turned slowly, not wanting to startle anyone into firing their weapons. The elderly couple before him were nothing exceptional to look at. Had he not known they were psychopathic killers, he wouldn't have pegged them as such. They were the typical grandparent type, but he kept his guard up—they may look old and frail, but so far, they had done a pretty good job of holding their own.

"Yes, dear, he was supposed to bring you here so you could join us," Job Lincoln replied. Clara looked crestfallen at the confirmation.

Moving around him to unlock the door, Jonathon didn't have a good feeling about allowing himself to be locked away, even if Allina should turn up at any moment now. Fingering his gun, it appeared only Ruth Lincoln was armed, and he thought he could get off a shot at her before she could do anything about it.

He was going to risk it when something suddenly slammed into his head.

Stumbling, he fell to his knees, his vision cloudy. Clara's screams echoed in his head. He clung to consciousness because he didn't want to leave Clara alone and vulnerable.

Fighting to get back to his feet, he had just managed to get halfway up when the second blow had him dropping like a rock.

~

9:34 A.M.

.   .   .

Clara couldn't stop screaming.

All the bottled-up fear and pain she'd been holding back came bubbling out as she looked at Jonathon lying unconscious on the basement floor.

"Don't be afraid, dear," Job's voice cut through her terror. "He's not dead. Not even hurt badly. Ruth just needs him unconscious while we open the door because neither of you understands yet."

That didn't stop her screaming.

Jonathon looked dead.

What if Ruth had hit him harder than she'd intended and had killed him?

As Ruth unlocked the door and dragged Jonathon through it, Clara knew she should do something—somehow take advantage of the situation. But all she could do was scream and sob.

"Stop," Ruth shrieked, storming her and holding the gun to her forehead. "Stop. Just stop that squawking."

She pressed her hands to her mouth to try to physically stifle her sobs, but the cold metal of the gun against her skin wasn't helping.

"Just leave her be, dear," Job said. "She's upset; she'll calm down. We've had our morning walk, let's go and have breakfast."

"I hate shouting," Ruth muttered, but left the cage, locking it behind her.

As soon as they were alone, Jonathon sprang to his feet. His face was white, the blood that dribbled down from a small cut on his forehead stood out in stark contrast. Her shock-addled brain thought fleetingly that he must be a ghost. Which was odd, she considered, since she didn't even believe in ghosts.

"It's okay, Clara, I'm okay," she could just make out his voice through her screams. "I was just faking; I was never unconscious. The blows stunned me; that's all."

His arms were around her, and she was crushed against his chest. The pressure of his body against her raw burns made them sting, but she didn't care. There wasn't a single other place she wanted to be right now than in Jonathon's arms. Her whole body was trembling violently, the kind of shakes she knew she didn't have a hope of controlling. She was losing it, she realized dismally.

"Shh, it's okay, baby. Shh," he soothed. His hand smoothed her hair just as he had the first day they'd met. His voice and his hands had calmed her that day, and they had the same effect on her now. Slowly her sobs quietened, her tremors stilled, and she sagged tiredly against him. "Come, sit down." He led her to the table and eased her down into one of the chairs. "Let me take a proper look at you."

As soon as he released her, her shakes returned. Jonathon grabbed the blanket from the bed and wrapped it around her, then tilted her face so he could examine the bruise on her jaw from where Ruth had hit her earlier. The bruise was painful but nothing like the burns. Next, he lifted one of her arms, examining it, then her other arm, and her chest and stomach.

"Some of these look like they might be getting infected," he told her, tucking her hair behind her ear. "Allina should be here soon; then we can get you out of here. You're still shaking. Let's try and warm you up some. You're not properly dressed for the cold, and I think you're going into shock. Just hold on a little longer."

He picked her up and sat with her on his lap. His hands carefully rubbed her arms, trying to warm her, as she rested heavily against his strong chest. *Home.* The word had never sounded so good. She wanted to see her sister, make sure Naomi was okay, then go home, climb into her bed, and sleep for about a month. Jonathon's presence was so comforting that Clara could feel her eyes growing heavy. She had barely slept since she'd been kidnapped. She was just drifting off to sleep when she suddenly remembered something. Wiggling out of Jonathon's grasp, she gasped out, "I have pins—from Katie's hair—that's how we got out of the attic."

"You picked the lock?" Jonathon looked both impressed and amused.

"Naomi will be thrilled she taught me. I didn't think I'd remember what to do, but I did." She offered a weak smile as she reached into her bra and retrieved the pins.

"You are amazing." He gave her a quick kiss, slid her off his lap, took the pins and hurried to the door. He had it unlocked in less than a minute. "Wait down here until I come back for you. Try to find some-place to hide."

Jumping to her feet, she exclaimed, "I'm not staying here on my own! I'm coming with you."

He looked like he wanted to argue, but instead he said, "Stay behind me."

Dropping the blanket, Clara kept as close to Jonathon as she could without actually climbing onto his back.

"They must have taken my gun," he muttered as they started up the steps.

Clara couldn't remember seeing Ruth take Jonathon's gun, but she had been preoccupied with thinking that he was dead.

At the kitchen door, Jonathon held a finger to his lips to make sure she knew to keep quiet; then he pressed his ear to the door. Waving at her to tell her to stay where she was, he inched the door open. Jonathon's broad shoulders blocked her view of the room, but he crept through the door then partially closed it again.

Peeking through the gap, she saw Job in his wheelchair over by an open fireplace. The flames were dancing about, a bright mix of oranges, reds, and yellows, and Job was either mesmerized by the fire or else asleep. Jonathon crept over to him, arming himself with a knife from the counter on the way.

Clara knew that Jonathon wouldn't hurt Job unless he had no choice, and once the old man was restrained, they could find Ruth and get her restrained, too. Then it was time to go home. She wasn't expecting any trouble from Job; she didn't think the man was violent. Jonathon was almost upon him when he suddenly sprang from his wheelchair, wielding a knife and lunging for Jonathon.

Terrified, she screamed and barged through the door.

At the same time, another scream echoed through the house.

Ruth appeared in the kitchen doorway, a gun in her hand.

Jonathon reacted quickly, grabbing Job just as Ruth fired the gun. The bullet plowed through Job. Blood blossomed on his cream sweater, right over his heart.

Ruth's howl of pain was worse than Job's.

The old man dropped to the floor when Jonathon released him and didn't move.

Face contorted in anger, Ruth howled in rage and flung herself at Jonathon.

Jonathon moved forward at the same time, and the bullet Ruth fired missed him, slamming into a wall.

Wrapping his arms around Ruth, she squirmed frantically, desperate to get free, but thankfully, with her arms pinned to her sides, she couldn't get aim at Jonathon.

Clara couldn't just stand by and do nothing. She grabbed another of the knives from the counter and ran to Jonathon and Ruth.

"Clara, go—get out of here. Wait for Allina outside," Jonathon ordered.

Using Jonathon's momentary distraction to her advantage, Ruth stomped on Jonathon's foot and managed to get free of his grasp.

A shot went off.

Pain burned through her left shoulder.

It took Clara's foggy brain a moment to connect the two.

Jonathon screamed her name.

She wobbled, sank to the floor, and pressed her hand to her shoulder to try and stem the flow of blood.

"You're both going to die," Ruth raged as she held her gun pointed at Jonathon's head. "You killed him. Now we'll never be together again."

"Ruth," Jonathon began, his voice was intended to be soothing, but it seemed to have the opposite effect on her.

"Shut up," she screeched. "You're going to . . ."

Another bang shattered the room.

Clara expected to see Jonathon drop down beside her, but instead when she looked up she could no longer see Ruth.

She assumed it was Jonathon's partner who had just shot the old lady, but when she turned in the direction the bullet had been fired from, she saw her sister.

"Naomi?"

"Is she dead?" Naomi asked breathlessly.

Kneeling, Jonathon replied a moment later, "She's dead."

"Good." Naomi swayed and toppled over.

"Naomi! Jonathon, go see if she's okay," she insisted when he crouched beside her.

"You're bleeding," he gestured at her shoulder.

"I'm okay; it's not that bad. Naomi is unconscious. Go make sure she's all right," she pleaded.

Looking torn, Jonathon did as she asked, going to Naomi and pressing his fingers to her neck. "Her pulse is weak, and it looks like the stitches in her shoulder have popped. She's bleeding. She's supposed to be in the hospital. I have no idea what she's doing here or how she even knew where we were. I'll bring her over to you so I can keep an eye on both of you." Picking her sister up, he carried Naomi over to her and laid her down on the ground. Clara grabbed one of her sister's hands and clutched it tightly. Then Jonathon grabbed a tea towel from the counter and held it to her wound. "Are you really okay?"

She let out a long shaky breath. Her shoulder throbbed, but it didn't seem to be bleeding too badly, and relief that Job and Ruth Lincoln were dead and the Doll Killer murders were over forever far outweighed the pain. "I'm really okay."

"Jonathon, I heard gunshots," Allina's voice called.

"We're in the kitchen," he yelled back, his hand pressing more firmly to her shoulder. "We need at least two ambulances, maybe three. Clara was shot, Naomi is unconscious, and I'm not sure if Job Lincoln is still alive."

"Naomi Candella?" Allina appeared, assessing the scene. "What is she doing here?"

"I have no idea, but she saved my life. Is Job dead?"

"I've got a pulse, extremely weak. He's bleeding out. I don't even know if he'll make it till the ambulance arrives. Are you okay with Clara and Naomi while I call for backup?"

"Yeah," Jonathon hadn't taken his eyes off her during his exchange with his partner.

Adrenalin was seeping from her body along with the blood. She was crashing quickly now that everything was over. Her eyes met Jonathon's, held his gaze, tried to decipher the mess of emotions swirling around them. The fear and relief were obvious, but there was something much deeper—respect, admiration, attraction, maybe even love.

"You hanging in there?" Jonathon asked as he adjusted his hold on the towel at her shoulder.

Sleepy now, Clara managed a nod as her eyelids fluttered closed. Too tired to open them again, she let them remain shut. "Stay with me," she murmured.

"Of course, I'm not going anywhere."

Whether she should say it or not, she wasn't sure. Whether or not it was too soon or not, she wasn't sure of that, either. She *should* be embarrassed, but she didn't have enough energy left for another emotion. Regardless of the consequences, the words slipped from her lips, "I love you."

CHAPTER
Eight

February 14th
7:52 P.M.

Nervous anticipation fluttered through her as the doorbell rang.

Clara hadn't seen Jonathon again since she'd closed her eyes back in Job and Ruth Lincoln's kitchen. Exhaustion had taken hold, and she'd passed out, remaining unconscious throughout the ride to the hospital, and while being examined and treated in the emergency room. When she finally woke up in the early evening, Jonathon had left to tie up the case.

Her brothers had coerced her into spending the night in the hospital, but she hadn't gotten much sleep. The bed wasn't her bed, and nurses kept coming in to check on her, plus she couldn't relax properly without Jonathon's arms around her. First thing in the morning she had insisted that the place where she was going to recover the best was her own home. Dylan and Davis had brought her home, but when they'd offered to stay with her, she'd declined, saying she needed some alone time to process everything that had happened.

Clara had used the hours alone to over think and obsess.

She was worried that she'd scared Jonathon off with her shock-induced declaration of love. What had she been thinking? No guy wanted to hear that after dating for a couple of days. And she and Jonathon had never even actually dated. She was just going to blame it on being shot—it was a pretty good excuse, after all. Or hopefully, Jonathon was just not even going to bring it up.

"Hey," he grinned at her when she'd garnered enough courage to open the door. "Happy Valentine's Day."

"Oh, yeah, it is. I totally lost track of time," she smiled back.

"These are for you." He held out a bouquet of dandelion puffs and a fluffy white teddy bear.

"Dandelion puffs?" she giggled, half-amused, half-confused.

"They remind me of you—whimsical and free. Plus, now whenever you see dandelions, you're going to think of me and of this day, our first proper date," his grin grew wider.

Raising an eyebrow, she asked, "Our first real date?"

"I owe you one, remember? Now you take these." He gave her the flowers and the teddy, picked up the basket that sat at his feet, and headed for her kitchen.

While she was interested to see what Jonathon had planned, there were some things she needed to ask. Clara knew she needed closure before she could move forward. "Jonathon, before we do this, have our first date, I need to know about the case—is it really over?"

"Job Lincoln never made it through surgery; he's dead. They're both dead. They killed the couple who owned the Hyatt Estate, the Reebs. We found their bodies buried in the backyard. It *is* over now, Clara."

"Yeah," she nodded, wishing it *felt* like it was over. "How's your mom doing? Has it helped her to know the people who killed your sister are dead now?"

"She's happy they're dead, but in the end, it doesn't bring back Dora."

"How're you doing?"

"I hate them for killing my sister; I hate them for hurting you." His fingertips touched the bruise on her jaw, then lingered on her cheek.

"And I'm a little jealous that Naomi was the one to kill Ruth Lincoln and not me," he joked lamely. "How is Naomi?"

Her sister had also insisted on leaving the hospital, even though her doctors wanted her to stay for at least another day or two. Discharging herself, driving halfway across town and shooting a killer, had weakened her already weak body. Not that Clara could be angry with her sister about it—if Naomi hadn't arrived when she had then Ruth would have killed both her and Jonathon. Since Naomi was going to discharge herself regardless of anyone else's opinion on the matter, they'd gotten her to agree to come back to Clara's house. Dylan and Davis had given her painkillers and a sleeping pill and put her to bed in the guest room before leaving. That she'd agreed to take both was a testament to how exhausted Naomi was.

"She's okay, pretty weak, she doesn't really have enough energy to do anything, which is driving her crazy, but it also means she has to sleep."

"She staying here while she recovers?"

"Yeah, she's upstairs asleep."

"How are you doing?" His hand hovered above her bandaged shoulder. "Are you in a lot of pain?"

"I'm all right. The bullet didn't do much damage. It hurts but it's not so bad, and the burns are already healing." She knew they'd leave scars that would forever be a reminder of her ordeal. "I'll be fine. I'll need some physical therapy once the wound has healed to get back full movement in my shoulder, but the injury isn't anywhere near as bad as Naomi's. I'm okay. Really," she added truthfully. She felt a little like a mummy since her stomach was bandaged and her arms were wrapped from wrists to shoulders to protect the burns, but considering what she'd just been through, she felt pretty good. "I'm being a good girl and taking plenty of painkillers, and I haven't done much of anything today, just relaxed and re-read some of my favorite books." Absently, her fingers moved to the bandaged wound on her shoulder. It was true painkillers had numbed most of the pain, but it was odd that both she and Naomi had been injured in the same place.

"How did Naomi know where we were?"

"She said that somehow she just knew. But she knew everything I remembered from the hypnosis session. I think she just managed to put things together and figure out the killers' identities. Apparently, she'd been looking through copies of Tommy's pictures. He must have drawn something from the Hyatt Estate and it just clicked for her. Now why she didn't just tell someone rather than leave the hospital a day after she nearly bled to death, that I couldn't tell you."

"Honey, you're not really angry at your sister—what's bothering you?" Jonathon took her hand and led her to the living area where he sat her down on one of the sofas.

She shrugged fitfully, then winced at the pain that shot through her shoulder.

"You can talk to me, Clara, I hope you know that. I *want* you to talk to me. Clara," he took her chin and gently angled her face toward his, "what you said to me right before you passed out . . ."

Embarrassed, she looked away. "Obviously I'm not in love with you, you can't love someone you just met. It's just that I've just stepped over the ledge ... I'm falling for you."

"Look at me." He waited until she reluctantly lifted her eyes back to his. "I'm falling, too."

"What?" Surely her overly medicated mind must be misunderstanding him.

"I'm falling for you, too." He leaned in close, his lips hovered just above hers.

"Really?"

"Really." His mouth took hers and everything else faded away.

Clara could feel heat brewing between them, it sizzled and bubbled, and she lifted her hands to curl them into Jonathon's hair. She'd never felt anything this intense before, it eclipsed any feelings she'd ever had for a guy, and somehow she knew that things were only going to get better between them.

"We should stop," Jonathon said. His breathing was heavy as he gently circled her wrists with his hands and touched light kisses to each of her fingertips.

"Why exactly are we stopping?" Her body was already throbbing with a need that only one thing could quench.

"We go much further and I reach the point of no return."

"What's wrong with that?"

"We only just met it would be presumptuous of me to assume you were ready to sleep with me."

She didn't have to ask him to know that he was clinging to restraint. That touched her, Jonathon made her feel safe, she knew that he would always consider her feelings and put her first and that made her feel bold when she otherwise would have shied away. "You should presume."

His smile was tender and he reached out to smooth her hair, letting his fingers brush across her cheek. "Are you sure?"

"I can honestly say I have never been more sure of anything in my life."

Jonathon gave a guttural groan and then his hands spanned her waist and he lifted her up and set her down on his lap so that her legs straddled his thighs. "You're beautiful, you know that? I love this silky hair, I love your big green eyes, and I love this mouth." His thumb swept across her bottom lip before he kissed her again.

The kiss was hot and hard, and it set her body alight. She shifted restlessly against his growing length, she needed to be closer, needed to feel him against her without the barrier of their clothes. "Hurry," she begged, the pressure inside her so strong, it was begging to be released.

"Impatient aren't you?" Jonathon smiled against her lips before kissing his way down her neck, making her squirm.

"Only for you." Because she had a feeling he intended to draw this out, and she was pretty sure she would lose her mind if he didn't hurry up and get inside her, Clara reached for the tent in his pants, stroked him once, and then unzipped his jeans. When she shoved his boxers aside his impressive length sprung free and she licked her lips, her body clenching in anticipation of how good it was going to feel with that buried inside her.

When she went to touch him again, Jonathon snagged her hands. "Unless you want this to be over *really* quickly you better stop doing that."

"Who said I don't want it to be over quickly?" she asked, shifting restlessly.

Jonathon chuckled, then he slipped a hand inside her panties, teasing her with feather light touches. "So wet," he whispered, before his mouth found hers again and he began to plunder her mouth as she wished he would ravage her body.

She gasped when he slipped a finger inside her, and then another. He curled them around stroking a spot inside her that she'd heard of but doubted really existed because she'd never been able to find it.

Jonathon seemed to know exactly where it was though.

His thumb pressed on her little bundle of nerves, as his fingers stroked her, and she rocked her hips trying to get more of the amazing sensations he was creating inside her.

"Stand up," he said, pulling his hands out from her pants, making her whimper a protest. "Condom?"

"Don't need it, I'm clean and on birth control."

"I'm clean too. I've never done it without a condom before."

"Me either," Clara admitted, realizing the gravity of her feelings for Jonathon. She'd never felt connected enough to a guy, never trusted one enough or cared enough about one, to let them enter her body without protection.

But Jonathon was different.

He set her on her feet in front of him and shoved her jeans and panties down her legs before lifting her up and setting her down on top of him. His length slid inside her like he was made for her, and already she could feel pleasure rippling towards her.

One of his hands held her hip while he thrust inside her, his other hand continued to work her little bud and bright lights began to shimmer before her.

"I'm going to come," she said, clutching at his shoulders as an overwhelming tsunami of sensations came down on her.

Jonathon's lips came down on hers, swallowing up the scream that would have fallen from her lips as the bright lights burst in a colorful display of fireworks behind her closed eyes lids.

"That was amazing," Jonathon said, touching his lips to her temple.

"Yeah it was," she agreed, nuzzling his neck.

"This is the end of all the dark stuff. From now on, your life is going to be full of light. *Our* lives are going to be full of light."

Clara liked the sound of that. She followed Jonathon to the kitchen where he bustled about preparing their first official meal as boyfriend and girlfriend.

It was time.

She had lived in the shadows for twenty-three years.

But now it was time.

Time to let go of the dark and let the light in.

"So," she said slowly, her fingertips drawing lazy circles on Jonathon's chest. "I want to know everything about you, and I mean *everything*. Favorite color and food, book and movie, and ...

Candella sister Agape is desperate to find love and thinks she's found it in the sexy man who saves her from a mugger, unfortunately he's keeping a secret that will destroy her.

<u>Little Hearts (Candella Sisters' Heroes #2)</u>

Also by Jane Blythe

Detective Parker Bell Series

A SECRET TO THE GRAVE

WINTER WONDERLAND

DEAD OR ALIVE

LITTLE GIRL LOST

FORGOTTEN

Count to Ten Series

ONE

TWO

THREE

FOUR

FIVE

SIX

BURNING SECRETS

SEVEN

EIGHT

NINE

TEN

Broken Gems Series

CRACKED SAPPHIRE

CRUSHED RUBY

FRACTURED DIAMOND

SHATTERED AMETHYST

SPLINTERED EMERALD

SALVAGING MARIGOLD

River's End Rescues Series

COCKY SAVIOR

SOME REGRETS ARE FOREVER

SOME FEARS CAN CONTROL YOU

SOME LIES WILL HAUNT YOU

SOME QUESTIONS HAVE NO ANSWERS

SOME TRUTH CAN BE DISTORTED

SOME TRUST CAN BE REBUILT

SOME MISTAKES ARE UNFORGIVABLE

Candella Sisters' Heroes Series

LITTLE DOLLS

LITTLE HEARTS

LITTLE BALLERINA

Storybook Murders Series

NURSERY RHYME KILLER

FAIRYTALE KILLER

FABLE KILLER

Saving SEALs Series

SAVING RYDER
SAVING ERIC
SAVING OWEN
SAVING LOGAN
SAVING GRAYSON
SAVING CHARLIE

Prey Security Series

PROTECTING EAGLE
PROTECTING RAVEN
PROTECTING FALCON
PROTECTING SPARROW
PROTECTING HAWK
PROTECTING DOVE

Prey Security: Alpha Team Series

DEADLY RISK
LETHAL RISK
EXTREME RISK
FATAL RISK
COVERT RISK
SAVAGE RISK

Prey Security: Artemis Team Series

IVORY'S FIGHT

PEARL'S FIGHT

LACEY'S FIGHT

OPAL'S FIGHT

Prey Security: Bravo Team Series

VICIOUS SCARS

RUTHLESS SCARS

Christmas Romantic Suspense Series

CHRISTMAS HOSTAGE

CHRISTMAS CAPTIVE

CHRISTMAS VICTIM

YULETIDE PROTECTOR

YULETIDE GUARD

YULETIDE HERO

HOLIDAY GRIEF

Conquering Fear Series (Co-written with Amanda Siegrist)

DROWNING IN YOU

OUT OF THE DARKNESS

CLOSING IN

About the Author

USA Today bestselling author Jane Blythe writes action-packed romantic suspense and military romance featuring protective heroes and heroines who are survivors. One of Jane's most popular series includes Prey Security, part of Susan Stoker's OPERATION ALPHA world! Writing in that world alongside authors such as Janie Crouch and Riley Edwards has been a blast, and she looks forward to bringing more books to this genre, both within and outside of Stoker's world. When Jane isn't binge-reading she's counting down to Christmas and adding to her 200+ teddy bear collection!

To connect and keep up to date please visit any of the following

www.ingramcontent.com/pod-product-compliance
Lightning Source LLC
Chambersburg PA
CBHW031958240626
47153CB00003B/1022